RUNE

A Fantasy Epic

Toni Gorkin

The characters and events portrayed in this book are fictitious. Any similarity to real persons, living or dead, is coincidental and not intended by the author.

ISBN-13: 9798727829653
ISBN-10: 1477123456

Cover design by: Toni Gorkin
Library of Congress Control Number: 2018675309
Printed in the United States of America

Dedicated to Travis and Robin

CONTENTS

CHAPTER 1

Morat High-Lord of Rune eased himself from his saddle and bent to examine his cornua's front hoof. He could see no injury, no stone caught in the tender part, no swelling of the leg. The animal stamped its foot, moving skittishly under his firm fingers moving up its leg. He could find nothing amiss.

Yet the mount had been limping for some time.

The High-Lord grunted, eased himself to his feet, and looked around. They had been climbing into rougher and rougher terrain. The soft, rolling ways had given way to steep, trackless slopes. He saw around him now dark, lowering pines sighing in the wind.

Lower down the slopes the mountain maples and aspen had been beginning to open trembling new leaves to the spring's call. This far upslope, the pale red of their buds was only a faint wash against the bare branches. The tiny streamlets rushing headlong down courses of wet, black boulders were cold with the chill of high melting snow. Indeed, there were still patches of snow to be seen gleaming under the shelter of the pines. There were touches of beauty; carpets of white and pink flowers underfoot wove a magic that occasionally distracted the High-Lord from his weariness.

But these woods—there was no mistaking it—this was not the forest of Runegladden in which they had begun the morning and the hunt. Not the same forest at all.

Morat was worried.

He pushed aside a few branches, trying to see what lay ahead.

Had he caught the faint sounds of the hunt party? Had he found the companions who had started out with him early that morning? Redd, his cross-cousin; Amran-an, Wizard Lord of Rune's Deld-Deeps Portion; Heller Jade, who ruled Kai-Haluu, the seacoast trade city; the rest all gathered in to Rune's spring festivities?

All of them had followed the white stag-beast, shaggy with its partially shed winter coat, its wide-spread antlers still covered in spring velvet, with the same abandoned determination as the hounds, leaving Morat High-Lord of Rune far behind with a lamed mount. Cursing, his calls snatched away by the wind to blend with the voices of the pines, Morat had seen them lost from his sight, lost like the strange gleam of the unnatural white of the beast, the incredible reach of the branching antlers on its noble head.

A strange weariness had fallen over him; he had sat on the cornua, unable to muster the strength to follow.

He wondered what spells the pines were murmuring now to the cold, wet boulders.

There! He heard it again. The hunt! And coming this way! He shook himself free of lethargy and ran up the slope, drawing his mount along behind him by the reins.

From the crest he looked down into a bowl-shaped depression of land. Cupped in the hands of the rocky slopes lay a turbulent pool, dark at its center, catching the melt water in its hollow and spilling it forth into a tiny, roaring streamlet. Heavy gusts of wind tore down from the towering cliffs, giving the pines savage voices, shaking the shaggy shadows beneath their boughs. Beneath the cliffs a battle was in progress.

Morat poised, hand shading his eyes from the glare of the pool. He couldn't seem to make out clearly how many were fighting, but it was clear his party was under attack. Redd and the Deld wizard stood back to back, fending off attackers with the light, short-bladed swords that were all they carried forth that morning besides their hunting spears. Heller Jade stood over the senseless body of a page, laying about with his huge double-bladed sea-ax, the only real weapon among them.

Morat squinted, trying to see more clearly the dark-clad attackers. There seemed to be dozens of them, but the tossing shags of pine-shed shadow, the flickering of the light on the agitated pool, confused his eyes. He could make out no runes on their tunics.

But his party, his kin and close as kin, were hemmed in between cliff and pool and pines and in desperate straits. Morat snatched his hunting spear from his saddle. He held it high, shoulders tensed to throw. But his vision kept clouding over. His head buzzed and the cliffs kept wavering in the strange light from the glittering, turbulent pool. Then Redd was down, his sword knocked from his hands. He held his empty hands up to ward off the blow of the attacker looming over him.

Angrily Morat shook his head, muttered a rune, and cast the spear with all his might, leaning his body after it. It struck the nearest attacker, the one raising sword at Redd, squarely in the back.

The attacker fell without a cry.

Morat stood transfixed, as if he himself had been struck by the spear, his arm still thrust forward with the follow-through of the spear-cast. Below him, equally motionless, lay Redd, stood Amran-an, the pages. Heller Jade swore softly, eyes bulging from his florid face at the empty space before him.

Now Morat could see clearly. Now the buzzing was gone from his brain. The cliffs were still dark, but ordinary; the pool no longer cast flickerings into the air. The pines were silent. The air was crystal clear. Morat breathed it in in a great gasp that made his chest ache. He lowered his arm.

There was only one attacker to be seen. He sprawled on the cold, rocky ground, silent, still, Morat's spear sticking from his back. The rest had been . . . illusion.

The High-Lord walked down the steep slope, the scree of pebbles under his feet making the only sound. He knelt at the side of the body. With an angry groan he pulled the spear from the middle of the dark stain spreading across the attacker's back and turned the body over. Young green eyes stared lifelessly from a face not many years older than Redd, his young cousin. The beard on his face, as fair as his almost white blond hair, was the short and soft beard of youth. The shoulders were broad, the arms strong; the man had stood as tall, perhaps, as High-Lord Morat himself, and without the help of illusion. But the frame was unfinished, the look of him still coltish. Not at all the burly seasoned warrior Morat had thought he'd seen menacing Redd when he cast the spear.

Morat tasted sadness, felt sick shame inside him. "Why?" he croaked.

He fingered the wooden amulet that hung about the young man's neck. A wizard's amulet: though not the fine-made sign of power of an advanced adept, it was intricately worked, inlaid with what must be runes of power. He shuddered, drawing back his fingers suddenly; the wood was warm. And its shape had penetrated his awareness. The crescent moon, thin and cruelly pointed, holding the round full moon in its arms. He made a protective rune-sign between himself and the amulet and looked around uneasily into the woods.

"The Mother." It was Amran-an who spoke beside him. His long, thin face looked gaunter than usual, the cheekbones showing under the skin. "How? How can we have come to the lands of . . . to Her forest?"

His voice was a hoarse whisper. His own portion of Deld, and the lands of Near and Far Renden, and the Wastes of Maia, climbing into the northern foothills, all lay between Runegladden's trees and the Mother-Mountains, realm of the goddess Mother-of-All. Ancient was her power, primordial; she had birthed even these most ancient of rocks on which they stood.

The High-Lord looked around. "Where are Tellit and the rest of the pages? And the hound-master? And the hounds?" He was suddenly anxious to disturb this forest as little more as possible.

*****

The baying of the hounds was turning away, the hunt moving upslope. Willow breathed again, easing the ache in her chest. Her heart's pounding abated, no longer stirred by the frightful belling of the dogs. Yet she cowered as still as she could, ignoring the tickle of pine boughs on the back of her neck. She bit her knuckles, trying to stifle back a sob.

Rowan! Where was Rowan? Oh, Mother-of-All, keep him safe!

How she ached to rise and go after him. She had her knife. Perhaps she could find a stout pole. She could help him if the interlopers attacked him; she had some little power herself. But he had told her to hide, and built an illusion around her, giving up some measure of his own self-protection to do so, and told her not to waste his work. He had sealed the gift with a kiss.

Rowan! She had argued with him, angry at his determination to deal with the interlopers.

"We can go back down the path, circle around them . . . reach help from other Woodwaynim in the settlement from which we've come."

She had pleaded, frustrated with his pride, so easily aroused, that surety in his newly trained powers that so often irritated her.

"No," he had insisted. "We can't let these intruders move unchallenged through our holy woods like this."

With an effort Willow turned her mind away from her betrothed. It had occurred to her to worry that these interlopers might be wizards, too, and able to follow the thought-scent of a name to its caller. She retreated inside the illusion, banking the fires of the stillness of her heart.

She startled. A tremor ran through her body. The hounds of the strangers had turned, were coming toward her! She stared unbelievingly out through the branches of the pines, seeing dimly through the needles how the hounds topped the crest of the hill. They stopped to sniff the air, the ground. She could see their spotted sides heaving. The men came up behind the dogs.

Fear squeezed her heart, urging her to leap up and run. Rabbit! she cursed at herself. Rabbit-heart! Rowan's protection would hold if she stayed still.

The dogs looked down into her covert; their noses dropped surely to the ground. They loosed a baying of triumph that climbed in pitch, spiraling unbearably in Willow's ears. One of the interlopers pointed straight at her, his finger an arrow that wounded her heart.

Astonishment, pain, grief took Willow, overwhelming her like a landslide. She felt them bruising her as if with down-tumbling rocks, chilling her as if cold snow slid down the mountains and buried her. They saw her! The illusion had failed!

She did not even try to move as they approached, hounds and men slipping down the steep slope toward where she cowered. She barely struggled when hands seized her roughly, haled her forth from among the pine boughs and rocks and away from the panting tongues and gleaming teeth of the snarling dogs. The illusion had failed!

Hallon, High-Lord Morat's hound-master, had his hands full

restraining the pack of hounds. The girl's fear was a scent in the air to them, a scent that drove them to wild, high-pitched howling. He swore at them; these strange woods they had strayed into had turned his pack half wild. He was too busy to pay much attention to Tellit.

Tellit had a streak of bully in him. He smelled the girl's fear as clearly as the dogs did. It made him smile and feel the desire to handle her roughly. And these days he was capable of being rough; in size and burliness he surpassed the growth of his age-mates of sixteen summers. As a small boy, he'd had the gentle temperament of his mother. But being the not-quite-acknowledged bastard son of Evmorat, the High-Lord's brother, Tellit had needed of late to prove himself capable of handling all kinds of taunts. It seemed, Hallon thought sadly, he had acquired a taste for blood in doing it.

And looking on the girl he had pulled forth out of the hiding-place at the foot of the cliff, Tellit found himself feeling a rough randyness. One hand tightened on the girl's arm. The other made a teasing reach for her breast. Now the girl struggled.

"Well, now, we seem to have found ourselves a proper kind of doe," Tellit jeered. He pushed the girl to the ground, commanding the other pages to help him hold her down. They backed off, protesting, but he swatted the nearest one, and they edged to do his bidding.

"Let her alone!" cried the hound-master, struggling as the hounds nearly dragged him off his feet. He beat at the dogs with the leashes. "Tellit, you fool! Do you want to wake whatever rules these woods? We'll never get free then!"

"Damn the boy," he cursed to himself. "Damn this forest! The boy's gone as crazy as the dogs." The wrongness in the air made him nearly giddy.

Tellit laughed.

The girl struggled silently, biting her lips, not even weeping, though the hound-master saw terrible grief on her face.

"Tellit, I will loose the hounds on you!" cried Hallon.

"Let the girl up."

At this new voice, Tellit froze. It was the voice of the High-Lord.

The youth, cowed, got up and helped the girl to her feet, but kept a firm grip on her arm. The pages hid behind Tellit, who put on a shamefaced, apologetic grin for his uncle. Morat frowned down at him. He knew full well how artful Tellit could be these days, how he could manage to appear the overgrown child when he willed it. He gritted his teeth on the notion that the child was only being his father's son. He climbed wearily down from his mount.

Tellit knew better, this time, than to say anything.

"Are you hurt?" Morat asked the girl.

She shook her head. "No," she whispered, in a strange-accented but understandable variant of Rune's tongue. "Not by him." She cast a withering glance at Tellit.

Morat turned to help the hound-master. "Tellit, Jor, the rest of you, help Hallon with the hounds. Let us rejoin the others. Quickly. I want no more splitting of our party while we are in these woods." He led them forward, drawing the girl along with him. They walked silently under the dark, old pines. The wind hummed a sad note in the tossing branches.

The sky was clouding over, the wind growing brisk, when they turned down into the cup of lowland that held the pool and the rest of their party. They had grown so careful of the silence, so careful to lay their feet softly so as not to disturb it, that the girl's shriek cut across their minds like the blow of a sword.

"Rowan!" she cried. She broke loose from Morat and ran down the slope to throw herself on the body of the man Morat had slain. At the sight of him all the wild grief that had seemed to sit like fever on her brow burst forth in wailing.

The forest stirred as if it heard her cries.

Redd went to her side, tried to draw her from the body; Lord Amran-an, too, tried to turn her aside gently; but she fought them, clawing at them. The High-Lord moved to stand before her.

"It was an accident!" he cried, suddenly overcome with a wildness of heart that rose to match hers. He tried to grab her shoulders, make her hear him. "We did not mean this harm—I didn't know—"

With a flash of motion, she drew a small knife from her blouse, dove at him with it. It was a strange-shaped blade, almost as broad as its short length, sickled, crescent-moon form to its cutting edge. It flashed in the glitter from the pool. Morat grabbed her arm, but not before the knife's edge slashed at his jaw, leaving a shallow but bloody cut. He forced her fingers open; the knife dropped from her hand, stuck in the soft earth.

Her voice rose shrilly; she spat words at him he didn't understand now. But the forest heard. It was a curse.

The pool rippled and exploded into spray as if its roots had suddenly tapped the hot core of the earth. Crescent-shaped ripples echoed from rim to rim until the rocks gave forth a high, singing note of vibration that Morat felt in his marrow. He gritted his teeth, tried to outshout her.

"It was an accident!" he shouted. "I did not want to kill him! He deceived me, with an illusion!"

The rocks trembled beneath their feet. The trees lashed their limbs, reaching scratchy-barked, sharp fingers at him. The wind keened uncanny echoes of the girl's high-voiced word-runes. Morat heard Amran-an chanting some wizard's words, but they seemed to be blowing away on the wind gusts with no effect. The light was seeping out of the sky.

Morat shook the girl, groaning with frustration and helplessness.

It was Tellit who silenced her. He stepped forth, shoved Redd aside, and drove the hilt of his hunting sword across the back of her head. She crumpled, and the pool, the rocks, the trees, the wind fell with her into silence.

*****

Morat sighed. A great weariness sat on his shoulders like the weight of the darkness, and he let his eyes lose their focus on the page who walked at his mount's head, leading the animal in silence, sharing with the animal the small circle of bobbing torchlight. He was glad his mount had regained its surefootedness. Ahead of Morat rode Heller Jade, also torch in hand, the great ax laid across his knees. Behind, he heard the hooves of the rest, the soft, plodding sound sucked quickly away into the still darkness. Slowly, steadily, they were making their way down out of nightmare. He hoped that dawn would come and bring the sight of home with it.

The High-Lord remembered how he had looked down at the still, crumpled form of the girl at his feet. He had, beyond all rationality except animal rage, raised his own arm to strike down Tellit.

But the boy had stood straight before him, his face for once clear of impudence. "I had to silence her," Tellit had said in a whisper. "I had to."

Morat sighed again, a deep sigh that stirred the girl resting against him. He looked down at the figure that he held before him on his saddle. She stirred in her sleep. A tear welled from beneath the long eyelashes and ran down her cheek. One of the braids of her hair, loosed from her woods-dress kerchief and bronze in the torchlight, lay across his hand that held the cornua's reins loosely. Her hands lay limp in her lap.

What else could he have done? He could not leave her injured and unconscious, to wake alone beside the dead body of her man. He could not leave her alone to the cold and the coming dark. She had not stirred while they worked in silence to build a cairn of stones over the slain man. And so he had taken her up, limp and unconscious, before him on his saddle. Ridden with her in his arms, down and out of the Mother-Mountains.

She had awakened, softly moaning the name of Rowan. Realizing where she was and who carried her, she had pulled stiffly to sit upright, letting as little of herself touch him as possible. For long hours after nightfall she had sat thus, in silence, flinching whenever the steepness of the path and the cornua's gait threw her against him.

He had felt only her tears dropping onto his hands.

Finally she had given way to weariness and fallen asleep, slumping against his chest, her head falling on his arm. That had made him feel better. He had drawn his cloak around them both, against the chill darkness.

Morat opened his eyes with a start. He had fallen asleep to the rocking of the cornua's gait. He looked around, seeing in surprise that the sky was graying slightly above the trees, and the trees themselves were taking on shape beyond the circle of the torchlight. Shapes, he realized, that he knew. The landmarks of his own familiar Runegladden woods.

He had not believed air could be so sweet, or dawn's light such a blessing.

CHAPTER 2

Willow woke slowly, the light of late morning warm on her face, coaxing her eyes open. It filtered through high, narrow windows, and the dust motes dancing in the shafts of light seemed for a moment to carry the impress of her pain-ridden dreams. Then the strangeness of the room intruded on her, and the real weight of grief constricted her throat with a sob.

She lay very still for a while, trying to get hold of the grief, staring around at the high ceilings and square corners. So strange, such wide, level expanses of floor. Her eyes were used to the bowers of Woodway. There the curving, enclosing wooden walls of her tree-home wrapped around one, the floor rambled over terraces, up and down, the eye constantly met artfully framed vistas, unexpected nooks sheltering a treasured object, blossoms and birds close above, echoing bridges beneath the feet ever up-stepping and down-stepping.

And it was so silent here! No wind-runes chiming in the breeze, no scent of green or tart odor of resiny wood, no whisper of leaves.

Willow shivered, drawing her chin under the coverlet, chilled by all the stone. There was a strange kind of beauty to the mosaics, she had to confess. The stone had intricate patterns, cut and pieced into interlocking chains and loops, almost like runes, patterns that teased her eyes. The large square flags of the stone-paved floor, the veined stone of the polished pillars—she had never seen stone so beautiful with its marbled veins and glittering flecks of color. She had never seen stone so beautifully worked, so polished to shine.

But there was so little wood! None at all except the carved chair, the chest by the wall, a paneled screen. What little wood there was, was also carved into patterns, burnished with handwork and age and inset with stone. All tamed and somehow unalive, so that it might as well have been stone. She shivered again, feeling diminished, powerless, lying cold under the weight of numbing loss, thinking that here they might even bury their dead in crypts of worked stone.

She started at the sound of footsteps sharp on the stone and clutched the coverlet tightly under her chin. But it was only a girl who appeared out of the shadows beyond the screen. Her arms were laden with clothes.

The girl dipped in a brisk curtsy and laid the clothes across the chair.

"Good morning, my Lady. 'Tis high morning; I hope you are well rested. I am Ranna, but they call me 'little frog,'" she chattered brightly in a speech heavily accented and fast, but Willow caught most of the words. "The High-Lord Morat sent me to wait upon you."

The girl saw Willow flinch at the mention of the High-Lord, saw the grief well into her eyes. She came to touch Willow's hand.

"It's all right, my Lady. No one will harm you here. See, I have brought you clothes to wear. I took your woods-clothing yesterday, and they are being washed. But I think you will find these more fitting for Highrune's halls."

She spread out the rich fabric of a gown across the coverlet for Willow to examine.

"Or this. They belonged to the Lady Lilliamne, the High-Lord's sister, but she has grown more . . . ah . . . matronly of figure since she went to be wife to the Lord of Provens. I will have to lengthen them a bit." She whirled, holding the dress against her so that the wide skirts swirled. "Ah! How long it has been since we had a pretty Lady to fuss over!" she exclaimed. Then she faltered into silence, fidgeting nervously before Willow's wide-eyed stare. The dress hung limp from her arm.

"My Lady?"

The serving maid looked so crestfallen. Willow swallowed her grief, letting it settle like an animal curling up to hibernate beneath her breastbone. She was a daughter of Woodway's highest Branch, had been betrothed to a green-wizard Prince; she had her pride. She smiled, as brightly as she could manage.

"The blue one . . . that one." She chose the least ornate one, dark blue, the Woodway color of mourning. She didn't think she could bear to wear the green. Not ever again.

Ranna smiled radiantly.

*****

The bath had warmed Willow, but the wide, open stone chambers had quickly made her feel chilled again. These rooms did not wrap themselves around her; the sunlight did not penetrate into the deep corners, nor carry the sweet scent of mountain pear blossoms and new leaves.

Ranna had noted her shiver and brought her a shawl to wrap around her shoulders. She sat now, on a small bench, with the combs in her lap, waiting to comb out Willow's wet hair.

But Willow walked restlessly through the suite of rooms, feeling awkward in the long blue dress, missing the loose, free clothing of Woodway, the split-skirt pants, the loose-belted long-blouse, the soft boots. Her hand closed over the pendant that hung on her breast, the carved wooden locket, Rowan's betrothal gift. Absently she fingered the luck-runes carved in its grain.

Hesitantly Willow approached the wood screens, looked beyond them. There stood high, heavy metal doors—closed. She turned, glanced questioningly at Ranna. The serving maid looked down at the combs in her lap, her neatly-pinned brown hair all that Willow could see.

"The High-Lord felt it best if you remain here in these rooms for a while, my Lady."

Willow's hands tightened.

"He meant it as a kindness, my Lady. Highrune is large and confusing. And the court is very much stirred up. We were all so anxious when the hunt party didn't return. A whole twelve-day they were gone!" she exclaimed. "Though they say it only seemed like one day and a night to them."

The serving maid looked up, then down at the combs again. "We were frightened to see them ride out of the dawn mist. They looked like ghosts. They rode right out of the easiest way of Runegladden, which the Runeguards and the Foresters had searched every which way.

"Since then, the High-Lord and Lord Amran-an and the rest have been closeted, talking of it. And though they have told very little of what happened to them, there has been nothing else whispered of, in high folks' chambers or servants' tunnels."

She added softly, "They would all be over-curious, I fear, to see the Lady the High-Lord brought home under his cloak."

Willow read the runes of the girl's message beneath the light-spoken words. So he meant kindness, did he, the man who had brought her here to these stone halls. She supposed she should feel gratitude. He at least understood that she grieved; if he had given her a large and well-feathered nest, he meant it to be a haven rather than a prison.

But gratitude was brief, grief and anger more enduring. "The

Lady he brought home under his cloak," she thought to herself, "Yes, that's what I suppose I'd be, to such a murderer. A prize of the hunt, only somewhat better than a hart or a horn-doe."

With an angry abruptness Willow paced the room, up and down, then suddenly she went to the window. She put her hands on the sun-warmed stone sill and leaned out. The sill was wide, too wide for her to see the base of the wall or much of the courtyard below. The window was high. Close below her she could see the walls of the court, and the city beyond them, a maze of streets and houses that spread out like a quilted coverlet. Willow could see the ordered pattern of the streets of the city, its gridwork of streets embraced by a new high wall; closer in, the remnants of older fortifications encircled an only slightly less orderly old quarter. The clean rectangles of its array, the straight avenues radiating out from some center that lay below her window, the gradual heightening of the buildings closer to Runehall's domineering towers, all were an unreadable rune to her sight.

Her eyes sought the distance. Beyond the city's ring of walls, she could see out over the land of Rune. Fields spread like striped, brown cloth over gentle hills; in some the new green already ran its rows across the brown. Great dark cloud shadows grazed over the meadows, chevvied by the spring winds. A wide river wound a lazy course into the mist of distance, sparkling in the sun; squat, square barges rode it, towed upstream by oxen on the banks.

"No mountains," she whispered, half to herself.

"This faces east," Ranna said softly at her elbow. "The Mother's Mountains lie to the north."

Willow sat down on the window bench, feeling the cold of the stone seat. She longed to lay her head on the sill and weep out her grief for Rowan. Would she ever forget his body lying cold among the crushed bloodroot flowers, his pale hair stained with their blood and his? His green eyes staring with his death?

But she couldn't weep in front of the serving maid. She couldn't weep in this flat-floored, sharp-cornered, stone-walled, echoing chamber that was the unwanted kindness of Rowan's murderer. Some strange shred of pride kept her stiff-backed, her hands folded in her lap, sobs choked back behind tight lips. She would act like the Mother-born Woodwaynim she was, scion of one of the highest Branches, destined to be Xyl, the bride and widow of Rowan Green-Wizard, and not a waif of the woods brought home under his murderer's cloak.

*****

Ranna was combing out Willow's hair.

It was thus that Morat saw her, entering through the door from his own adjacent chambers. He was still preoccupied by the questions they had tossed fruitlessly among themselves in the council. Whose had been the trickery—or more seriously intended act of sabotage—that set them astray from Runegladden to the Motherwoods? How had it been done? And why? Who had the power along with the intent? Even Amran didn't carry that kind of sway over space and time.

Why had they been attacked in the woods? When they hadn't intentionally done anything to menace? What would be the consequences of killing the Woodwaynim man? He was, after all, a wizard of some kind and obviously highborn.

And why was Tellit becoming such a problem right now? Why had the boy's father Evmorat gone off wandering again, and where? Why did Morat's suspicions rest on his brother? When, Morat thought wryly, had mischief *not* had Evmorat mixed in it? Why did Evmorat always have to meddle with things he ought not? Contrive to appear so guilty if he was innocent?

Morat stopped. He stood for a long time, staring at Willow. The soft yellow of her hair beneath Ranna's combs reminded him of the gold of pollen dusted on the surface of a still pond where the spring willows overhung. It was a fine cloud on her graceful neck and shoulders, hung past her rounded bosom to her slender waist, covered her hands in her lap.

He saw the straightness, the supple dignity in her, enhanced by the simple lines of the blue dress. He watched the fine, lovely stillness of her face, pale and unutterably sad profile, haloed by the sun-brightened mist of her hair. Helplessly he watched the strokes of Ranna combing, over and over, from crown of head to fine, wisping ends.

And then she felt him there, the woman he had mistakenly thought was a rough girl of the woods. She turned to stare back at him with eyes the green of new leaves, the green of the eyes of a dead young Woodwaynim wizard.

*****

"You have closeted yourself in here for most of a week, my friend," said Morat, "and you look it!"

He smiled as Amran-an ran his fingers through disheveled hair. The wizard rubbed his eyes, drew long fingers down his face, feeling the stubble that roughened his cheeks. Amran-an smiled back.

"I guess I didn't feel the time passing. But I felt something here in this library when we came here before. It wasn't clear, with everyone stirring the air of the place, carrying their foment in here from the outer council chamber, looking for books that would explain what happened."

"But with quiet," asked Morat, pulling out a chair, dumping the books on it onto the floor, and sitting down across from the wizard, "did the room speak to you?"

"Aye, it did. I felt Evmorat's trace. In these rooms. He was here. And I felt his trace on some of the books. Fingerprints, though not the kind your Head Guard could see with his tools of investigation, not like those of a regular thief."

Morat sat quiet and patient. He was familiar with how hard it was for Amran-an to describe how his wizard senses worked.

"It's like I can see a small bit of color on things. Sometimes, if it is really quiet, I hear a sound, a word or two that was spoken." He paused, steepled his fingers before his face.

"I think Evmorat wanted at first just to do some small mischief. He was bored after a long, quiet winter, I imagine. He started poking around the books, thinking he'd try a spell or two." Amran-an smiled. "I sense him whistling as he poked around, that little tune he used to sing to annoy you and Ellienne. But he got adventurous and dug a bit deeper into the stuff stored here."

He gestured at the maze of shelves and chests. "When is the last time you spent any time back there in the old rooms? Really poked around the really old stuff? Not recently, if ever. I didn't think so," he smiled at Morat's shake of his head. "Well, we know Evmorat's ability to get into trouble. And there were some things here no one has looked at in Rune knows how many generations."

He paused, then laid a hand on Morat's arm, and the High-Lord could feel a tremor in his friend's fingers.

"I don't know exactly what Evmorat found, not yet. I need to keep looking. I *will* keep looking. I think it's important that we find out. Because I sense more moiling in the dust and agedness of this place than I can get a clear picture of, not yet. And I am afraid of it."

*****

Morat stood when Ranna slid the glass door aside and drew Willow into the garden. It was a space flooded with sunlight and exotic flowery scents that teased at Willow's nose, making her breathe the humid air deeply into herself. She closed her eyes briefly, comforted by the tangible greenness that filled the place.

Morat came forward and took her hand. "I thought you might like this place. It's a green-garden, glassed in to keep out the seasons. My mother had it built for the plants that come from the far southern boundaries of Rune that she loved. This," he pointed to the tree that grew in the center of the place, its branches just touching the glass roof, "was her favorite. It's called the Sensitive Tree." He reached out and brushed one of the feathery fronds with his fingertips, and it drew away quickly, curling tightly into itself.

Willow let herself be drawn to the little table set beneath the Sensitive Tree, laid with a brilliantly embroidered cloth and dishes touched with gold. She sat in the chair that Morat pulled out for her. She looked around at the plants, keeping her eyes from the man that sat himself across from her. A lump of grief sat stony in her breast, and she felt as if she curled as tightly around it into herself as the disturbed frond of the Sensitive Tree.

Smaller plants hung from the Sensitive Tree, reminding her of the wish-runes that her Woodwaynim folk hung in their home-trees. Sprays of flowers hung from them, of riotous hues and shapes like butterflies and other insects.

"They're orchids," Morat told her, "brought up from the rain forests near the Kai-Haluu coast. They're why it must be kept so humid in here."

Willow looked down at the paving, glad to see how small plants had disrupted the straight seams between the stones and moss obscured the runes inlaid there.

Morat took the lid off one of the plates, and gestured, offering her the fruits and sweetcakes it held. He poured a golden liquid into the glasses.

"It's juice of a fruit from the South, not wine, I hoped that would be fitting for the morning."

His smile was cautious, small, when she looked up at his face. She took one of the cakes, took a small bite, then put the rest on the dish in front of her.

"Has Ranna brought you everything you need? Is there anything else that I may provide for you? Clothing that is suitable? My sisters have gone to live with their husbands in other Portions, but I remember they liked books . . . embroidery . . ."

"I'd like to have my Woodwaynim clothing back, and be taken back to the Mother's Woods," Willow answered softly, trying not to be hostile, trying not to let begging creep into her voice.

Morat looked down, fingering a peach on his plate, then back at her, a hint of the greenness of the place touching his dark eyes. "I cannot get you back to the Woods . . . to your home . . . not now," he said gently. "The distance is very great; Deld Portion and the Wastes of Maia lie between Rune and those mountains."

"But we came here in one night," she whispered, questioning.

"There was magic . . . some trick . . . and well filled with harm were the runes that made it happen," his voice was a growl. "We don't know how it was done. We are studying . . . but are still in the dark. I have some fear that the force that overtook us might somehow harm you."

I have already been harmed beyond reckoning, Willow thought to herself, but she bit back the words. She touched briefly the medallion, the token of her betrothed, that lay on her breast beneath the blue cloth of the Runerin dress.

"I am sorry. Sorry for all of it, beyond words," Morat took her hand in his, across the small table. "There are not words I can find, no runes in my heart or on my tongue, that can possibly say enough how sorry I am."

"The distance is not impossible," she said.

"No, but there is turmoil in the lands, perhaps left over from the magic of that day, perhaps stirred up by new runes. There is sickness in Rune itself, problems with the spring planting. Rumors of blight in Deld. I cannot take you abroad now and cannot trust the task to anyone else who is not already taken up with problems. Please try to understand. For safety I'd have you stay here, in Highrune, for now.

"Now, what else can I provide to make your stay more comfortable?"

CHAPTER 3

Springtime was a busy time in Rune, and this particular spring season seemed to be taking its cue from the mishap of that winter's end hunt and was birthing a strange array of oddnesses and troubles along with the lambs and the new calves. These weirdnesses and bothersome events gave the inhabitants of the court something to talk about beside the quiet Woodwaynim woman. And since Willow was at last growing restless, Ranna bullied the High-Lord into giving leave for Willow to leave her quarters, though he still set the limit that she remain within Highrune Hall's walls.

"The faces all have a touch of Lord Morat in them," Willow gestured at the portraits that lined the long hallway, life-size in ornate rune-marked frames.

"Yes, even there, in that one there," giggled Ranna, pointing at a rotund lady seated, in her portrait, on a gilded chair, with a small dog in her lap, long hair over its eyes. "See the nose and the hairline? Is that not like my Lord?"

"Do you mean the lady? Or the dog?" teased Willow.

"The Lady Marjala would be insulted," cried Ranna, "probably fussing in her crypt. Legend has it that the Lord Morat's great-great-grand aunt ruled these halls with very firm hand. The kitchen staff still tell stories of her refined palate, not to mention the fussy tastes of her seven daughters. It's a phrase they use, 'Oh, that'd *almost* be good enough for the Madame Marjala and her daughters,' when someone spoils a soup or burns a roast."

Willow turned to the serving maid. "Why, then, if the halls of Highrune were so full of people in these by-gone eras, are they so thinly populated now?"

"Well," said Ranna thoughtfully, "I hadn't thought about it. There are as many of us keeping the household as there always were, it seems. But the Lord's sisters Liliamne and Saralinne have married and gone to live in their husbands' Portions. Both of them are expecting children; Lady Sara already has a son. We hear she hopes for a daughter."

"You hear?"

"Well, word travels between the household servants along with the wagons of produce and the travelling merchants' wares as well as by letters among the high folk, you know," the girl said pertly.

"In Woodway everyone knows everything there is to know; if you don't hear it from the mouths of your friends or relatives themselves, the windrunes we hang in the trees pass messages in the tones they sound. We hang runes we construct everywhere . . . they're sometimes flags, sometimes bunches of flowers, sometimes wreaths and decorations we hang on our doors, sometimes more elaborate constructions for public places and great events. Tie a bunch of grass and flowers on a girl's door-tree, and it tells her you like her and want to walk with her. Leave a pot of herbs at a doorstep, you tell someone you are sorry their arthritis is paining them. They all give out messages, depending on the kind of blossom or leaf that is woven in. But we live close, and if we need to send word over a distance, we have the birds carry the message."

"That would be nice," sighed Ranna. "The birds. My sister has gone with the Lady Liliamne to Provens Portion, and I miss her; my mother gets word from her so infrequently."

Willow touched the medallion at her breast gently, remembering the bunch of spring beauties, tiny, fragile early flowers, wrapped with a rowan twig in spring wine vine, that Rowan had tied on her door on the day he invited her to walk with him.

"And I'd like to tie a message rune on the door of a certain gardener's son," smiled Ranna. "I'm too shy to talk to him, a bunch of sprouting seedlings would be so much easier."

"Maybe I could ask for some new plants for the Glass Garden, and I could send you to him to pick them out."

"Oh, I would be tongue-tied! You'd have to write a note! Well, enough of that," she smiled ruefully. "Let's see. The High-Lord has cousins and cross-cousins. Redd is his favorite, who has come to be his page. Others live in the page's quarters, supervised by Hallon the hound-master and being trained in the use of weapons. Master Jade does that when he is here, or some of the Runeguards. A few female cousins attend one or other of the schools in Highrune, to learn their letters and artsy things. The rest live in the Portions, though they will all gather in for the holidays."

"This painting here, who is it?"

"Lord Morat's father, the High-Lord Reyno. And his Lady Wife Mariela the Kind. They were much loved, and Rune prospered under their reign. We had such fine festivals, even us servants had fine food to eat at the harvest festival, my mother tells me, the fields and folds were so overflowing in their time. Mam worked the fine tapestries then, in their workshops. They died within a brace of days of each other, the Lord of a disease that came on him and ate at him over far too long, and his Lady of grief. The Lord Morat was a young one to be High-Lord, but he put on the circle crown and took Rune Kingdom in hand strongly and wisely." Willow heard the respect and devotion in Ranna's voice.

"And Lord Morat has a brother?"

Ranna shivered. "The Lord Evmorat is his twin, though they are alike in face only, not in their hearts." She caught herself, "I am just a servant, I say no more. Come, I'll show you more lively corners of Highrune," she said briskly, and drew Willow away.

Today Ranna was showing off the Great Hall of Highrune. They paused at the entrance to Highrune's audience chamber, while Ranna gave Willow the stories behind a few of the many ornate carvings up the walls and across the overarching entrance. Large banners hung from the high ceiling inside the entrance, and Ranna pointed out the signs for each Portion.

"The one with the cloud and lightning, that's the banner of Deld Portion. The Lord Amran-an holds it; Deld's had a long line of wizards ruling it over the ages. That one with the triangle and the sword and axe, that's for High Havenn. The triangle stands for the mountains, where they dig metal ores to make the finest metalwork and weapons. The Lady Lithen-al-Thenda rules there; they say she's a smith herself, brawny from working metal, not at all the delicate lady her name sounds like. But the Lord Morat's sisters had some very wonderfully worked jewelry from Havenn."

Ranna drew Willow along the row of banners. "That one, with the orchid chain across it and the seashell, that's for Kai Haluu, it's the furthest coastal portion and includes some offshore islands. It's tropical, with rain forest; that's where Lord Morat's mother got the plants to fill the Glass Garden. Master Heller Jade rules it, though some of the servants say he's more of a sea pirate than a land lord, but then, that's the way of a land that is made up of islands and mostly deals with ships and cargoes and such, I'd think."

The little maid blushed under the look Willow gave her, but continued her chattering. "The banner with the sheaf of wheat and the olive branch and the grapevine, that's Provens Portion . . . lots of large farms and orchards and vineyards. Lord Morat's sister Liliamne lives there with her husband Lord Jerral. Of course, the best wine comes from there, and they send it often, so we get news most often from there. And Lord Morat's other sister wed the Lord of Fabria, they live in a castle with towers like the two towers on their flag. It's mountains, too, where they power great mills where paper and cloth are made, with the waterfalls that tumble down toward the coast. They dig the many kinds of stone we use from large quarries. The next one, with the thistle on it, that's the flag of Lancia. It's known for its harsh weather, but the best wool comes from there. The last Portion is Yan-tsse in the far east, the land of jade and dragons; it's got the dragon and three stones on its banner. The legend is the three stones are the jade hearts of three dragons that lived there long ago, giving the first men fire."

Ranna curtsied, proud of her store of knowledge, and Willow smiled at her.

There was a lot of noise inside the high-arched chamber of the Great Hall, now that Ranna and Willow stood further inside . . . contentious voices and calm, calls of messengers for Master Merchant So-and-so and calls for scribes and tally-keepers echoing back and forth from stone wall to stone wall, from high coign to polished stone floor. But toward the other end of the hall, where Morat sat, it was quieter. Ranna led Willow around the outside of the room to where they could see and hear better.

"This is a special spot," Ranna told Willow softly. "Not too many of the high folk know about it, but the serving folk use it to keep an ear to the High-Lord's needs. If you stand exactly here," she showed Willow a stone slightly darker gray than the others, a slight bit off from the perfect pattern of the ornate tiles paving the great hall, "you can hear even the lowest whisper from the Lord's seat. It's a trick of the architecture."

Morat sat on the slightly raised dais that had been the center of the Great Hall for dozens of generations. The chair on which he sat, oversized and ornate, had obviously been meant as a throne, but he had thrown his cloak casually over the arm of it and leaned forward in total concentration on those who had come before him. Amran-an sat on one side of him, on a bench brought there for the occasion, not part of the original regal setting. And Redd and several other pages stood at Morat's side. A pair of scribes sat cross-legged at the High-Lord's feet, to record the official doings.

The dispute before the High-Lord at this moment might have seemed trivial to any observer, but Morat was treating it with his entire seriousness; the two cousins had come halfway across Rune to bring their case before him. Willow found their accent hard to understand, despite the clarity with which their words came to her, almost as if rising out of the imperfect stone in the floor.

"Every year 'a scants me ma half o' the harvest," the one man pointed to the other. "Ahr fathers lef' the land ta us jointly, ta kaip t' family and t' holdings together. But every year 'a makes the dividin'. A' is older, so 'a insists it be 'is duty. But every year for t' five years since ahr fathers died 'a scants my half."

The speaker was obviously younger than his cousin, but he was earnest and had his dignity, and did not whine.

"'A be jealous that I manages ma half more wisely," countered the cousin. "I feel 'tis ma right as t' older to make the division; even if 't didn't state so in the will of ahr fathers, I was left the exec'tor of t' wills because I was t' older."

"I suggested we take turns making the dividin'," the younger cousin said, "but 'a refused."

"'A insulted my honesty. Tha insult has led to a quarrel between ahr two households, and na one will speak t' another. I made the division as fairly as I knew how."

"But 'a refused t' allow a third party t' measure the lots," countered the first cousin. "How could I prove 't if I couldna measure both portions for myself?"

Morat waved them silent. He sat thinking, apparently giving the matter a great weight of consideration.

Ranna whispered to Willow, “It’s a small case; not the kind of matter usually to be brought all the way to Highrune. The Lords of each Portion hold courts, and usually these kinds of problems are handled there. But High-Lord Morat has never turned a petitioner away. Still, it’s difficult for him. Any evidence he might examine lies far away. And both cousins seem honest.”

Morat sat back, hands on the carved arms of the throne-like seat. The cousins straightened before him to receive his verdict.

“Highrune speaks. It shall be thus. You two will take turns making the division of the harvest, the younger of you this year, the older one next, and so on thereafter. However, whichever one of you does *not* make the division shall have the right to select first which half he will take. Doth Highrune give thee satisfaction?” he added the traditional formal conclusion to the verdict.

The cousins were thinking fast. Then both smiled. They bowed deeply before Morat. “We thank Highrune f’ hearin’ us,” they answered. “We be satisfied in th’ High-Lord’s wisdom,” they gave the traditional response, as Morat motioned the scribe to write down his verdict, signed his rune to the parchment, and gave it to them. And they walked out together, talking happily with each other.

A smile crossed Morat’s lips, then he regained his seriousness.

Ranna nudged Willow. “He’s good, our High-Lord. The answer is what every nursemaid knows to use with two squabbling children and one jelly cake. But he gave it to them with dignity and honored them, even though they were backward folk from a far Portion.”

The next person in line was moving forward to present himself to the High-Lord.

"Sire, I am a messenger sent from Lithen-al-Thenda, Lady of the High Havenn Portion. My Lady bids me greet you with the High-Lord's due respect and a dear friend's affection, and to show you this." He unwrapped a heavy bundle and laid a piece of metal, apparently a piece of a plow, in Redd's hands, to be carried up to Morat. "My Lady bids me show you the strange blight that has appeared on this metal."

And indeed, the surface of the metal was pocked and discolored. When Morat handed it to Amran-an to examine, greenish flakes came off on his hands.

"My High-Lord, this plow was made only last season, and should have lasted a decade."

Amran-an looked up sharply and frowned. He rubbed his long fingers across the pitted surface, murmuring a few runes even the special acoustics of the place failed to carry to Willow and Ranna.

"Has this blight affected other articles?" Morat asked, leaning forward.

"Aye, my Lord. All metals except gold and silver seem to be affected. Shoes fall off the cornua's hoof; swords have crumbled that were in households for generations without tarnishing. Doors fall from deteriorating hinges. The articles were all made with the finest ores; as you know well, we in High Havenn are in the foothills of the mountains from which the best ores and first-smelted metals come. Our metalwork is famous, the best in all Rune."

"Morat, may I question—"

"Of course, Am."

The wizard stepped down to the messenger. "The blight is not limited, then, to articles that are used to till the earth, that come in contact with the soil?"

“No, Sire.” The messenger was clearly in awe of High-Lord Morat’s wizard. Even having stepped down from the dais, Amran towered over the man. “My Lady Lithen bid me tell you it affects articles which have never touched earth.”

“Have protective runes been tried?”

“As you know, the Lady is somewhat adept herself, and has a Wise One and several very experienced metallurgists in her employ. The blight has affected articles which had simpler protective runes inlaid in them in an attempt to protect them. But not articles having runes of higher complexity or articles having runes inlaid at their smithing rather than afterward.”

“Is the blight widespread?”

“No, it has appeared only recently and in only a few small areas . . . here and there across the Portion.”

“Not apparently from one single source, then . . .”

Willow watched Morat watch Amran-an question the messenger, and something chilled her heart, something in the idea of metal being blighted. She had little sympathy for the runes of metal, being Woodwaynim; her heart ran to those of wood. But still, she felt fear at anything that blighted.

Eventually Amran-an had satisfied himself that he had asked all the questions in his mind. He took possession of the blighted metal sample, wrapping it up again and speaking seals over it while Morat called the scribe to him and composed a brief message to be carried back to the Lady Lithen.

And then another person stepped forward to take his turn. His clothing and his features were strange to Willow, and she asked Ranna about him. “His skin is so golden. His face seems so wide and flat, and his eyes are different. I have never seen his like before.”

“He is Yan-tssian,” whispered Ranna. “It’s said they ride

dragons in his Portion and dine on fire and green jadestone." Willow looked askance at Ranna, and the serving maid shrugged her shoulders and let a look of credulous simplicity show on her face, but there was a twinkle in her eye.

"Sire, I am here to report that the powder sample you provided for trial in Yan-tsse was successful," he spoke in an accent even stranger than the two farmers. "It succeeded in eliminating the sample of winged locusts that was plaguing the red rice fields, and our field-elders believe it will stop the infestation sweeping in from the hills."

Morat was clearly pleased. "Well, at least one problem may have a solution. Am, can larger quantities of the powder be manufactured quickly enough to meet the emergency?"

The discussion proceeded to logistics of timely manufacture, emergency transportation by pack animals, and so forth.

Willow yawned, lulled by the buzzing of the voices at the far end of the hall. She and Ranna took refuge on a bench near enough to the special focal point to hear a few of the words of the High-Lord's interviews, though by now their interest was waning. Willow wondered aloud how Morat could manage to keep his interest in so many detailed matters, not at all the kind of thing she imagined a High-Lord spending his day dealing with, while Ranna pulled a cloth from a pocket in her voluminous skirts and unwrapped some small cakes to share with her. Their attention was drawn to a small uproar at the entrance to the hall, where a bundle of goods in dispute had fallen and broken open, revealing contraband bags of spices spilling from the folds of plain muslin cloth.

Now it was Hallon the hound-master that stepped up to stand before Morat. A large brindle hound stood at each side of him, and his hand rested on the head of one. Morat stood up and stepped down off the dais to his level.

"Old friend, what brings you here in so formal a manner? You don't have to wait for council to bring a problem before me."

The man seemed embarrassed. "High-Lord," he persisted in his formality, "The problem I bring before you is difficult to broach. I felt—" He stopped, swallowed hard.

"Hallon, there is nothing I will not hear from you. As High-Lord or as friend."

"It's Tellit. The problem is Tellit."

Morat stiffened for an almost imperceptible instant. Then he took Hallon's arm. "Come, it's been a long session, and I'm thirsty. Let's go and sit and talk this one out over a cup of wine." And he led the hound-master to the side of the great hall, where he bid a servant bring the wine.

"Now tell me."

"Until recently he's been a good boy. Seemed to have the sweet nature of his mother—I mean—"

"Go on."

"But something's gotten into him. Now he's grown almost to full size, he's not just a boy. He's been bullying the other pages, been involved in some incidents of not so minor mischief—and I fear he may be instigator, not just tag-along."

"I take it there's something specific."

"Oh, aye. A bit of a fuss with a girl . . . a meeting in the woods . . . She was na so willing when it looked to be more than Tellit who was waiting for her."

Morat lifted the High-Lord's circlet from his brow and ran his fingers through his hair, as if trying to free some frustrating tangle from it. He sighed.

"Her family accepted some recompense . . . as a bridal gift . . .

and she accepted one of the young stable grooms for a husband. So it's settled more or less to everyone's satisfaction, though the girl obviously had her sights set on a higher target in the High-Lord's nephew, even if he is a bastard. But . . ."

"But . . .?"

"Morat—Sire—the boy isna manageable. He's gotten wild. The hounds cringe around him, and the cornuas shy . . . it's as if he's got a smell on him of something not exactly evil, but it's more than just mischief."

"You want him taken away from the pages." It wasn't a question.

"I canna keep him with the other boys, not all the time. I've got ma hands full," he held his hands up apologetically, "with the straying hounds. I canna manage straying boys as weel."

"Send him to me. I'll see if Redd can take up some of Tellit's training. I'll keep him closer to myself." Morat patted the hound-master's shoulder, to let him understand he had done well enough with the burdensome problem. "I thank you for what you have done."

As the hound master bowed briefly and turned away, followed at his heels with precision by the two large hounds, Morat sighed and looked into his winecup.

"Where is Evmorat?" he asked, to no one in particular. "Where in the wasted hells is he?" He looked up and saw Willow and Ranna walking out of the High Hall into the sunlight, and he smiled. Then he went back to the dais, and the throne, and the petitioners.

"Morat, I am worried."

"Why, Am?" Morat threw his cloak over his shoulder and started walking down the steps from the dais. Hours had passed, and uncounted petitions had been dealt with, and Morat was tired and hungry. Amran-an followed closely, talking quietly so the people remaining in the hall would not hear.

"It's as obvious to you, I think, as it is to me that we have more than the usual number of problems coming before us. And the nature of them has me deeply concerned, too. These are not all people problems, to be solved only with a good knowledge of the law and understanding and firmness. These are problems with the earth, the plants, the animals, the sky."

The wizard stopped walking. The pair stood in the doorway of the great chamber, and the sounds of the courtyard, cornua's shod hoofs on cobbles, the calls of squires and grooms and other outside sounds, mingled with the hall's inside sounds of commerce, as if all the business of Rune hung on the threshold.

"They are little problems, no one overwhelming in its consequences. But what of all of them at once? And now the sickness that has started up among the people . . . the work will not get done if many more fall ill. At least no one has died," he said, making a warding rune sign with his fingers, "yet."

"Old friend, I hear in your voice there is something more you have to tell me."

"Morat, you know I have gone back and taken a closer look at the library," Amran-an said. "Alone, in the quiet of the night, and during this last dark-of-moon. You know some forms of my wizardry are stronger then. My doppelgänger came to me in a dream, three nights in a row, and told me where to check again. And I fasted and performed deep meditations."

Morat adjusted the pin that held his cloak. "And . . ."

The wizard raised his long fingers in front of his face. "I used the Touch. It took time, and concentration in the deep quiet of most of a night, to let the deeper Touch take hold. I let myself run fingertips over the books I suspected. I looked more thoroughly. There *was* a book out of place. A small one, but a dangerous one." He paused.

"I have a feeling I won't like this."

"Not at all, no, you won't. It was a book from Deld. From *Deld*, of all places. A book I didn't know had been taken astray from my Portion. One I thought had been buried long ago where it could do no harm. A book of Deld, of course, to take us haring off in that direction, to the far side of Deld and then some."

"And did the Touch tell you for certain Evmorat had used it?"

Amran-an grimaced. "Ay! It verified it was Evmorat who had handled that book."

"Of course it was," Morat said, swearing.

"But I suspect he found himself in way over his head," the Wizard said. "I think he thought to try a small trick . . . but it went far beyond his intent. That's why he's gone wandering, I would think, away from you and your anger."

"And now we've got a Woodwaynim dead, and another far from home here in Rune."

"And perhaps something worse. Something in the land-runes themselves is shifting. Sometimes they appear to me, like lines of force, like the lines of a magnetic field . . . and they are not where they have always been . . . it is different, in a way I wish I had words to explain. The wizard who wrote that Book of Shaping—the wizard Maara-ap-nan—called the Great Shaper, Seeker of Perfection—was one of the most powerful that ever ruled in Deld. And one of the most ambiguous."

"How so? I don't think I've heard of him."

"His balance of good and evil . . . It did not hold steady. He is not one we are proud of; we do not speak of him, especially outside of our Portion.

"As his story begins, he was poor, a woodsman who eked out

a living gathering ice from the frozen lakes in winter, and wood for the builders of cottages in the summer. As good wood became more and more scarce, he went deeper into the forest, until he came to the place where it met the edge of the Wastes of Maia. And there he found a tree unlike any he had ever seen before. It amazed him, having both flowers and fruit on it at the same time, and the flowers perfumed the air with sweetness, and when he tasted the fruit, it sang on his tongue. And between the scent and the taste his mind was opened, and he saw ways to do magic.

"Some say that was how wizardry first came into the folk of Deld.

"At first he did small things, the kind of things expected of someone who was poor . . . conjuring gold coins and gems with which to buy comforts. But as he experienced the admiration of the townspeople, he became enamored of finery. He built a house, then a larger one, then a castle, striving always for greater perfection. He conjured fine coaches and horses. And, initially, he was generous, sharing with those less fortunate. The best discovery came when he found he could teach the making of magic to others, at first by giving them to eat from the fruit of the tree, but in time out of his own power. He started schools in which he could teach some of the wizardry for the benefit of all.

"He went back again and again to the tree, though he kept its existence, at the far side of the Deld forest, a secret. And he noticed that as he created more and more good things, and shared the gifts it gave him, the tree flourished. It grew taller, and its flowers gave forth even more splendid perfume, and its fruits became golden.

"And then he fell in love. The object of his love was a young woman who came to study in his school. She wasn't particularly beautiful; in fact, she walked with a limp, having a twisted foot. And she was dark and not shining like the other women who were drawn to him. But her mind was keen, and she challenged him. Together they began to create deeper wonders, exploring the nature of nature itself . . . finding out the chemicals of which the world was made, finding out the way of the forces which bound objects to one another, even to the motions of the planets.

"Eventually they married. And had a child. A son.

"The child, like his mother, was born with a twisted foot. Now that had not bothered Maara in his wife, as it was only a part of the composite that he loved. But it bothered him deeply that his child, the child of such a great wizard, should not be perfect. And he undertook to find a way to fix the deformity.

"He took the child into the forest, to the far side by the Wastes of Maia, to the tree. And he took the fruit of the tree, and the flowers, and he made magic upon them, and created salves and chemicals he deemed would be therapeutic. For days and days he worked, beneath the branches of the tree. He tried several salves on the child's foot, but it was not mended. He gave the child potions to drink, but the foot did not heal. Maara did not notice that the tree suffered damage from the fumes of his fires, and shrank its branches from his incantations, as they became more perverse.

"He did not see how he was trying to change something innate, essential, natural in its way, in the child. He lost sight of his love.

"Finally, he had a potion he was certain would heal the child. The poor child shrank from its odor, and clung to the trunk of the tree, crying, "Father, why do you not love me as I am? I am what I am . . . I cannot be changed." And the tree bent its branches down, trying to protect the young creature.

"Maara insisted, forced his son to drink. "Ah, it burns," cried the child, as he fell to the foot of the tree, clinging to its roots. In a flare of light, the child's foot turned straight. The child was perfect, now, to Maara. But the child sighed and gave up its breath to mingle with the scent of the flowers and died."

"Amran-an, that is one of the saddest and most terrible stories you have ever told me," cried Morat. "Is this Maara an ancestor, then, of yours?"

"Not direct. But he is said to be the source of our Deld wizardry."

"What happened to him?"

"It's uncertain. It's said that in his grief over his child he turned away from shaping to unshaping. He did write that cursed book that Evmorat found, astray in your library in Highrune, and much of it is focused more on unshaping than shaping. That's not always an evil thing, you know; the book's scope is beyond simple classifications like good or evil. Sometimes there's a need for unshaping, so that reshaping can happen.

"Some say he lives still, wandering, that the tree that had given him so many gifts died with his child and he looks endlessly for another. Other stories say he lives on the edge of the Wastes of Maia, hidden in a secret landscape, cutting ice from the lakes that are always frozen there.

"In any case, whether it's the spirit of Maara or no, I think Evmorat, in his meddling, raised out of sleep something buried so deep beneath the heart of Deld, and thus of all Rune . . . something so old . . . that we can't even imagine it."

"Ah huy," sighed Morat. Of course it would be that particular kind of mixed thing that Evmorat's impulses would discover. Ever ambiguous, ever setting aside the obvious rightness of things, those were the runes of the nature of his twin.

"Yes. And since it's in Evmorat's nature to be devious and

meddlesome, and since this thing answered to his presence, I've got very deep misgivings about it. I fear whatever unshaping impulses he has allowed to emerge again into our world for us to deal with. I don't think a misdirected first hunt of spring is the last thing we will see go awry.

"I have taken possession of the book Evmorat tampered with. I promise to put it safe again in Deld. And to watch it as best I can.

"But there's more," Amran-an hesitated. He put his hands out, fingers splayed, for Morat to see, as if there were something the High-Lord might perceive there like stains, though there were none.

"Morat, my dreams have changed, in a way that makes me afraid. I used to get such clear images, sometimes, that helped me, as if the wizardry could come to me better in my dreams. But the Good Shadower, my spirit mirror image, seems lost. The spirits of the elements, the magic objects, the paths I found up dream mountains, the boats that came and took me to my well-springs . . . all these images come no more. Or worse, come in perverse form, corrupted and corrupting, so that I am afraid to use what they teach me. Morat, this unshaping thing is, I fear, at work on my wizardry as well."

Amran-an was trembling, despite Morat's steadying arm.

"You alone know how the wizardry works in me, for me, how much I depend on my dreams, waking and sleeping. There are no living wizards of my blood to teach me."

"I know, Am. Few could bear the loneliness you have. I know what it costs you to come here to Highrune and have us all make demands on you, when you could stay in Deld . . . take your own pace and rhythm with your magic . . . live at least in some peace."

The terrible trickery of the hunt gone awry, the Green Wizard dead amid the spring flowers, Willow in grief, were all foremost in Morat's mind. He blinked to hear Amran-an put such fears into words.

"If my wellsprings are tainted, how can I be sure that whatever action I take will not bring on more harm?"

"Am," Morat said softly, to the wizard's back, "Am, yours is the truest heart, yours are the surest instincts, the most caring soul among us. Whom could I ever trust more?"

*****

"I can see why you find embroidery boring, then," said Ranna, "if you were training to make Woodwaynim Mother-runes." The maid tied off her last stitch neatly and bit off the trailing needle and thread.

Ranna was stitching small flowers on quilt squares, making them for a wedding quilt. She had caught the eye of that young man apprenticed to Highrune's master gardener, and she was hopeful, although matters hadn't yet proceeded beyond the hand-holding stage, under the watchful eyes of her mother. He was an earnest young man, was Lexin, and had dutifully asked Ranna's mother Peggin for permission to "walk about" with the maid. And under the admiration of his eyes, the little frog was blossoming into a little swan, thought Willow.

"But you can use threads like these?" asked Ranna.

"Sa, that purple there, with those soft blues, would be lovely to use for a Binding, to catch some lovers' dreams at late evening," she said, teasing Ranna gently. She sorted through the basket of things Lexin had brought to Ranna for Willow's work, sorting in her lap the bits of wood and stone, the small objects Lexin had brought her from his garden work. "Rune's dyes are deeper and more varied than I've seen. Ours are made from plant extracts and other natural sources, so they tend to be paler."

"Oh, those come from Yan-tsse, my Lady, and not from here. They are rare, and I may use only a little of them. I'm lucky my mother saves some aside from the tapestry work for me. My quilt will be quite splendid because of them, and Lexin does love the purple flowers."

Ranna's mother Peggin was steward of the linen rooms at Highrune, presiding over the sewing of the regular linens. But she and her seamstresses were a major force in the highly skilled work to create and maintain the tapestries that lined Highrune's stone walls.

So far, most of Ranna and Lexin's handholding had taken place at the far end of the big sewing room, while the stitching maids giggled quietly at them and her mother watched carefully. Twice or thrice they had sat under Willow's eye, in the Glass Garden, which Lexin insisted needed pruning regularly.

"I think my mother has dreams I will become fine enough with the needle that I can join the tapestry work," continued Ranna. "You know, I think that might be very nice. I imagine myself someday walking into the ballroom of Highrune and seeing the fine new tapestry on that bare eastern wall, and knowing exactly where are the few small flowers and leaves I put into it." She sighed. "To be part of some large masterwork . . . that would be a fine thing."

"It takes four to make a Woodway rune," said Willow, twisting a few colorful threads about her fingers, "a Finder, a Maker, a Binder, and a Tuner. I was training to be a Binder. It's always a woman, just as the Maker is always a man.

"The Finder seeks out the special wood, the clay, the threads, the seeds, shells, and all the other natural objects, sensing their secret powers. It seems there's a bit of the Finder in your Lexin," said Willow. "This is a fine bit of wood he's brought. And the grapevines will do nicely. He's even brought some feathers—and look, here's some small stones with holes drilled in them—agates, I think. I wonder where he got them, drilled like that. I've rarely worked with stone, but then, it seems more fitting to be using it in Rune."

"That wood is driftwood from the beach at Straand; the Master Gardener has had them send it up from the coast for the meditation garden he is redesigning with Amran-an," explained Ranna, turning the gnarled bit in the light. "And I think the feathers are from the more exotic birds in the bird-ponds; they've gathered those birds from all over Rune, over the years. The Master Gardener's brother breeds the rare birds for ornament."

Willow twisted the grapevine in her fingers, her fingers moving swiftly, devising networks with the brilliant, purple-colored threads, working in a feather here and there. "Sometimes the Finder spends a lifetime seeking some special element he or she knows the Mother-rune requires. Sometimes it is something you just are born to do, the Finding, and you have a special luck that no one can teach or learn. Sometimes, even, rarely, the objects for the rune find the Finder.

"The Maker carves the wood or works the clay. His work holds the rune; it is the foundation on which the magic rests. His carvings may catch the wind just so, or cradle a feather or a pebble at just the right angle. It's easier to be the Maker; so many Woodwaynim carve wood from the time they are children and can handle the blade with the wood as naturally as they cut their bread. But only the best carvers can work the Mother-runes.

"The Binder ties it all together, weaving in the feelings, the heart of the magic. That's so hard to put into words. It's done with colored threads, grasses and vines, spidersilk—and with dream's threads and trains of thought and linked memories. I had studied for years, since I was a child. The Binding is something that grows as a woman moves through her life stages, changing as she moves from Maid to Bride to Mother to Matron to Crone. At each stage she can bind something different that makes the rune speak praise to the Mother in another one of her manifestations."

To herself, Willow thought, "I was only a maid. I was walking up the mountain with Rowan to pledge our marriage. I was to become a bride, and that would not only have joined my path with his for life, but taken me to higher work as a Binder. And now . . . I'm still just a maid, and frozen here alone in a prison of stone." She shook herself inwardly, to free herself from the sad thought. It wasn't something she could share with the cheerful maid stitching her wedding quilt squares.

"That's why we build them, you understand, the Mother-runes. To pray and praise the Mother, and the earth her body, and all the trees and flowers and animals and Woodwaynim that are her children."

Ranna looked at her, puzzled.

"There are many kinds of Woodwaynim runes, just as there are many runes here in Rune. 'Rune' . . . even its name is a rune. There are small runes in the patterns of the mosaic in that patch of stone floor there, that weave messages of enduring strength, and runes on Morat's High-Lord crown that make it the symbol of inherited authority it is. You are embroidering the runes of your hopes for a long, happy, fruitful wedded life on those quilt squares. Highrune itself is possibly a rune that binds the law and order of the ruling city."

"And the High-Lord Morat himself, he's a rune that binds the land," Ranna said thoughtfully. "I never saw it that way before, but that's what he is, to me and the likes of me, here in Rune and all through the land."

"Life's a rune, Ranna, that you work as well, as artistically and as truly as you can. And when you spend it building something higher, larger than yourself, something that praises the force of Life itself, then you are part of something much larger, much more beautiful than you could do alone. It's like your tapestry, and you can take joy in placing your own few flowers and leaves within it.

"I had already done some praiseworthy Binding work, and I was moving forward in my training. They said I had promise. I already had a piece in the Xyl Hall. I wish I could show you the Xyl. It's the greatest Mother-rune of all. It has been growing for generations, under the hands of hundreds of Finders and Makers and Binders. Each small rune has its place in the whole. Each one creates some blessing, captures some hope or dream. Some capture and repeat the songs of Woodwaynim hearts; some hold and bind the scents of our most beautiful flowers. Some hold the cries of newborn babes, and others the love pledges of newlyweds. Some enfold the green of spring buds from generations past. There are even some that hold the flashing wings and shining pelts of creatures that have long disappeared from the Mother's woods.

"But all of them together! Ah! It's a living work that keeps Woodway alive, keeps the years turning, keeps the Mother birthing and growing her abundance of nature and all the generations of Woodway.

"What of the Tuner?" Ranna asked. "What does he do?"

"The Tuner? That's even harder to put into words. Once we have bound the rune, the Tuner sets it to sound, to echo, to speak its praise. The Tuner is most often, though not always, a man. He has his male stages of life, as well as we have our female ones, and his Tuning may change as well as he moves from Youth to Hunter to Husband to Maker to Sage.

"He sets the rune to speak . . . to speak to the eye, the ear, the fingertips. Without the Tuner, the rune just *is*. With him, it *speaks* to all Woodwaynim, and to the living trees, and most especially to the Mother."

And again, to herself, Willow thought of Rowan, who was to have been the Tuner to her Binder, who was to have moved through the stages of his male life as she moved through her female stages, together. And she fell silent, twisting threads of green and purple embroidery yarn around her fingers.

CHAPTER 4

There were times when High-Lord Morat was so straight of mind, so lacking in the tendency toward artfulness, that he was blind. He did not know enough to recognize what was growing in his heart and had to do with Willow. True enough, he fashioned opportunities often to come sit with her in the Glass Garden, even though he sensed she didn't feel comfortable in his presence. Being with her did something to counterbalance the stress of ruling Rune in these complex times, something he didn't find otherwise in his duty-filled life.

It's true he was distracted. He had always been a dedicated steward of the land he ruled. He read its runes as necessarily as he breathed. And it was awakening with all the force of summer. He felt Rune's soil warming to the sun like his own flesh; he tasted its needs and concerns rather than the bread he ate for breakfast. The messages of his land were like secret runes on the insides of his eyelids when he pressed his fingers against his closed eyes, weary both with the joy of his burgeoning land and with the concern that lay like dark skeins through it.

Since the mis-happening in the Mother's woods, he was troubled more and more by the mounting signs that something was not as it should be.

Amran-an had once said, with the perceptiveness of a loving friend as well as the sight of an adept rune reader, that Morat saw the world differently. Where his twin Evmorat breathed deviousness, selfishness, Morat openly and directly cared for the concerns of his land and for the needs of others. On the behalf of Rune he could peel away the layers of meanings that lay around things like the layers of an onion, to get the important truth, but he lacked that perceptive skill completely with respect to himself.

It took a wizard like Amran-an to make him see that his own heart, as well as the land's, was waking.

It happened that Amran-an came to find Morat one day, to tell him that more barges had come upriver on schedule to dock at Highrune. Amran-an had been at the ford, and seen them already being unloaded with the blocks of sea salt, the bags of guano fertilizer from the Bird Islands, the wine from down country, and the metal for the smiths sent from the mountains by sea until the high passes were open of ice. Heller Jade had sent with his most trusted barge-captain a gift for Morat, something found by one of the pearl divers exploring the sea caves at Straand.

Amran-an had looked everywhere in Highrune's public halls, but he had not found the High-Lord. Finally he had come to seek Morat in his chambers.

"Morat? Morat? Ah, there you are."

Morat motioned him to silence. He had pulled his chair over to the edge of the balcony, between the pillars, so that he could see over the stone railing into the courtyard below without being noticed. Amran-an stood at his shoulder and looked down.

"Morat, look what Heller has sent! I haven't parsed all the runes on the wrappings yet, but it looks like it may be the lost Runebook of—"

Morat took his arm, shushed him, pointed down into the courtyard.

The courtyard was filled like a pool with sunlight. Sheltered and pampered under glass all winter, now that the glass panes were pulled aside, the Glass Garden was in a glory of bloom far ahead of the countryside. Morning trumpets bloomed blue amid the dark green of the ivy; tulips and windflowers crowded the beds. The large yellow flowers of the Allamanda, imported from the tropical islands off the eastern coast of Som-a-Nissen, were glorious. The lacy Sensitive Tree at the center of the court hung its branches low, heavy with the frail feathers of its strange blossoms. They brushed at the yellow hair of Willow, who sat on the bench built around the tree trunk.

At her feet sat Ranna, mending spread in her lap. And across from her sat Wayland Wordsmith.

Morat had given instructions for Ranna to do whatever she could to make Willow comfortable and happy. The maid had her own inner doubts about how "happy" Willow might be, but she had told Morat Willow had shown no signs of great distress or extravagant behavior. Rather, she had been reserved and quiet, though she often paced the length of her large room and back. She hadn't told her Lord that the Lady Willow called the quarters a stone cage.

But Ranna had quickly run out of things to keep Willow amused, going from one to another of the pursuits usual to a highborn Runerin lady, from embroidery to reading to more embroidery. She had dug out several musical instruments, including an old samisen from the Isles of Som-a-Nissen, which had too much stone inlaid in it to tempt Willow, and a flute which Willow had rejected because it was made of metal rather than wood. Digging out the Lady Liliamne's harp had been an inspiration, and Willow spent long hours playing minor-scaled Woodwaynim songs, laments by their tone, whispering lyrics to them softly.

That inspired Ranna to bring together Willow and the one person in Highrune castle who was the most expert in the art of the harp: the Wordsmith Wayland.

The old bard no longer sang much; age had roughened his

voice, and he had a streak of vanity that impelled him to preserve his reputation for his golden voice. But he had a truly wondrous collection of song lyrics and long lays in his head. He was expert at the harp. And he loved to tell stories, which Ranna loved to listen to. Soon Willow and Wayland and Ranna were spending long hours in the sunny inner garden, amidst the hothouse flowers that ran ahead of the burgeoning season, exchanging songs and stories.

Now Amran-an looked down where Morat pointed. Willow held a harp in her lap; her fingers were flying surely over its strings. The old wordsmith was making notations as she played, taking down the runes with pen and ink on parchment while Willow sang the Woodwaynim lyrics:

"... for April is the cruelest month,

And I was born for May.

I'll wash away with tears of love the long, cold winter's pain;

I'll shelter you within my arms from April's bitter rain,

For April is the cruelest month, and I was born for May,

And when the summer's come to bloom, I will have my day.

May's the month of tender fires, just begun to burn,

May's the month of sky's desires, I've just begun to learn.

But in April's seed is promised winter's cold return;

Past and future blended still, say I will lose, will come

to yearn.

For all's a bitter cycle, come to find and come to lose,
And past and future merge in patterns, lost in repetitious views.
If you'll be free of all beginnings, never bound to time to part,
Abandon April, come and love me; you must clasp May to your heart."

Amran-an nodded appreciatively. "Not bad. But she could use a better harp than that old toy of Lilliamne's."

Morat looked up sharply. "Think you so? I will have to find one . . . yes, that would be a splendid gift. I have been trying to think of a gift for her."

Amran-an looked wryly at Morat's eager face; he found himself shaking his head. "Morat, see what I have brought you; Heller sent it upriver to you. The message says he thought it might be the lost Third Lorebook of Kelsin-ta. Imagine! If we can get it open, we might find some of the finest rune-smithing—"

"Hush! I just want to listen a little more. Put it on the table, and we'll look at it later."

"Morat!"

"I'll come in in a while. When she finishes this song. It's one I've heard before, but she does some marvelous things with the minor harmonic scales in it. She won't play for me, so I have to eavesdrop."

"Morat! Kelsin-ta's Third Lorebook! By the fires of Tran . . ." He dumped the cloth-wrapped bundle in Morat's lap.

"I heard you. You take it in; I'll be in in a few minutes." Morat returned to listening, his chin on his hand, intent, his eyes fixed on Willow.

Amran-an took the bundle back, muttering something to himself. Something about a three-centuries dead rune-wizard, however famous, hardly being able to compete with the magic of a lovely face and an enchanting voice. "I don't need rune signs to read you, friend."

"What?"

"Morat," the wizard gave an exasperated laugh, laying a hand on Morat's shoulder, "You have fallen in love with her."

Morat looked back at Amran-an, thunderstruck.

*****

Once Morat realized that he loved Willow, he saw no way open to him except to tell her. Once Amran-an showed it to him, the truth of his heart was so evident to him that it never occurred to him that she might not understand it.

It wasn't that he *forgot* he had killed her betrothed. No, in the deepest part of the night, he would wake and stare, chest heaving with pain, at the fading dream-image of the young man falling, Morat's spear in his back. He saw in the darkness of his sleeping chamber the young green eyes wide with shock at the tragic error. But the Mother's Mountains seemed as far away as they were, and the truth of Morat's life was here, close at hand in Highrune. He was too ensorcelled by the newness of his love to read the runes of Willow's sad eyes.

And so, the first thing he did was to search through every shop and trader's stall in Highrune for the perfect harp for Willow. It did not seem odd to him, although it gave Amran-an more than a moment's pause, when the perfect harp turned up. It was exquisite, of Woodwaynim manufacture, no less, with a clarity of sound even Morat found impressive.

And the second thing he did was to take it to her.

"Ah! What love does to the most serious of men," Amran-an would have groaned, had he seen Morat High-Lord of Rune, checking his rush and falling suddenly silent at the entry to Willow's rooms, struck dumb at the sight of her kneeling hastily to gather up the spilled balls of her embroidery yarn. He picked up the ball that had rolled to his feet, went and knelt beside her, putting it in the basket she held.

"I'm sorry I startled you," he murmured.

She took the yarn from him, let him help her to her feet. He didn't let go of her hand again.

Ranna, entering silently from the servants' door, saw them standing thus. She smiled and tiptoed away again.

Willow sat looking at the harp. She had set it on the table, afraid to trust herself to hold it, and the afternoon sunlight fell on it, setting aglow its inlaid highlights of varicolored woods. It shone with splendor. Any Woodwaynim, she thought, would recognize a harp manufactured by the Master of Ash-and-Ebony. How in the Mother's name had this outlander come by it? Its value was unguessable. Any harper would give a dozen summers of his life for it. No, the High-Lord could not know what he had given her. But the gift had, in its way, fit his intentions, for they were extravagant.

"I am shaking like a new birch-leaf," she whispered to herself.

She pressed her fingers to her cheeks, feeling their coolness soothing against the heat that flamed her face. The heat of anger, of dismay, of confusion, of what?

He found her harping beautiful; he wished her to have an instrument more suited to the beauty of her music. He wanted it to be a condition of the gift that she consent to play for him.

Thus had the High-Lord begun to speak with her, awkwardly and hesitantly, while he held her hand in his, and looked down at her with those intense dark eyes.

As always, she had felt deeply uncomfortable in his presence. The sight of him stirred grief, resentment, pain in her.

He didn't seem to see how she felt. He was too preoccupied with his own feelings.

He loved her!

Tears leaped into her eyes, blurring the sight of the harp. He had dared to speak such words to her, he who had come upon her and Rowan as they made their way up Mother Mountain to join hands before the Mother. He who had murdered Rowan, her first and only love! Rowan, in the mirror of whose eyes she had seen herself grow to womanhood. Rowan, who had filled her world with his youthful power, his wizard's dreams. Rowan, who lay dead beneath a cairn of rocks.

He, Morat High-Lord of Rune, loved her! Wanted her, she whom he had made a widow before she was a bride. He had taken the gold band of High-Lordship from his brow and held it out to her, swearing the truth and honor of his love upon its run-e-engraved metal. Truth! Honor!

Her heart was overwhelmed with the memory of it. It made her chest hurt, so desperately did she want to let the tears forth, pour out the pain. But she still could not cry.

She had snatched her hand from his grasp, turned her back on him, left him holding his Lord-crown in cold fingers. She had called him a murderer.

And then she had fled from the hurt blossoming in his troubled eyes.

The harp sat before her; she reached out to touch its fine-wrought inlay with a tremulous fingertip. But she didn't really see it. Her eyes still saw the hurt in the High-Lord's eyes, the bewildered, uncomprehending, then all too knowing pain that had whitened his face, as he put his Lord-crown back on his brow, straightened his shoulders, turned, and left her.

*****

Morat watched Willow from afar when he was free to do so, from his balcony looking down on the garden. He watched Willow and Ranna trade stories with old Wayland. He watched as Redd came and sat with them when his page's duties allowed. His young cousin had a voice just deepened, putting him well out of the boys' choir that sang in the High Hall at festival, but what he lost he exchanged for a growing timbre and range, and he had begun to study singing and harping under Wayland's instruction.

Willow did play the Woodwaynim harp, to his great pleasure. Her voice and Redd's voice blended well together, bound within the magic voice of the harp. And Wayland was teaching both young people songs of Rune from his vast collection, often bringing old parchments along to reinforce the lessons.

As a few days passed, and Willow seemed to maintain her calm demeanor, Morat tried again to reach out to her. He found a moment when she sat alone in her rooms, fingering the harp softly. He held out the small bowl of tropical fruits he had brought from the latest shipment Heller sent up from the coast, hoping she would appreciate their rareness. He spoke softly of the weather, of the small goings-on in the castle. When she seemed to bear his company well, he spoke his heart.

"Willow, I didn't *murder* Rowan."

"I don't want to talk about it."

"I do! I must!" Morat put his hands on Willow's shoulders, turned her to face him. "I want you to understand how it was."

"I don't *care* how it was." But Willow stood still in his grip, eyes downcast; Morat couldn't tell if she were listening or not, but he talked anyway.

"You have to believe me. We never intended to intrude into the Mother's Woods. I still don't know how we got to Her mountain. We had only been riding for a day, for Rune's sake. We were set on a spell-path. We were ill at ease, frightened; things were very confused. I became separated from my party. When I found them again, the fighting was already started. I saw my hunt party, ill-armed, besieged by a large party of warriors. Many well-seasoned, well-armed attackers."

Willow looked up suddenly, a flare of anger on her face. "Defenders!" she retorted.

"Against what? A few lost hunters? I saw what I saw. My men hemmed in against the cliffs. Redd on the ground, about to die. Amran-an says they were ambushed."

Willow made a harsh sound.

"You have become acquainted with Am. Do you think he'd lie about something like that?"

She didn't answer.

Morat felt like shaking her. With an effort he spoke quietly. "I saw what I saw. I could not let my men—my best friends, my own cousin—be killed. Above all, I was responsible for them."

"So you killed him. Killed a wizard of Woodway with a hunting spear in the back."

"I threw my spear at a seasoned warrior in armor. One like the rest. They *all* looked as solid as he did; I picked him because he would've killed Redd."

"Your vision must have been keen," Willow said with a sarcastic edge to her voice. "You say you were confused! Yet you threw your spear at the one real man, and not the illusions. How perceptive."

Morat sighed, let go of her shoulders while he still could control his hands. He turned away abruptly, began to pace up and down.

"I claim no particular perceptiveness," he muttered. "Whatever put my foot on that spell-path must have guided my spear arm as well. The same runes of stupidity that made Rowan make his particular illusion to deal with us. The same evil rune-spell that made him see us, a poor lost band of hunters, as invaders desecrating the sacred Mother's Woods."

Willow had turned away again to stare out the window. Morat came to a halt behind her.

"It wasn't murder," he whispered. "And I am as sorry for it as for anything I ever did."

"It doesn't matter," Willow said. "I have listened to this same tale from Amran-an. You should not be surprised that he pleads your case. And from Redd, too." She shook her head angrily. "But it doesn't matter. Rowan is dead. At your hand."

Morat stared at her. He stared at the braids of her hair, hanging down her back, at the fiery white-gold of her hair in the shaft of sunlight streaming in the window. A dozen dozen fragments of sentences whirled in his brain, trying to come together so that he could ask her forgiveness. But the runes of persuasion wouldn't come to his tongue.

The silence grew long between them.

"I love you, Willow," desperate, Morat threw words into the void between them. He thought he could almost see them dancing in the sunbeam like the dust motes.

A tremor shook Willow. She steadied herself with both hands on the stone window ledge. Then she turned slowly to face him. Bright color sat on her cheekbones; against the paleness of her face, it gave her a fevered look.

"This window doesn't look north, does it?" she asked. "To Woodway?" Morat could barely hear her, she spoke so softly.

"It is a dozen days ride and more to Woodway. Even if it did face north, you could not see even the highest of the Mother Mountains from here."

"Will you send me home to Woodway?" She stared at him, pale, eyes wide above the flush on her cheekbones. "Please?"

"No." She had asked before, worn him weary. He no longer tried to make excuses for keeping her near him.

"Will you give me a room with a window to the north?"

"No." Morat clenched his fists, trying not to see the paleness of her face.

"You leave me no room for honor," she told him, her voice trembling for the first time. "How can you ask me to forget? How can you ask me to dishonor my betrothal? My love? My grief? If I were in Woodway, I would throw myself off the cliffs into the chasm of the Mother's River, before I would be so dishonorable. And everyone would understand!" She was shaking.

Morat took hold of her shoulders again, gently. He touched her cheek, brushed back the hair from her brow.

"I don't ask you to forget Rowan. I don't ask you to forget his death." He took her hands, felt her fingers cold in his. "I only ask you to leave the past in the past. I only ask you to know me. Know that I am not an evil man. Not a vicious man. I am only a man who can make a mistake." His eyes sought hers.

"There is no dishonor in loving a man who loves you," he said softly.

"How much? How much do you love me?"

"I would lay Rune at your feet."

Morat's heart was a pain in his breast. He held her hands as gently as he could, hoping.

But she freed her hands, suddenly, and stepped back. She fingered something at her neck, and Morat saw it was a necklace she wore hidden within her dress. Now she clutched the pendant in her hands, looking down at it.

He had seen it only once before, worn openly around her neck in the Motherwoods. Intricately carved, inlaid, it matched the one with the crescent Mother signs Morat had found on the breast of the dead Woodwaynim wizard.

"Do you love me enough that you'd bring back Rowan to me, if it lay in your power?"

Morat felt as if she'd slapped his face. "That," he pointed at the necklace, "it was his gift, wasn't it?"

She stepped back, cupped hands over the pendant. "A betrothal gift," she said defiantly.

"There is no more betrothal. There can't be any marriage to Rowan for you. It's done!" He felt anger like a rushing sound in his ears. "Let go of the past! Let go of the useless past!"

"You ask me to let go of my honor!"

"I don't ask!" he cried. "I demand!" he cried, who had never demanded anything for himself, since he had come of age and taken on his brow the crown of the High-Lord of Rune. He grabbed suddenly for the pendant. The chain broke, and he had it from her. He held it high, blood rushing in his ears, astonished at his rage, but powerless to fight it. Willow flung herself at him, clawing for the necklace, but he held her off easily, with one arm, while he held the necklace high out of reach with his other hand.

"Give it back! It's mine!" she sobbed angrily. "Please, oh please, Morat, give it back!"

He looked down into her distraught face, feeling a crazed kind of power, a mad thrill of hope. It was the first time she had called him by his name, the first time she had called him by anything other than formal titles, "High-Lord" or "Sire."

He stood like a rock against the wave of her distress, thinking, "As long as she had this, she could see nothing but the past, nothing but Rowan. Now she'll see me. Now she'll see me."

She was sobbing, truly crying now. Suddenly the anger, the defiance was gone, and all that was left was grief. Pent up all these weeks, the tears finally came.

He thrust the necklace into his shirt. Then he took Willow in his arms and held her, carefully, whispering soft, comforting words to her. He let her beat at him, let her scream wild words, but he held her.

"We weren't just betrothed! We were to re-unite two of the highest Branches of the Xyl. We were to study to become rune-builders together, him Tuner to my Binder. He was becoming one of our greatest wizards. And he loved me," she sobbed. "Oh, Morat, we had loved each other since we were children! I can't remember when he wasn't beside me. I don't want to live without him!"

Morat began to realize he had made a deep mistake about the depth of Willow's feelings. "You seemed so calm, so accepting. I thought—"

"What do you know of me?" she cried, explosively. "I am Willow Lythew of the Greenwillow Branch, destined to be Xyl! I'm Woodwaynim! Do you think I'd bare my heart to alien outlanders? To murderers?"

"You never cried—by the Runes, Willow, have you never wept for him?"

"I couldn't," she sobbed. "Oh Mother-of-All, forgive me, I couldn't cry. I didn't want him to be gone forever."

Her hysteria was changing. Now she didn't struggle against him but clung to him. And wept with heartbreaking sobs. He smoothed her hair, held her close. "Go ahead," he told her softly, and held her tenderly as she shook with her grief. "Weep for Rowan. Weep for him. It's all right, it's all right."

After a long while he felt there was an end to the heaving sobs that seemed too large for her body to endure. She was exhausted. He lifted her in his arms and carried her to her bed and laid her down gently. He smoothed the damp hair back from her brow, wiped tears from her flushed cheeks, kissed her on the forehead.

Then he left her. She was still crying softly.

By the time he got to his own chamber, his knees were trembling, and the necklace was a hot lump of fire against the skin of his breast.

CHAPTER 5

"I always liked 'The Invisible Prince' the best," said Ranna. "Perhaps it's because the heroine is a servant, like me." She looked hopefully at Wayland.

"Aiee, that's a long one," the old wordsmith sighed. "Must it be that one, little froglet?"

"It's my turn to choose. You promised. If I got the steward to let me have some of the wine from Kessen, the special vintage from nine summers back, the one that was so crystal clear and fine-tasting that it's put aside in Lord Morat's special store." She brought the sealed bottle, wrapped carefully in a cooled cloth, out from behind her back.

Willow smiled, and with a wink at Ranna, took a corkscrew from her pocket. "It's the agreed-upon bribe, Wayland."

"Conspirators! Well, if I promised, I promised. Actually, it's a favorite of mine, too, for a lot of reasons. It has a lot of levels of meaning . . . I like what it says about the creative power of art. I added my own bit to the tons of commentary on it in my day. But I must have a little of the wine to clear my throat now, and some more when we get to the point where they take the treasure to the gate of the Invisible Prince's castle."

He sipped slowly, with appreciation, at the goblet of wine, while Ranna and Willow settled comfortably on the cushions the maidservant had brought out to the stone benches under the Sensitive Tree, and while the bees hummed in the blossoms above them, he began to weave his tale.

"Now the young king looked upon the rich forest that neighbored his own, and he saw how abundant the animals were in it, how wide the antlers of the harts reached, how majestic were their leaps. He saw the fat sleekness of the smaller game, the fineness of the plumage of the plump pheasants, and he grew envious.

"'Why shouldn't I hunt there, and you my favorite lords with me?'

"And the younger lords, catching fire from the king and eager to please him, now that they had finally got to have their day from their old fathers, since the old king had passed away, answered, 'Why not?' Only the few elder lords in the party frowned and hung back.

"'We beg your pardon, o King,' said one, carefully, 'but you know as we do this forest belongs to the Invisible Prince, and no one else may hunt here!' And with great tact he reminded the king of the story that was old when even he was young: that the king and queen of what was now the forbidden forest had finally been granted the child they longed for. But at his birth all the ladies attending the queen had been struck blind. The king forbade all others to enter the child's presence, and when the child was grown to young manhood, he had built a high wall around the castle and its wondrous, widespread gardens, and leaving his son inside, he had taken his queen and all his people to seek new lands far to the west.

"'That place and the forest grown up around it have long been held in awe and fear. Some say the prince was invisible, and hence his name. Others say that his queen-mother birthed a monster so hideous none could bear to look on him.'

"'But that's an old tale,' replied the young king, frowning at having his whim questioned. 'You can see as well as I can how old this forest is, how dense its trees. If there ever was an Invisible Prince, he is long dead. It would be a discourtesy to this forest, would it not,' he turned to his younger comrades, waving a gallant hand toward the tempting lushness, '*not* to partake of its abundance.' And he spurred his mount forward with a cry to the hounds, and his young favorites sped hot on his heels, leaving the old men behind to shake their heads and cluck their tongues.

"Now the forest tolerated the young king well the first day," continued Wayland after a sip of wine, "and courteously yielded him much pleasant sport—and the largest horn-beast he had ever taken, with antlers as wide-spreading as the tree branches themselves. And on the second day. And on the third, and so on, the forest continued to be a courteous host to its guest.

"But by now the king's crowd of hunt followers had grown large. The dust they raised coated the rich green of the leaves; the flowers they trampled bled upon the ground; the great noise of their chase affrighted the birds. And on the seventh day the young king and his party met not with horn-beast hart or doe, but with a huge black boar, who when cornered with difficulty, gored the hounds and tossed them back at the king, and melted away into the forest after a glaring look and a shrug of his bristled shoulders that said as eloquently as a man's words, 'Enough! I have been a courteous and generous host with my forest. Do *you* be a courteous guest and depart well satisfied!'

"When the young king rode back out of the forest that evening and saw the looks on everyone's faces when no huge horn-beast was tied across the pack-pony's back, his heart was sorely irritated.

"'Be ready at daybreak,' he commanded. 'I will hunt one more day in the forest of the Invisible Prince.' And he stalked off to his chamber while those who had seen the boar shuffled their feet and gave each other uncomfortable looks.

"But the king was the king, and they gathered in a rather chilly, gray, blustery dawn, though a somewhat dispirited hunting party it was. All morning they rode through the forest, and they saw no animal, not even the smallest ptarmigan. The wind blew coldly through the trees, which seemed to be shedding early showers of autumn-reddened leaves. At mid-day, they had reached the heart of the forest, and paused. Even the king was looking around him uneasily.

"The storm broke upon them with a force that nearly swept them from their mounts. The hounds cowered, tails between their legs, and then bolted for home. The wind swept their masters after them, the tree branches lashing at them to hurry them on their way. There was a strange timeless time when none of them could see clearly for the rain and hail and the din of the thunder, but fled as best they could. And then they were out of the forest, its fringes thrashing threateningly behind them; and they found themselves on the high hill overlooking the king's castle.

"Before them was a sight that froze them in their tracks. A huge, great whirlwind was sweeping down before them, towering like a dark and monstrous pillar from a storm-moiled sky hung with pendulous gray breasts of lightning-streaked cloud. It swept the fields clean, wasting the harvest-ready grain, scattering it like sand. Houses, barns, crofts, all in its path disappeared into its darkening mass. It swept onward, scattering people and flocks, toward the king's castle.

"The king watched white-faced as the whirlwind paused at the castle gate, then moved in a grand circle around the castle reaches, flinging debris at the walls, but leaving them unbreeched. Three times it circled the king's castle, a screaming demon of pent-up destruction, and then, all of a sudden, it was gone, sucking itself back up into the dark clouds. In the abrupt near-silence, the king listened to the cries of lamentation mounting to the hilltop where he and his party sat still on their trembling mounts."

Ranna jumped up to refill Wayland's goblet almost before his sentence ended. Willow unknotted her fingers and sat back and smiled. "Ah, Wayland, your word-weaving has worked its spell on me again. You should be declared a national treasure."

"He has been," said Ranna. "He's got the medal to prove it. On a fancy striped ribbon. They gave it to him in a fancy ceremony. But he keeps it in the chest in his room."

"I am suitably refreshed and rebribed," said Wayland. "Shall I continue?" He bowed to the small crowd of servants who had quietly taken seats at the edges of the courtyard, spinning, shelling peas, sewing, or at least pretending to. Word had gotten around.

"Well, the king's elders persuaded him easily that he must make reparation to the Invisible Prince, lest he send the whirlwind again. Once had been enough to bring the threat of starvation before spring, so much of the harvest was destroyed. And so they gathered gifts to present to the Invisible Prince of the forest, or to whatever reigned there.

"They took antique gold chalices from the cellar coffers, and the finest trophy armor (they left the first-best hunting spears in their racks, though they did gather up the second-best). They combed the guildhalls and crafteries for the best workmanship: leather shoes like silk, so softly worked and brilliantly dyed; enameled and inlaid boxes of exquisite design, by the new artisans come from the East; the glass colored like flower-petals that came from the best glass-blower's pipe; a chariot with ornate harness-work, and the best two white cornuas in the king's stable to draw it. The king's high counselors ran from here to hither, in haste and self-important urgency, commandeering this or that, hurrying an artisan here to finish off a piece, digging there into traders' coffers of antiques.

"It was the king himself, though, who, after selecting the best tapestries from the weavers' hall, had an afterthought.

"'Bring these,' he pointed to the weavings still being trimmed from the looms, 'and bring the girl, too,' he pointed to the youngest of the weavers.

"The counselors lauded that afterthought. She was a pretty enough young woman. And better to send her to the Invisible Prince to do his will with, than one of their gentle-ladies, just in case his will *was* to eat her. She'd look the same, properly robed, even if she were just a servant girl.

"And so quickly, not too well organized, they made up their gifting procession, and rode to the edge of the forest. They were not too easy in their hearts at approaching it. But it presented a fair aspect to them, with only a sighing late-summer breeze rustling the leaves. And a path opened before them, a wide grassy avenue that rolled out before them though no one saw any of the dense-growing trees move aside.

"With wide eyes and uneasy glances to the side, they made their way deep into the forest, reaching at last the gate itself of the Invisible Prince's keep. It was hard to make out the walls, so ingrown with huge trees it was. And the ornately cast bronze gate itself was so green with age it almost blended with the vegetation.

"It opened silently for them. Quickly they piled the gifts just within, daring to go no deeper, tethered the chariot cornuas to the gatepost, thrust the frightened girl inside the gate, and hurried away, back out of the forest, as quickly as they could without entirely losing their dignity.

"Amalee—for that was her name, the weaver girl they had dressed so quickly in her finery they had not let her wash the weaving wool's dye entirely from her fingers—Amalee stood without moving, feeling uncomfortable in the stiff brocade she'd been given to wear. She looked around at a courtyard; whatever was beyond it was almost hidden by trees with tiny leaves and feather-like flowers, arranged in a square around the court.

“Beneath the trees were stone-paved paths, lined with flowerbeds, with stone benches placed here and there. Moss grew between the large paving stones dappled with shade. She could see another gateway, a glint of water beyond; the thin trickle of a fountain sang softly in the stillness. A bird trilled briefly, then fell into silence.

“Behind her, a bolt of silk slid off a coffer, rattled something metal. Amalee jumped at the sound and looked fearfully behind her. She clenched her hands behind her, but stood her ground.

“For long moments she stood, and there was no other sound, no movement but that of the feather-blossoms in the smallest of breezes. The moments stretched out. ‘Perhaps there’s no one here, after all,’ she thought. But there was a small tension to the air that contradicted that thought. ‘Well,’ she decided, swallowing the lump in her throat, ‘I might as well get eaten and be done with it.’ And she walked beneath the trees, went to the gate, and peered through.

“Another courtyard, its walls barely visible for the trees . . . pebbled paths through beds of star-shaped flowers in pinks and purples . . . the fountain’s sound a little closer, not much. She picked a path and followed it, unconsciously trying to make no sounds with her footsteps. It led her into a maze of hedges and vines that closed in around her. She rounded a turn and gave a small cry as she came face to face with a monster’s visage—of stone, spilling cool water from its lips. There was a small silver cup, engraved with fine scrollwork, on the stone edge of the catch-basin, and she dipped it in the cold water and drank. The water tasted green and sweet, of moss and cool stone.

“Amalee wandered courtyard after courtyard, garden after garden, through shade and sunlight . . . she came to nothing that looked like the castle itself. Perhaps there was none, for one could easily sleep or eat under the many porticos and small galleries roofed here with grapevines or wisteria or other exotic blossoms, or there with red brick tiles. There were stone grottos, artificial caves with hummocks of moss as soft as cushions, worked with tiny flowers like living embroidery.

"At last, weary and hungry and overwhelmed by the silence, Amalee stood in the middle of yet another courtyard, in the middle of a formal pattern of hedges and herbs, clenched her fists at her side, and called out, 'Is anyone here?' And being a servant, and accustomed to deference, she added, 'May I please know where you wish me to go and what you wish me to do?' And to herself, she whispered, 'And I would be so happy to have something to eat!'

"Her voice echoed in the silence—and was answered by the softest tinkling of a bell, a wafting of sweet perfume that stood out even in the fragrant garden, and the gentlest motion of leaves at one end of the garden. She went toward the signs eagerly, turned a corner, and found a soft, grassy patch of lawn, in the sunlight, spread with a cloth. On it was spread a feast—fruit, small cakes, cold meat and cheese, a small flagon of wine.

"Disappointed, Amalee noted there was only one goblet, one plate.

"But she sat on the grass and ate eagerly, though she strained her senses, all the while, for some sound or other hint of the being that had placed the food there for her. The food was far finer than she was used to, even finer than what she had helped to serve the king at the castle's best feasts.

"It grew dusky as she sat and ate. Her only company was the slight sound—she couldn't decide if it was a bell or a bird—that hovered in the air, sourceless and directionless. Finally, in the last light of the evening she left the little feast on the grass and walked on, in the direction she hoped was the one the sound seemed to lead her.

"Wearier than she had ever been from a whole day of weaving, she wondered aloud what she would do with night falling. And again, rounding a corner, she found a gate, walked through, and found a roofed grotto, with cushions and fine cloths spread among the flowers. She lay down on them and fell asleep, with the dark air sweetly fragrant around her, the gentle, almost not-there tinkling of the bell/bird mingled with the soft breeze.

"And so it went, for days. Amalee wandered the garden, searching for its owner. She soon understood that if she voiced her wishes aloud, the garden would provide what she needed. She never quite saw anyone, but the sense of a presence grew stronger and stronger. Sometimes she saw birds or small animals, when the bushes rustled. She saw peacocks and egrets and other rarer birds she did not know. She saw squirrels and groundhogs and even a fox or two. But sometimes, when the bushes rustled, she saw nothing. But she knew, more and more certainly, that something, someone, was there.

"It felt peculiar, to know she was being watched. She took to talking out loud often, as if she could make the presence more and more real by communicating to it. She didn't know if the presence was the Invisible Prince, and it didn't matter. She wasn't a princess and had no idea what royalty talked about. So she talked about her work as a weaver. She told the invisible almost-there presence which plants in the garden made good dye sources, and what colors they made the yarn, and how dying the yarn in an iron kettle or using certain chemicals would mordant the wool so the dyes would take strongly.

"She told the rustling bushes how it felt to fall into the rhythm of the weaving, feeling the shuttle fly back and forth and back and forth across the wide reach of the great loom, with the pull of the reed to firm each row of weft between each cast. She put into words, for the first time, what it felt like to fall into that familiar pattern of motions until her body moved like the rhythmic lilt of a song. She told about the joy of feeling the pattern grow under her fingers, how it felt to know the pattern so well she didn't need the written drafts anymore, but could just let it flow across the growing cloth. She told the bell/bird/hum in the sweet-smelling air about the special pleasure of working the small tapestry loom, fingers playing the weft across the warp strings like a harpist playing a harp, to create the detailed likenesses of the plants, animals, and people around her.

"You must remember," Wayland raised both hands, fingers spread, earnest to explain, "That Amalee was an artist, even if she was only a weaver. And being an artist, she knew how to notice and to appreciate the garden's play with color and texture and composition. And, as she walked, in her loneliness, she forgot herself and put her appreciation, her artistic sensitivity, into words. She told the garden how beautiful it was, how splendid its flowers and vines and branches would look if she could only capture it on the warp and weft the way she knew, in her artist's heart, she could. Being a true artist, not a simple craftswoman (and being more than a little lonely for the busy companionship of the weaving hall), she let her yearning show, to capture the beauty of her surroundings in her art form.

"And that afternoon, when she turned the corner in the pebbled path she had chosen to wander, she found the loom of her dreams.

"Set in a vine-sheltered portico, in dappled shade, it waited for her. It seemed almost alive itself; the uprights were wood carved with vines and leaves. It was already threaded, as she would have liked it, with fine linen warp. And in baskets at its foot were skeins and skeins of fine linen, silk, and wool yarns. They were brilliant in color and sheen unlike anything she had ever had to work with.

"From that day Amalee felt truly at home in the garden. She sat and wove the riches of the garden into brilliant cloth, and her heart sang with the joyous satisfaction that only an artist knows, when the mind's image is realized in the work of art. She wandered the garden freely, and now she always knew where she was, for the loom was the heart of the garden, and like a compass needle to a pole, she could always find her way back to it, her arms laden with the flowers she translated into images on the cloth. The peacocks followed her back, and sat by her, and she wove them into the tapestry. The doves sat in the tree above her, and she wove them in. She wove in the fox and the grapes, the mouse and the berry, the exotic lilies, and the homely semi-wild asters.

"And somehow, she wove in the presence that sat just beyond her sight and watched her weave and listened to her. It was becoming more and more actual to her, as she worked and talked to it. She felt it walking near her. And the garden itself seemed to blossom more and more abundantly and richly, as if her artistry had awakened its own ever-changing artistry, and it strove to outdo itself for her.

"Perhaps it was as artist to artist that they communicated, or as artist and truly appreciative critic. Whatever it was, the garden grew more and more beautiful, and its secretive presence more alive to Amalee each day. And she, in her turn, captured its beauty, its abundance, its artistry, in the new order, the higher art, of her weaving, as she had never done before.

"When she finished the first tapestry, it was almost painful to cut the threads and loose the cloth from the loom. It was like she cut some kind of umbilical and held forth something rare and newborn. Carefully she tied off the ends into an intricate, knotted fringe. Her heart beating hard in her breast, she took it and laid it out in the grass at the center of the court next to the one where she worked the loom, just beyond the fragrant privet hedges. And in the morning, it was gone.

"She began another, happy at the exchange of gifts, the work of art for the gift of letting her be an artist as she had never been permitted before, as mere servant in the weaving workshops of the castle back there in the almost unreal distance, beyond the magic forest of the Invisible Prince.

"But this second piece did not go as well. It seemed more of a struggle. There was uneven tension in the warp; the weft did not sit properly. The images Amalee wove emerged with more difficulty. She did not know why, but she felt a restlessness in everything, in the weaving, in herself, in the presence in the garden. The air in the garden grew hot and dry with summerness, even though there seemed to be no real progression of seasons in its everblooming present.

"The garden grew parched. It was only a lessening of its lushness, not a true drought. But the fountains sprang less far into the air. Dust sat on the foliage. Here and there, leaves turned brown and grass turned dry. It puzzled Amalee. She asked the invisible presence, voiced her concern into the air, but it seemed to be uncentered, less tangible even than usual, and she felt no response. Paradoxically, she felt more and more watched than ever before, and she worked at the loom in quiet embarrassment. And the tension grew.

"The thunderstorm struck the garden the night the garden made love to Amalee.

"The air had grown heavier and heavier and stiller and stiller as late afternoon deepened into dusk. Restless, Amalee left her loom to walk, even though it was growing hard to see in the darkness. Fast-moving clouds covered the full, low hanging moon when she was in a glade of small trees, and the darkness closed in around her, trapping her. The perfume of the garden was like mist droplets in the heavy air, clinging to her face and her arms uncomfortably. She stood still, unable to see, afraid for the first time since she had entered the garden. The tree trunks loomed like obstacles she felt rather than saw. The white blossoms that hung from their branches glowed, ghostlike.

"Then the wind rose, and the branches began to move. They brushed at her, pushing her, and she began to walk, slowly at first, unsure where she was, then with quickening paces. The stones of the path were uneven, treacherous under her feet. A harsh cry behind her, a night bird or a peacock scream, set her running.

"The wind pushed her, and she ran, brushed by branches. The path seemed to glow; it was the only thing she could see, and she followed it. The garden moved her, urged her. Bushes clutched at her; vines swung across her face. Thunder boomed overhead. A crack of lightning split the darkness, and she ran toward what seemed like a familiar gate revealed for a moment in its glare. She crashed into the gate, fell through it as it opened. Heart pounding with the thunder, the agitation of the garden in the wind fevering her mind, she darted forward, tripped, and fell into a mass of vines.

"The vines tangled around her, and she struggled against them in panic. The wind seemed to be roaring through the branches, but that was high above her. Here, on the ground, the pocket of air in the vines was strangely still. But heavy, heavy with scent that drugged her and clouded her mind and smothered her panic. Lie still, the vines told her, gentle but firm around her wrists. Lie still, the blossoms' heavy scent whispered in her ear. You are in no danger, the leaves rustled at her neck. Despite the storm raging far above her, she lay still, in the embrace of the vines, feeling the leaves and blossoms caressing her skin, felt the kiss on her lips.

"Now Amalee was not totally innocent," Wayland paused. Not a needle moved in darning, not a pea fell from a pod. His listeners were as caught in his storytelling as Amalee was caught, entranced, in the vines. "Do not forget, she was just a servant in the castle full of young men. She was lovely enough for the king to have noticed her and sent her along with the other treasures in the gifting procession. She had kept to herself as much as possible, but she had been noticed once or twice anyway. And had little choice in the matter, when the eye that fell on her was a lord's.

"But now the garden whispered to her, in scent and sound and strength of its presence. The vines around her wrists gentled their touch, having gained her attention. The garden did not command—it asked.

"And Amalee thought of all the gifts the garden had bestowed upon her, of how she loved its beauty. She felt its loneliness, and it matched her own, fit it like one puzzle piece fit into another. And she said yes.

"'Yes,' she told the garden, and she tasted the utter sweetness of the blossoms and felt the gentle embrace of the vines and heard the soft caress of the leaves. And the storm broke, and rain poured down upon the bower where she lay among the vines, and it was the weight of the invisible presence of the garden that she felt in her arms, not the weight of the air.

"It was the dusting of pollen from the willows on the still waters of a pond that gave Amalee the idea for her finest weaving. The pollen floated down from the catkins like the golden condensation of the sun itself, shimmering upon the dark greenness of the still water in the new spring that emerged as the garden turned in its own special cycles.

"Amalee had woven several beautiful tapestries for the presence in the garden, and he had come to her and embraced her upon the beds of flowers many times. Each time he came, and they touched with the love that was growing between them, the invisible presence of the garden grew more and more solid, more and more real, to Amalee's touch. Her embrace made him more and more tangible.

"But to her eyes he remained only a deepening shadow in the fragrant darkness.

"However much they reached for and embraced each other, and found joy in each other, their love was incomplete. Or maybe it was *because* their love was growing so nearly complete, that they suffered. For Amalee, however much she could touch and hold and feel her beloved grow more solid in the darkness, could not help longing to see him. And however much she could sense his moods and his feelings and his wants, humming in the dark, flower-scented air, she longed for him to speak to her, to say her name. But when she pressed him, begged him to make himself visible to her, he made it clear he would not. Could not.

"It was almost enough, even with this incompleteness. In the wondrous idyllic timelessness of the garden, she felt his love so clearly that it was almost enough for him to be at least solid, real in her arms, in the sweet darkness. It was almost enough. But it wasn't quite. She loved him too much; she was too much the servant-weaver and not enough the magic princess to be satisfied with the fairy tale.

"So she gathered the pollen in her pocket, as unobtrusively as possible. And she threaded new warp on her loom, with the greatest of care, and began a new weaving.

"This weaving she worked in the true tapestry manner, using her fingers instead of the shuttle to thread the brilliant hues of yarn with infinite care in and out of the weft. And although she captured the porcelain blush of the pink rose, and the clear blue of the delphinium, and the greens of the fern and the fir and the ivy, the cloth's pattern was abstract, rippling from color to color in its own self-contained rhythms.

"Even the lavish pallet of yarns the garden's presence had provided did not satisfy her now, but she wandered every corner of the garden, to find and point to the flower or leaf whose color she desired, and spoke her need to her invisible lover. And he brought her what she wanted, in tune with the urgency of her artist's need, although she could feel the air hum with his mystification and bafflement at her new project. And when he came to her, in the darkness, and she could read his feelings almost as clearly as if he *could* speak them, she smiled and teased him gently away from the questions that hovered in the fragrance of the flowers.

"And she wove on. She wove faster and faster, seized by urgency that she tried to keep hidden in her breast, not understanding its source. She couldn't stop longing to see his face, couldn't stop longing to hear him speak her name. And he would not be seen, be heard. It was only a matter of time before it would start to harm the garden. Already, when he came to her each evening a thunderstorm came with him, the wind tossing the branches and strewing petals across the stone paths. She feared the stormy wind would blow down more blossoms and new leaves than could grow back; the paths would be littered with the debris of yearning.

"With trembling fingers Amalee finally cut the finished weaving from her loom. It was high afternoon, and the presence in the garden was not near. Carefully, as the sun moved slowly lower and lower in the sky, she finished the piece, tying off the threads and stitching here and there. She breathed a soft little song, wordless but haunting, absentmindedly answering the birds that called in the vines above her head, as she worked.

"Then, when the sun was low, but the evening still light, she called her lover. And with the wind tossing the trees, and large raindrops splatting the stone walk with the strewn petals, he came. She felt him come close, felt the familiar ripple in the air that was his daylight guise, then felt his arms close around her.

"And she quickly drew the handful of pollen from her pocket and threw it over him.

"Held motionless by his shock, he stood, limned by the golden powder, tall, misshapen, the one shoulder higher than the other, the body twisted, the hands that were so gentle opening and closing on the wind-tossed, petal-strewn air. And he spoke: 'Why?' he cried out in a wonderful voice, rich, sweet, despite the agony in it. 'Why have you done this? You have ruined —'

"But before he could finish, before he could move, Amalee drew her other hand from behind her back, and threw the weaving she had just completed over his shoulders. It was a shirt, and it fit him, misshapen, the high shoulder and the stooped one, the twisted body, like a glorious new skin.

"For Amalee was a craftswomen, an artisan, a true artist, above all things. Her hands were skilled and knowing. What her eyes had never seen, her hands had already learned, in the dark, in the loving. She had made the shirt to fit him perfectly according to what those hands knew.

"'You *knew*,' he cried, shocked.

"'Of course I knew,' she smiled.

"'And you loved me anyway!'

"'Of course I did. There was no need for you to hide . . . never was.' And she smiled and took his pollen-limned hands in her own.

"And that, of course," Wayland's rich voice rang out, and his audience, knowing the end of the story, nevertheless listened rapt with wonder, "was when the miracle happened . . . when the shirt Amalee wove, containing all her love and all her artistic passion, worked the miracle, and she saw the misshapen body melt, and reform, and grow solid in the late afternoon sunlight, the shoulders even, the body straight, the hands fine and strong, the features of his face clear and clean and beautiful."

CHAPTER 6

"Her fever has broken."

"Ranna's mother's words were almost a sob. There were tears as well as relief in the eyes she turned up to Willow. Willow sensed the fear the woman had held in bay for the long hours while Ranna tossed, raving at first in the throes of the fever; then ominously her words had faded to a soft mumble. Peggin put aside the wet cloths with which she had bathed her daughter's face, arms, and then her body to cool her, rose and hugged Willow, then shrank back at her boldness, embarrassed, and patted Willow's hands, then wiped the tears from her eyes with her apron hem.

Willow had had her own fears as well, that her Woodwaynim lore might not work as well here in Rune. She had quickly exhausted the range of herbs that were in Highrune's garden; Lexin had done his best to search out others, based on her descriptions, in the city's gardens and surrounding fields. But finally Willow had implored Morat to let her go to the more distant Runegladden forest to search for the things more familiar to her lore.

"Lexin has done well," she told him. "He's got talent, and his care for Ranna has driven him beyond his usual range. But I need to search myself. I don't even know if I can find what I need, here in Runegladden, but I have to try."

Morat resisted at first. Amran-an had confided to Willow that Morat was hesitant to send her into the woods where the trickery of the spring had occurred, afraid somewhat that the magic that had taken them awry might recur, somehow, and pull her away from him. "Tell him, Am, I will not leave Rune," she insisted. "Tell him not to fear. I'm tied here, by concern for Ranna, and by concern for his people as well." She didn't voice the inner tumult she felt at the idea of leaving Rune, leaving Morat. It puzzled her and moiled her peace.

And so Morat had sent her, accompanied by Amran-an and Redd, as far afield as she wanted, frightened for the little waiting maid . . . and for his citizens, among whom the fever was also spreading, in the excessive heat of high summer that burned as the solstice neared.

The scents of Runegladden were strong and came unexpectedly close to overpowering Willow's heart. Each tree and shrub, oak and maple, ash and birch, ninebark and snowberry (and even the rowan, she felt with a special twinge), had its own distinct message to her senses, so long deprived of forest. It took a few minutes for her to steady herself, her hand on the horn of the cornua's saddle, when she dismounted. Amran-an seemed to sense her discomfort and came to steady her with a hand on her shoulder that brought her back to focus on the task at hand.

"What I need will be growing near water," she told him, sensing in return his wizard's interest in her lore.

She brushed aside the spicebush undergrowth to make her way off the path, holding aloft like a lantern the woodrune she had made, listening to the soft chimes it made as she went forward. She had woven into it her deep need, with some of the purple threads that Ranna was using to embroider her wedding quilt squares and some of the herbs that Lexin had brought her. She whispered to it to take her forward to what she sought, letting Runegladden's woodsy breath filter through it, sorting out the healing scents.

It took a while to find a promising place. "First on that downslope to the creek, then on the upslope beyond, there," she pointed. She let her nose guide her rather than her eyes, and then, as she came to denser growth, she dropped to her hands and knees, handing the woodrune to Amran-an, and sorted the vegetation, her fingers, probing.

"Sa, golden motherwort, see here the shape of the trifold leaves, Am?" she pointed. With the small knife she had brought she dug deftly, bringing up the root. "And rosy feverbane as always, near it," she said as she cut the leaves. "The Mother watches out for us, in our need, growing these always together."

Stonecrop, alumroot, heart-leaved mistflower to clear the fevered mind, tall heart's-ease, Lady fern, lungwort for congestion; one by one Willow pointed out the healing herbs as she led Amran-an on and on into deeper glades. She took cuttings from the woody shrubs as well and unearthed rotting logs to seek out fungi, filling her basket.

"Now, if I could just find . . . ah, Mother of All, let it be here . . ." She reached for a small mushroom half-hidden in the greenery. She pushed Amran-an's hand aside sharply when he reached for another, "No, never that one, Am. It's deadly, not healing, be careful what you take." And Amran-an took note that he might have wizard's lore, but never the depth of the knowledge of the plants of this woods that this Woodwaynim woman possessed.

******

While the wizard took copious notes and made drawings of the plant samples, Willow made sufficient quantities of the concoction for Ranna. Amran-an gave instructions for more to be made for the other citizens of Highrune. Morat had thanked Willow, holding her hands in his, for sharing the cure for the fever. She sensed Morat wanted to embrace her, moved as he was by her help in the face of this yet one more danger with which he contended, but he had held back. On her side, Willow was surprisingly moved by having done something to help him help those he cared about. She had found some new solace in the gift of her Woodwaynim talents to the High-Lord of Rune.

The idea came to her that it might please him if she made some of the herbs up into windrunes to hang here and there in Highrune. To offer his household some protection from the sickness, she thought, and perhaps to add a bit of a touch of Woodway to the walls for her own sake.

How quickly the year had turned, Willow thought as she tied the herbs with some of Ranna's green thread to twigs from the Sensitive Tree. The solstice was upon them.

"It's hotter than usual," Ranna told her, "Even here within the halls of Highrune, where it usually stays cooler among the sheltering stones. I'm so glad the glass covers have been pulled back from the inner Glass Garden. Lexin says even these tropicals would suffer at the heat if we had not."

"How nice that Lexin comes twice a week now to give the orchids special care because of the heat," Willow teased Ranna. Lexin was with them now, sitting with the maid as they listened to Redd and Tellit try out some tunes on flutes.

"We'll be trying out the brass horns later today, after they finish polishing them up," Redd said. "These clarions are for the Midsummer parades, and they'll sound a lot better on the big horns. Don't worry, Tellit, there will be a drum for you," said Redd with a wry smile, as the flute broke in Tellit's large fingers. A dark look passed over the boy's face at the accident, familiar as he was with being so accident-prone.

The weeks had passed quickly. Willow considered how she had found growing ease in the company of Ranna, her mother, and the other women of the household; how she found comfort from her homesickness in the friendship of Redd and Wayland, and even Tellit, who hung on the fringes of Redd's company. She had come to enjoy the sweetness of watching Lexin carry out his shy wooing of the little maid as he tended the flowers of the Glass Garden from fragile spring blooms to heavier scented summer blossoms.

She even enjoyed the visits by the High-Lord; she perceived clearly the kindness in him toward everyone else, how much they all loved him, and that somehow made it easier, as time went by, to accept his kindnesses toward her, the many small gifts he brought, his careful, respectful words.

"Maybe more than just the year is turning," she whispered to herself, feeling something welling up from the woodrune that was taking shape in her hands.

Ranna explained to Willow how, for the Midsummer celebration, Highrune was divided into four quadrants, each centered on one of the major Guild Halls of the city, each given a color: red for the weavers and dyers; blue for the stone masons, metal workers, and builders; yellow for the fine arts crafters; and green for the grocers, brewers, and bakers.

"My favorite is the Infloria," said Lexin.

"What's Infloria," asked Willow, anxious to hear about something that sounded like it had to do with flowers.

"All year long, the wives and daughters of the Guildsmen gather and dry flowers," the gardener explained. "They crumble them up to make colored powders. And for the holiday they lay the powders out, like paint, in huge pictures stretching across the whole floor of their Guild Hall. They are incredibly detailed . . . magnificent," he said, eyes glowing, "all made out of dried flower petals."

How like Runerin folks, thought Willow sadly, to dry and powder their flowers and lay the dust on stone.

She thought with a bit of homesickness of the way Woodwaynim folk wound live flowers around their door posts and railings and in pots on ladders everywhere, to spread the runes of their scent and share the message of Midsummer and the Mother-of-All's generous bounty.

“What do they depict, these Infloria?”

“They are scenes from our history,” explained Redd. “There is a contest among the Guilds, of course, and the winning Guild keeps the trophy in a place of honor through the year. They are full of majestic knights and brave explorers and fair princesses and mythical beasts. And there are lots of symbolic things incorporated in the images that the spectators are invited to parse out the import of, rune puzzles and references to literature, and even new poems. The more complexity, the more points are earned in the contest.”

“But I always feel a bit sad,” sighed Ranna, “when the week of Midsummer celebration is over, and the pictures are swept away, just colorful dust swept up and out into the streets of Rune, to blow on the wind.”

“All’s not lost,” said one of the older women. “Us older folks think the dust spreading through the streets helps keep our stones remembering our history. And maybe it spreads some good luck toward the harvest gathering at Autumn-Turning.”

“There will be a parade each evening of the five-day celebration, presided over by High-Lord Morat,” said Ranna’s mother. “The ladies and I have made up some special cloaks for you to wear, each day, as you will be sitting on high stage with the High-Lord, won’t you?”

No, thought Willow. In front of all Rune? Please, do not let Morat ask that of me, at least not yet.

“There won’t be a fair this year,” said Redd, “as the High-Lord has canceled it because of the illness. But there will be a foot race through the city streets, with the young men of each Guild Hall competing for the key to the city and the privilege to sit as High-Lord next to last evening, on the dais, and be served his meal by Morat himself.”

“And the food,” cried Ranna. “The food will be beyond splendid! In each quadrant an inn is designated to cook and serve the most magnificent holiday food. Again, it's a competition. The stews, the roasts, the *cakes*!" She shaped huge cakes in the air with her hands.

"I hear Heller has sent seafood up from Kai-Haluu for the blue team this year," said Redd.

"He has," Morat said as he entered; he motioned them all to sit again, after they rose hastily in respect. "And they will concoct a huge mermaid with seaweed for hair and scallops for the scales on her tail. And I know not what to cover her breasts," he winked.

He set two containers down on the table and opened them, releasing the salt-scent of the sea. "I've brought samples, sweet marinated octopus and spicy pickled fish, for you to try. The blue team cooks are anxious for your opinion."

He took a morsel, put it in his mouth, and made a large mocking gesture of smacking his lips with enjoyment. "I prefer the spicy fish, myself."

"All in all it will be splendid," Morat declared.

******

Once again, Morat and Amran-an had ridden out to survey the fields, to take stock of the growing things, some of which had developed their own fevers and blights . . . as well as to monitor the fevers that had abated in the city. The reports from the fields had been mixed . . . whatever had been troubling Rune since spring had kept up its alarming pace . . . crops stunted without apparent cause . . . insect hoards inexplicably devouring whole fields . . . rusts long ago cured by Amran-an's wizardry resurgent on grain. The celebration would be tempered a bit by the onging blights.

Ranna, still recovering from her illness and taking advantage of the scare she had given her mother and her High-Lord, had won permission for herself and Willow to join the other girls of Highrune, freed from the rigors of school, to go out beyond the city walls to gather flowers to decorate the city. Chaperoned by their teachers and their aunts, the girls went off in donkey-driven carts to gather huge bunches of flowers.

They were returning with the carts full of honey-scented clover, sweet heather, and the huge sunflowers that would symbolize the sun's solstice fullness, that had grown up in drifts on the hillsides. The girls wore bright summer field dresses more abbreviated than the usual garb, and large straw hats. They waved scarves and flags with large sun shapes painted on them, in full mood for the Solstice celebration. They were singing the Solstice songs, practicing for their procession through the city.

And they came upon the boys practicing in their own way for the parade, in which some of them would march for the first time as full-fledged pages. A few of the girls waved their flags and scarves to the boys.

In Morat's absence, Redd had gone along with Hallon to help keep the boys in order. But excitement was high, and somehow, they had gotten themselves into a boisterous form of practice for the parade that was giving Hallon and Redd trouble managing. And now, with the girls watching . . . well, that encouraged their antics.

Someone among them came up with the idea to form into squads and take up battling with each other, using sticks they had taken up by the roadside. One squad was led by a large, muscular youth who had grown past his age-mates surprisingly early. And of course another squad was led by Tellit, the next largest among them. They were begging scarves from the girls and attaching them to the sticks to make flags. "We are the red team," taunted one; "we'll beat the blue team for sure."

"Yeah, you better win now, because your team sure won't win the foot race or the contests of strength on fourth day," answered another.

For the fun of it, the largest boy took up the smallest one, and put him up on his shoulders and handed him a stick. The boys were arguing about that as an unfair advantage and pushing forward another smaller boy for Tellit to lift up on his shoulders.

Willow wasn't at all sure she saw it, some faint shape that came between Tellit and the other large boy, like a thin gray stray wind, and wound around their legs . . . or was it just a few bits of straw taken up and spun around by an eddy of air? But she cried out a caution, at the same moment that Hallon reached to pull the stick away, and at the same moment that Redd took Tellit's arm to exert control . . . and then there was a tumble of bodies on the ground, enmeshed dangerously with sticks.

The girls screamed.

Morat and Amran-an had taken that moment to come riding up, and they threw themselves down off their cornuas and joined Hallon and Redd, wading in, separating the factions, untangling the limbs, pulling the boys to stand, and yelling at them to be calm. But the small boy who had been atop his large fellow lay crumpled on the ground, shaking the head he'd hit on a hard stone and crying in pain at his arm bent at a not at all proper angle.

Hallon took up the boy, calling for one of the donkey-carts to come, dumped out the flowers, and laid the boy in it. The girls huddled around, but he shooed them away. "Redd," he called, "take him to the Healers. Have them give him something for his head," he instructed, "Make sure they watch for concussion."

"Sa," Redd agreed, "and that arm will have to be set and splinted."

"Stones of Rune," said Amran-an to Morat when the noise had

quieted. "Did you see that?" He was looking at Tellit, the boy standing aside, eyes wide, hands clenched at his side.

"I did," said Morat, running his hand through his hair thoughtfully.

"I also," said Willow, coming up to his side.

Amran-an muttered something about unshapers.

*****

Willow and Ranna walked slowly back toward Highrune. The Midsummer festivities had been enjoyable, and Willow had enjoyed exploring more of Highrune than she'd ever gotten to see before. She found the city of stone almost delightful. Flowers were everywhere, tumbling down from every window box, overflowing from garden boxes and flowerpots in front of every house, camouflaging the stones of the houses and the sidewalks. A glimpse of a garden through an alleyway had given her a jolt of homesickness for Woodway; the small fountain playing musically over stones beneath a rowen tree around which vines curled, heavily hung with wood roses, had seemed so familiar. The scent had wafted a memory to her. But it was walled off by an iron gate, and she walked on by.

"Did I not tell you the food would be fantastic?" Both of Ranna's hands held cakes, and a basket hung from her arm full of carefully wrapped treats she was taking back to share with Lexin. "I think the bakers of the Green team surpassed themselves this year. They made up for the scarcer than usual peaches with the dates and figs sent from Proven."

Willow murmured agreement around the cake that filled her mouth.

"My feet are sore from all the walking! But I had to show you all four of the Infloria. Aren't you glad you saw them? I am so glad Lord Morat relented, and let the fair be held after all. It's because of you he was able to do so, because your medicines controlled the sickness so well."

"The stories depicted in the Infloria were curious. I didn't understand most of the symbols in them," said Willow, after she had swallowed the last morsel of cake. "It seems the lore of flowers is the same in Rune as in Woodway, but there were some animals I have never seen."

"Oh, lots of them are mythical creatures," said Ranna. "And there are always a lot of ancestors depicted that I have trouble remembering much about. But the artistry is amazing, don't you agree?"

"And so much work involved, you say. Growing and harvesting and drying the flowers all summer long, then crushing them. Then laying out the design and coloring in the picture with all the crushed petals. And you said it is all swept away when the Midsummer festival is over?"

Ranna smiled. "Aye, it is all swept away, allowed to blow away in the wind. Like memories of the spring season. It's said some of the young girls and lads dance it away with their feet, hoping to see some omen of who will turn out to be their true love in how the colors stain their feet."

"And the year turns on, past the solstice," said Willow, growing thoughtful, and thinking of how the solstice was celebrated in Woodway.

"And now everyone's thoughts turn toward the tilling, the cultivating, and then toward the harvesting at Autumn-Turning. But I like Midsummer the best," said the little serving maid, pulling another couple of cakes out of her basket, handing one to Willow, and biting into the other herself. "I like the food!"

CHAPTER 7

The cool air of the garden felt good. Willow untied the ribbons at her neckline and bared her throat to the dark night air. She fanned her face with her hand; her cheeks felt so warm.

But it still wasn't that cold in the garden. It did not seem like Autumn-Turning, not nearly as cool as one could expect. The weather had finally turned warm and dry, after a worrisome summer of thunderstorms and damaging winds that had kept Morat often afield. Now it was finally fine for finishing off the growing fields of grain for the coming harvest. But warm. Too warm, indeed, to need fires in the great Runehall, even though the massive stones always seemed to cast a slight chill.

But tradition called for the new hearth fires to be lit this night, when the End-of-Summer Moon waxed to fullness and signaled the beginning of the harvest. And in Highrune, as everywhere else in the land of Rune, as even in Woodway, Mother-lands, and most of the known world, tradition was to be upheld.

Lighting of the hearth fires was women's task here in Highrune, just as Willow had known it to be in Woodway. In Highrune the full influence of the Mother's ways had long been overlaid with more masculine practices and wizardries, but Willow was surprised to find that the women's fire-song was the same crooning rune-lilt that she had known since early childhood. This made her feel particularly at home this night among the stones of Rune.

Willow and Ranna wore garlands of autumn flowers in their

hair, just like all the other women of the household: asters and chrysanthemums, with gold and yellow and brown ribbons, signifying the turning of the year to Autumn.

Holding to the traditions she knew, lonely in a strange land, Willow had made her own fire-gift to the Mother. She had woven in her favorite autumn Woodwaynim prayers when she used a few of the finer autumn-hued threads from Ranna's embroidery basket to tie the switches of the traditional seven woods into a bouquet. What she hadn't been able to find in the palace's gardens, Ranna had begged for her from Lexin.

Ranna had copied her, asking the meaning of each twig. Some she explained to the maid, like the bit of willow osier for her Branch; some she kept secret in her heart, the bit of dried everlasting and the dark sprig of berries for Rowan. A bit of a prayer for Morat welled up and surprised her, but she tied a knot for him, too, swallowing a tiny twinge of foreboding as she knotted the thread over the wood.

Each woman of the household stepped forth and laid her offering on the main hearth, the heart of Rune, laying their bouquets atop the traditional laying of oak, pine, and ash logs, adorned with wreaths of grapevine and the first sheaves of wheat. Willow was the last.

Willow was surprised when Ranna thrust the flint into her hand and nodded vigorously for her to advance and light the ritual wood. But when she looked around at the household women, they all smiled and nodded like Ranna. Willow supposed she was the one of highest rank among them. But it seemed she was a friend as well.

As she stepped forward to the hearth and lit the wood, she listened to the crooning women's-words rising softly around her to mix with the new smoke of the first-fire. She thought with a sudden new awareness, how sparsely populated the halls of Highrune were, that a woman of rank had to come from far Woodway to light the first-fire of autumn. She watched the flames catch in the wood, sending up in aromatic smoke the runes for luck and prosperity, for fruitfulness. And she thought: How empty these halls of stone were! Hardly ever the sound of a child's laughter. Only in the kitchen, or in the sewing room over which Ranna's mother presided, or in the other workrooms, were there voices. There was too much silence everywhere else.

All day long that emptiness had been concealed behind the clanging and hammering of the smithies in the low courtyard, where the men had gathered, in a kind of ceremony less formal than the women's, but as age-old—the honing and fixing of the implements of harvest.

But High-Lord Morat was away; he and his wizard and his cousin and his train of squires and pages had ridden out five days ago to survey the land's readiness for reaping.

As she stood still and silent before the roaring fire that signaled autumn, the crooning Mother-words all sung, Willow had considered again the emptiness of Highrune. Surely, once, she thought, these halls had been filled with the noise of several generations gathered together. In the flickering light of the first-fire, the shadows jumped and twisted until Willow could almost see an old grandfather High-Lord sitting in comfortable majesty in the chair Morat used now, his sons and daughters around him, wine cups in hand, a toast to a new betrothal . . . perhaps a woman held a baby to stand kicking on her lap, smiling at its bubbly giggles . . . a brood of younger grandchildren wrestled on the fleece-skin rugs . . . a small girl rocked a carved-wood doll to sleep with quiet play-woman dignity . . . older and with more serious matters on their minds, a couple sat with hands entwined and bowed heads together, whispering, a chaperone aunt frowning at them over her needlework . . .

Willow had stepped back, the heat of the blooming fire suddenly very hot on her cheeks. Was it the past she saw in the fire's lights and shadows? Or the future? It had almost seemed like a

Mother's-gift Vision.

High-Lord Morat's family was scattered. His parents were dead. His sisters raised their broods in their husbands' halls. His brother? Willow didn't know. They would all gather, as would the second and third cousins and the lords and ladies of Rune's Portions, to Highrune's halls for the great winter festival at Midwinter, the next Turning-of-the-Year. There would be great festivities then, according to Ranna. Baking and cooking and stitching of party finery for weeks beforehand. But after the dances and feasts and hunts and contests of skill were done, they would all return home to spend the rest of winter at their own hearths, the land quiet in the grip of winter.

Willow had turned abruptly away from the heat of the autumn's first-fire and gone outside to sit in the outer courtyard, under an ancient three-trunked aspen tree. She could not tell, in the silver light of the moon, whether its quaking leaves had begun to turn autumn-gold yet. She put her hands flat on the stone bench, at her sides, and felt the coldness of the stone. She was feeling the turning of the year, like a thin vertigo, and she steadied herself on the bench with her hands.

Something, she felt, had waned; something had thinned the air of Highrune over the years and years. Something—perhaps only the turnings of time—she shook her head, feeling a dizziness of doubt—had emptied the high-shadowed coigns of the ceilings of crowded laughter and noisy happiness.

Willow threw her head back and looked up at the sky, where the stars shone, hard and cold and beautiful—fixed in their places, yet whirling with the turning of the year. The Harvest-Wain, large, square constellation with its two bright oxen-stars had climbed well above the horizon as the night deepened. The moon was round and huge and orange above the walls of the courtyard.

"Poor Morat!" she sighed, not understanding the feelings that welled up in her. “So alone!” The rush of warmth that took her and shook her made her cheeks flash hotly again. She grabbed the cold stone edge of the bench and held on tightly. He had only been gone five days, and she couldn’t understand why she could miss him, long so much for him to come back.

The tears in her eyes blurred the stars.

And when she heard the scrape of boot on the path, and turned, her eyes were not yet clear.

“Morat!” she cried. “High-Lord! You have returned,” she added with more control. “You were not expected ‘til the morrow.”

She had stood and taken a few eager steps before something about the figure made her hesitate.

He emerged into the moonlight, and she saw Morat’s face. Or was it? Some trick of the moonlight, or the silly tears in her eyes, she thought. He doesn’t seem to know me!

A pang of anxiety squeezed her heart. Was this his shade? His ghost, come in advance of the couriers, to tell her of some dreadful mishap?

But the hand that took hers and raised it to his lips was flesh. And as she looked into his eyes, it seemed that recognition was waking.

“Lovely!” he said softly. “Moonlight lends beauty to most ladies, but you give the gift back again with your loveliness.”

Willow could find no words to answer. She tried to withdraw her hand, but he held it firmly. She felt her own fingers trembling, was embarrassed to know he felt them trembling, too.

He smiled, a slow smile that curled at the corners with a hint of arrogance. It was Morat’s face, yet not his at all.

“I am surprised to find he has such good taste. Surprised he had the sense, my dear brother, to bring you out of the wilderness of the Motherwoods, whatever his excuse."

A thread of understanding uncurled in Willow's mind, made her eyes widen.

"Allow me to allay your most pretty confusion, my Lady," he said, bowing deeply before her without relinquishing her hand. "I am Evmorat, brother and twin to Morat, High-Lord of Rune. And may I have," he smiled again, with more teeth showing this time, "the pleasure of your name?"

"I am Willow Lythew, Heart-of-Woods, of the Second Branch of Woodway," she whispered. She freed her hand from his at last.

"Lady Willow," he acknowledged with a nod and a look that made Willow's cheek flush again, as something in it made her feel as if she had given—nay, he had taken—something more intimate with her name.

"This garden is lovely," he said, releasing her gaze from his and looking around. "I have always liked it by moonlight, though our sisters hardly ever came here in the evening. But surely there are much lovelier bowers among the gardens of the Woodwaynim. The beauties of that fair fastness hidden between the breasts of the Mother's Mountains—why, they are too famous in rumor not to be true. Whatever attractions can you find to keep you here in old, musty Highrune?"

Willow didn't realize she was backing away from him until she felt the stone bench against the backs of her legs. She stood, feeling trapped. If she sat down, he might—*he* would—take himself an invitation to sit beside her. Her heart was beginning to hammer. This man alarmed her deeply. Perhaps it was the arrogance, that hint of playful cruelty sitting so strangely on Morat's gentle features. Perhaps it was that he invaded her body space, standing too close to her for her to feel comfortable, yet not close enough to permit her to protest.

She knotted her hands in her skirts and stood straight, determined not to show that he flustered her.

"Lord Evmorat—" she began.

"Nay, I am not Lord, simply Evmorat. Morat is the Lord here. My brother has always been such a serious sort. Someone told him when he was still too young that he was destined to be High-Lord, and he took it to heart. I can't imagine him being much fun."

It felt to Willow like Evmorat was much taller than Morat, even though she knew they must actually be the same height. She chided herself for her silly fear.

"High-Lord Morat's company is most pleasant," she said defiantly.

"Indeed?" His tone was insinuating, suggestive, almost a leer.

Willow blushed again.

He reached as if carelessly, touched the untied ribbon of her collar where it trailed down from her neckline, wound his fingers in it. Surely, she thought, he can feel my heart pounding beneath his fingers.

"Have you taught him to dance, yet? I always told him he ought to learn to dance," he said.

"Brother, you frighten the lady."

This time the figure that stepped into the moonlight was clearly the High-Lord of Rune.

Evmorat jumped. He dropped his hand. But he turned slowly.

"Why, Morat, my High-Lord, I didn't mean to frighten her." His hands opened, palms to Morat, at his side, and he bowed slightly. But the smile on his face, a mixture of innocence and mockery, denied the placating gesture. "I only happened on the lady alone in this chill, dark garden, and sought to offer her some company."

Morat stood rigid. His dark travel-cloak hung down, hiding his hands in massive shadow, but his face was white in the moonlight. Willow stood with both hands at her bared throat, watching the tight muscles jump in his neck, the skin tighten over the clench of his teeth.

"Evmorat," Morat said, "You were to wait for me at the Well of Urthumna. To ride the rest of the way in the morning."

"I arrived at the Well a day early," answered Evmorat smoothly. "You know how restless I get waiting. So I rode on ahead. I rode slowly, sure you would catch up with me on the road."

Morat looked at his brother, and it was clear in his eyes that he heard his brother's lie. The moon was high, and Morat had ridden hard on into the night to catch up. Evmorat tried to stare him down. But after several long moments his gaze dropped.

"I left word for you with the Well-keeper. Didn't I leave word?" Evmorat whined.

"You left word."

Willow watched them look at each other, their faces like mirrors of each other, yet different, too, the one hard with anger, the other mobile with slyness. She saw that somehow something was spoken between them, uttered without words, communicated nevertheless by the focus of eye and posture of body.

In Morat's look was a warning. In Evmorat's smile was an answer: "I submit . . . I leave your toy to you . . . for now."

"I warn you," said the grim line of Morat's cheekbone. "This is no matter for any of your games."

"If you say so, dearest brother."

Morat made a harsh sound in his throat. "Why can't you be—

why can't we—" His hands twitched at his sides with his exasperation. A sadness made his eyes even darker.

Evmorat looked up. A change flickered over his face, mirroring Morat's sadness. The sarcasm faded, and the sadness in his eyes deepened into a haunted, helpless look that startled Willow.

"I know no other way to be," Evmorat said softly. Then, the irritating smirk swept back onto his face.

"I warn you!" rasped Morat.

"If you say so."

Willow had wound her blouse ribbons tight around her fingers, in her tension, and she felt them cutting.

Finally, Evmorat moved. "By your leave, my Lord, and yours, my Lady," he turned to Willow briefly, "I am weary from my ride and will retire." He bowed once more, slightly, almost jauntily, and turned to go. "The night air grows cool, my Lord," he said, with the same suggestive softness of voice, "too cool, I'm sure, for the Lady. You should take her in."

Willow and Morat watched him go, heard the snatch of whistled tune he left in his wake. Willow went to Morat, stood at his side. She heard the soft growl in his throat.

She felt cold and tired and ached to cry; cry for the spoiled reunion with Morat that she hadn't even known she looked forward to. Now he was here, and she wanted to lay her hand in his, rest her head on his shoulder, but the hardness of his anger kept her from it.

A breeze rustled the aspen leaves and made her shiver. Morat saw; that stirred him from his preoccupation with his brother. He took off his cloak, put it around her shoulders. For a moment he stood looking down at her, cupping her face in his hands, and she thought he would kiss her.

She kept her face raised to him.

But he only hugged her, hard, crushing her to his chest and giving a small groan. “Ach! By Rune, I am happy to be home!”

Then he led her in, his arm around her shoulder.

*****

“Well, brother, so you have found yourself another wench to your liking,” Evmorat smiled, an ambiguous twist of his lips, “after all this time.”

He staggered back as Morat grabbed the front of his tunic; he spread his hands in his all too familiar placating gesture. “Na . . . na, brother, I meant no disrespect.”

Morat’s voice was tight, low. “If you lay a hand on her . . . if you so much as enter the same room with her, I’ll make you rue it!”

Despite the sameness of their stature, Evmorat was nearly lifted off his feet by Morat’s grip. Their eyes met, matched dark for dark, fierceness for fierceness. Then Evmorat’s eyes lightened, his head fell back, and he smiled a small, submissive pout.

“My, my! She's really gotten under your skin! Not a finger will I lay on your woman. We could swear it if you wish. Even on our identical blood. We could slash our wrists and let the blood mix to bind the oath if you wish. Like we did when we were children.”

Stung, Morat let him go, folded his arms across his breast to still his trembling hands. For the thousandth time he wondered at Evmorat’s ability to irritate him beyond endurance so easily. He watched, unable to trust himself to speak, while his brother set his tunic right again with elaborate care.

“Must you mock everything?” Morat asked at last.

“It is my way. What would you have me say? *You* got to be

High-Lord. You've got all the dignity. So I'm left with mockery. The court king and the court jester." He bowed to Morat with the high flair of a bowing performer, the ribbons of his sleeves fluttering.

"Why?" Morat cried, flinging the words into his brother's face. "Why are we like this? Like some whole split in two? Why should the splitting of a seed spoil the harmony of our souls? We are not like Nissyen and Evnissyen, in the old saga . . . our mother didn't conceive us during an infidelity forced on her to ransom her beloved husband's life. Our mother was true, our father noble and kind. Why, then? Why?"

"Fool," Evmorat looked at him mockingly. "Why do you persist in looking for order and reason where there is none?"

Evmorat turned away, his cape swirling mockingly. He put his hands on the railing, looked down into the courtyard and out over the city of Rune, white stone shining in the sunlight, reflected in the river. He went on, softly, a touch of bitterness creeping into his voice, "It is the times, the thinning of the blood, the winding down of the universe, the decay of the old high times into the farce of today.

"Maybe I fight you to keep us from falling asleep. Something has to keep us from the sucking, the leaching out of our souls in this tired, worn-out everyday."

His words touched something in Morat, reminded him of Amran-an confessing his fears over blighted metal plow shares and tainted dreams, of the unshaping and mis-shaping that had tasked him throughout the past turnings of the year. He laid a hand on Evmorat's shoulder. But Evmorat flinched away from the touch.

"Damn it, Morat, I haven't got any high battles to fight. But a mean battle's better than none at all."

"But why me? Why must you fight me?"

Evmorat laughed, a harsh, bitter, mocking sound. “Because you’re noble. Archaic, high-minded, pure-hearted, responsible. Hell, brother, the only real difference between us is the five minutes between our births, my most honored High-Lord.” He spoke Morat’s title with nasty emphasis.

“If that's really what you want—”

Evmorat ground his teeth, frustrated. “You rune-damned fool, you’d give it to me, wouldn’t you! Hand over that circlet you wear. You damn, high-minded, pure-hearted, stupid fool! If you thought it would fix things. You always have to fix things.”

“You’re still my brother. Above all things, you are still my brother. What we could do, standing together instead of at odds. What we could do for Rune!”

Stung in turn, Evmorat flushed with anger. “Well, let me give you some advice, High-Lord,” he said, changing the subject abruptly. “Don’t wait so long this time to make your woman yours. He who hesitates . . .”

Evmorat jumped back as Morat lunged for him, smiling that he had made Morat lose control of himself again, putting out an arm to hold off his brother. But Morat held back, stood still with a new stillness that made him like one of the stones of the wall Evmorat leaned against, cold and immobile and powerful with runes. Strangely enough, the conversation was taking its turn toward the matter he needed to broach with Evmorat. Maybe, if their guards were to be down, even if as a result of hostility, he might get somewhere with it this time.

“Evmorat,” he began, “we need to talk of Tellit. Na, don’t interrupt me yet. You owe it to me to listen. He’s not a child anymore; he’s becoming a man. And he’s having problems. He needs a stronger influence, to help him.”

Evmorat let him talk, let him wind down, gave him no help at all.

"Evmorat, you have to acknowledge him. Take him in hand. Be his father. Give him some steadiness for his life and you some for yours."

"Why should I? What need do I have for a brat trailing at my heels? And who are you to preach of it to me? He could as likely be your son as mine."

Morat's voice was cold as naked sword steel. "Do not dishonor Andellienne more than you already have, Evmorat. You and I, and 'Ellienne's ghost, and the boy, too, know he is not son of mine."

Evmorat leaned back, his elbows resting on the wide stone railing, the city beyond him, his hand resting on the head of a carved lion-head that looked out over the city with glaring stone eyes and snarling mouth. There was an insolence in his stance that made Morat's teeth grate. "He might as well have been yours. There's more to fatherhood than seeding, you know."

Morat found himself a step closer to Evmorat, his hands clenched.

"It was *your* name she cried out when we begot him."

The blood was humming in Morat's ears. He didn't know how he held himself in check, he wanted so badly to hurt Evmorat back. Why? he cried inwardly, why do you have to hurt me like this? Why, my brother?

Something flickered in Evmorat's eyes, as if he'd heard Morat's silent cry. He turned abruptly, looked out into the courtyard. "She accepted me as a substitute," he said softly. "She closed her eyes to me while I held her and pretended she had you."

"Aieee!" The sound escaped Morat's unwilling lips. He stared at Evmorat's back, wishing him to turn, wanting to strangle him, wanting also, perversely, to embrace him and comfort him.

“Why, Morat? You loved her! You knew she loved you! Why not take her! Too shy? Too busy with the affairs of your new High-Lordship? You fool!” he spat. “Which one of us has committed the greater failure of fatherhood? Me, for the thing I did and won’t acknowledge? Or you, for the thing you didn’t have the guts to do?”

It was too much. Morat turned and ran, through the stripes of sunlight and shadow made by the long colonnade, flare of hot rage and dark of cold pain. Evmorat’s mockery fluttered after him with wings like doves startled from the stone tiles of the eaves.

CHAPTER 8

"So you say he asked you if you knew how to harp the 'Song of Midhe.'" The old man frowned as if something tasted bitter to him.

Behind him Ranna stirred uncomfortably on the bench by the door. Her small face frowned even more severely. "Evmorat is meddlesome and—"

Wayland glared the waiting maid into blushing silence. She knew it was impertinence of her to cast words on the High-Lord's brother, even if . . . Ranna knotted her hands in her skirts to keep still.

"Tell me, Wordsmith," Willow insisted. "What is the 'Song of Midhe'?" Her voice held a quaver. "If I've been insulted, don't I have the right to know how mortal the wound is Evmorat has struck?"

Wayland sighed, looking from Ranna to Willow, and finally laid aside the scrolls he was holding, letting their heavy parchment curls roll up with a snap.

"I will not presume to harp the 'Song'," he shook his head as Ranna rose to fetch him the harp. "My singing voice has long ago lost its timbre and flexibility for the ornate passages in a piece of that period. And you will have to excuse the rather overdone, flowery language; it comes with the period in which it was written, not from me!"

Nevertheless, as he took up the tale of Midhe, his voice deepened into his long-practiced story-teller's cadences.

"In far past days, when wizards were men of very great power, and held the knowledge for the good of the people in young, healthy bodies, not in aged frames like mine, Elhad-Eln was the halest and most handsome of wizards. His shining fairness matched the strength of his wisdom like a casket proper to its treasures, and he was loved by all, everywhere in the land."

He smiled, gave a gentle wink. "Perhaps by the fair ladies was he loved most of all.

"For the most part he was blind to their adoration, though his known preoccupation with his arcane studies and his good nature kept any lady from taking insult at his inattentiveness. They watched him, and gossiped of him constantly, and put themselves in his paths, though in vain.

"But his heart was seized at last, and seized by the image of golden-haired, white-skinned, blue-eyed Midhe. Why he had never noticed her before, I cannot say. The daughter of the High-Lord's third sister surely would have been at court often, and Midhe would have held her place easily in the circles of the loveliest of the ladies, whatever her lineage. Perhaps she had just grown into her beauty suddenly, being so young, bursting out of girlhood with the astonishing flash of a comet. And perhaps Elhad-Eln had just reentered the world from some deeper than usual wizardly isolation."

Willow smiled. As usual, the old wordsmith enjoyed weaving a tale's runes properly. She leaned back in her chair, hands folded in her lap. It looked to be quite a while before she might understand exactly how Evmorat had insulted her.

"However it might have happened," Wayland went on, "the wizard's glance fell on Midhe, and he was smitten by the darts beaming from her eyes. Passion burned in his heart like a fever. She became his sun and he a love-sickened, waning moon. He was a prisoner, enchained by the gold wires of her hair; the snares of her long eyelashes had caught his look, wound tight around his brain. His heart was a wild animal, longing for the taming touch—"

Ranna giggled.

Wayland interrupted himself with a shrug. "I told you it was an old tale. Honestly, all those old cliches are really in the original song. I just wanted to give you the flavor of the period in which it was written."

"Is this going to be a session in literary criticism?" teased Willow gently. "Or do I get to hear the rest of the story before dinner?"

"Ah," he gestured theatrically, "But in those days, the cliches were not yet so tarnished with overuse. And they have a point in the story," he continued. "It was just becoming the fashion in those days, this business of wooing. Until then, it is said, a man and a woman simply recognized the gladness of heart they brought to each other and smiled and joined hands and lives. But from some dark, jealous realm had come this newfangled business of 'proving one's love'—a very different kind of proof required by woman of man than by man of woman, I might add. A lover must now be a swain, proving his adoration by the depths of his poetry, the melancholy quality of his sighs, and the desperation of his deeds.

"A lady must never yield easily, lest her heart be accused of an infirm temper, like a poorer quality of metal. And the daughter of the High-Lord's third sister had her place among the ladies to uphold. Exquisite beauty was not enough; charm and loveliness not sufficient factors where fashion ruled.

"And so Midhe set tasks for the wizard Elhad-Eln. That was a new idea, her very own, and a great of feat of imagination admired greatly and quickly adopted by the other maidens. No longer did one have to depend upon one's swain for the inventiveness with which he sought to prove his love—and thus one's worth as the beloved. One could assure one's worth by setting task after difficult task.

"The wizard Elhad-Eln was strong and straight and majestic of mind and body. He was foremost in command of the elements. He had charms and powers and could call all manner of forces to dance at his fingertips. He was, to put it simply (both Willow and Ranna smiled) the best of men.

"It was quite a task for Midhe to keep him busy proving his love. But the idea of demanding deeds of valor had been hers, and she had her position in the vanguard of this newfangled conceit of romance to uphold. She did quite well, actually, though Elhad-Eln presented her with quite a challenge." Wayland smiled wryly.

"Elhad-Eln rid the realm of most of its assorted difficult or irritating beasts. He slew eagle-winged gryphons . . . the hugest crafty old boars . . . three-headed serpent-dragons . . . wily all-trampling hornbeasts, who dined upon herbs that made them invisible. He dared the deepest of jungles to bring Midhe the feathers of the exotic Quetzal bird-serpent, and the furthest mountains to bring her the fruit of the Aeolian harp tree to sing in her window. And he brought for her to put beneath her tiny feet the furry skin of the deadly snow-gorilla, whose fangs were poisonous and whose eyes turned men to ice.

"Finally, he arrived disheveled and battered, to kneel at her feet and unwrap the delicate folds of silk from the greatest treasure of the heart of the earth. When he uncovered at last the astonishing diamount, heart-gem of the world's highest mountain, Him-al-haim, it struck all eyes near blind with its cold, soul-ensnaring radiance, and Midhe knew desperation.

"Elhad-Eln smiled in triumph. He had won.

"He truly was the wisest of wizards. He saw that he had won. But what had he won? It is the ever-unanswerable question, to an age-cooled heart such as mine, how so smart a man could not see that Midhe had never really loved him. How could he not see that her heart was shallow, with room only to hold the newfangled conventions that had come to replace the truth of love?

"He had won only her desperation. The game was all to her, not the man that was its prize. She realized with horror that she must now lay aside maidenhood to be a wife—a plain, ordinary, unsought, no-longer-admired wife. She knew a woman's power lay in her unobtainability, and he, the wizard Elhad-Eln, had obtained her."

Wayland leaned toward Willow and Ranna, the banter gone from his voice. He reached arms out beseechingly, even now, centuries too late, for an answer. Willow drew a hand to her mouth, her eyes wide.

"How could such beauty be so blind to such majesty of manhood as he? How could any woman not be happy to be won so dearly by one so loving?"

Wayland shook his head, sighed his dismay.

"Inspiration came to her," he continued after a pause. "She set Elhad-Eln one more task. And when the words spilled from her rich lips, even the conceit-maddened ladies and their posturing swains gasped in true horror, dropping from numbed fingers their poesy-scribbled scrolls and their love-tokens, the kiss-sealed lockets clasping locks of hair, the billets-doux. They were appalled.

"Perhaps now the wizard's sight was cleared; it's hard to know. It is said his eyes narrowed, and he looked up at Midhe long and hard, and that under his stare her smile grew stiff on a face like a pale alabaster mask. What was there to do?

"He rose from his knee, bowed deeply, sweeping his cap from his head to brush the floor. He stood straight and tall, nonpareil among all in the hall, for a long, silent moment. Then he turned and went to do her bidding.

"The task she set him could only mean his death. She knew it and he knew it and all the court knew it. He was the most powerful wizard in the land, but even such a wizard has his limits. His lore was land-lore, as had been the lore of all his race before him. He knew the secrets of the earth, the paths to its greatest riches, the words to bind everything from almost unliving rock to the most aerial and blithe clot of clay that ever took wing as bird.

"But Midhe sent the wizard Elhad-Eln against the sea, that last great reservoir of the primordial chaos that had held sway in allness before the Great Mother wrested the land from it and set it firm and formed for men to walk on. That chaos that ever after had lusted, in rage against that affront, to drag all that was formed back into itself.

"And into the face of its violence Midhe sent the fairest and most perfectly formed of men. For the sake of the fabled gem, heart-of-the-sea, aquamarine, never seen by man.

"The storms that raged that night were terrible. And even though the High-Lord's court lay at a safe distance from the sea, the castle walls trembled under the onslaught of the wind's heavy blows that pounded the stones like surf. It was a wind out of chaos, wet with salt rain and gusting from all quarters of the compass without even the sane disorder of an ordinary hurricane. In all their chambers they sat alone and afraid, each longed-for lady and each pining swain.

And in her high tower, at the most mercy of the storm, sat the Lady Midhe. The diamount on its pedestal cast an incredible light, but its fire was cold. Nevertheless, the fair Midhe sat unshivering, like a statue, perhaps not even hearing the mocking laughter of the chaotic wind."

Willow sat mesmerized by the old man's word-weaving, almost feeling the chill of Midhe's tower around her shoulders. She didn't feel any more like smiling at the storyteller's cliches.

By the door, Ranna had drawn her shawl around her shoulders and was staring with wide, sad eyes at Willow.

Wayland, too, paused to drink in a deep breath, as if the story had laid too heavy a hand on him. Then he went on.

"In the morning—such a morning! A cold, white, cheerless morning with no sun to call any color out of tree or flower or fair maid's cheek—and the fear in everyone's secret heart that there would never be sunshine again—the court followed Midhe down the road to the shore.

"There, amid the wrack of the angry tide, the refuse of shell and seaweed and broken ship's timber which the sea had spat up in contempt upon the sand, she found the broken body of the wizard Elhad-Eln. She took him into her arms, laying his head on her breast, soothing the wet, matted hair from his eyes. And she knew the hopeless pain of having no tears to wash the bruised cheeks, the torn lips. She knew the shame of her own emptiness, before the eyes of all the court, whose ladies and swains alike wept shamelessly and without restraint.

"The wizard was not yet dead. His chest still heaved with wracked, painful gasps. He opened his eyes, once the bright blue of the sky, now the green of the stormy sea and pain-filled. He smiled, a ghastly, crack-lipped smile that was somehow gentle, at Midhe. And he opened his hand to her. There lay his gift, his ultimate love-prize—the fabled aquamarine. Its surface, seemingly bubble-thin, held the opalescent, blue, green, gold, shifting highlights of the color of the sea-tide at dawn; its depths defied the eye.

"All stared at it. Everyone gasped—a single drawing in of wonderstruck breath.

"Midhe could not touch the gem. She raised a hand to it, fingers trembling, and dropped it again to her lap. Shame would not let her reach again. She lowered her eyes.

"Elhad-Eln smiled, and with a sudden clench of his fist, crushed the aquamarine in his fingers. The sharp cry of a seabird shrilled like the voice of the sea itself, crying in pain, and everyone drew back with an astonished shudder.

"Then Elhad-Eln, mightiest of wizards, most magnificent of men, drew breath into his racked and sea-broken body and cursed the beautiful Midhe: 'May you know now what you did not know before, cold beauty—the burning fire of passion unappeased, never-to-be-appeased. Take man after man to your heart and to your bed, but never know the rest of love requited, of passion granted the gift of surcease.'

"Thus," spoke Wayland, and even he shuddered, even as Midhe and all the foolish conceited love-playing puppets of the court must have shuddered, and Willow shuddered, too, "thus did Elhad-Eln curse lust into being and cast it upon the world."

For a long moment they sat, the old wordsmith, the waiting-woman, and Willow, who understood at last the subtle nature of the insult Evmorat Morat's brother had set on her. "Not fair," she cried inwardly. "I am not like Midhe!" She choked back a sob, looked down at her hands knotted in her lap, so that Wayland should not see how affected she was by the tale.

But before the scene had quite faded that old Wayland had conjured up, before she had quite been able to stop seeing in her mind's eye (would she ever stop seeing it?) Midhe at the sea's edge, dying wizard-lover's head in her lap, the old man spoke again.

"The story does not quite end there. For now, when Midhe had heard Elhad-Eln's curse, and the court had quailed before the words of power that echoed with the old majestic strength from his broken breast, Midhe wept. Now she wept, understanding how she had perverted a true love.

"And around her, maiden after maiden took up swain's hand,

raised it to lips cold with sorrow, and kissed it. Swain after swain took maiden into sheltering cove of arms and wiped tears from frightened, weeping eyes.

"Only Midhe remained alone, weeping, her face flushed with fever of unquenchable desire for what she could now never have.

"At the last the wizard looked on her with pity. At the last he remembered how deeply he had loved her. At the last his love was true.

"With a final wave of a dying arm, he cast his last spell, spilling carelessly from his fingers a blinding radiance. When the weeping maids and swains could see again, fair Midhe and the dying wizard were gone. In their place stood a gnarled, broken, near-dead tree, bending its limbs into the wind from the sea. And twining about those limbs was a delicate vine, too delicate, it seemed, to endure the cruel sea winds. But it clung to the gnarled, broken wood; weeping from pale white flowers, from their red-hued centers, fell large tears of nectar, opalescent blue-green as the aquamarine Elhad-Eln stole from the sea.

"And still it grows, to this day, along our shores, the vine Midhe's-tears, clinging to old storm-whitened branches of almost dead trees. A few still gather the blue-green tears of nectar, the most powerful and irresistible aphrodisiac known, although it has long been outlawed to do so, on pain of death, for even the noblest of hearts cannot resist the lust this potion, Midhe's-tears, inspires."

CHAPTER 9

"My master Heller Jade said to place this in your hands only, High-Lord Morat. He believes it to be one of the rarest of the finds he has ever made in all his travels. He has other items on route to you, sire. I believe his letter will explain. But this one, I am to tell you, he has no clue about, and it is thus a special puzzle for you and for the wizard, sire."

Heller's messenger handed Morat a flat bundle, about two feet long and several hand's spans wide. It was wrapped in cloths soft with age; gilt threads in the cloth were tarnished black. The seal on its wrappings had no obvious means of opening. Morat looked at Amran-an questioningly.

"Let me try."

Amran-an took the bundle, ran his long fingers over the bindings and the seal, and soft words came to his lips. Morat opened the letter the messenger held out. Generally he enjoyed the benefits of Heller Jade's peculiar passion to collect the unique, the fanciful baubles and the items of power cast up on his shores by the flux and flow of sea tide commerce and exploration. But Heller's packages were coming more frequently. Heller's stewardship of the sea-lanes, like Morat's stewardship of the land, put his finger on the pulse of the world's fluxes, and according to his letter, Heller was convinced something unprecedented was astir.

"As you can see from this list, items of curiosity and power are turning up at a rate I've never seen," the seaman wrote. "Odd items have been appearing in cargoes, unlisted on the manifests, and no longshoremen can remember loading them. Strange gems are turning up in the hands of the merwomen or the nets of fisherfolk. Old useless maps suddenly show fresh, untried clues that lead to true finds."

There followed a list with details that made Morat purse his lips and whisper softly.

"Perhaps," Heller's letter continued, "this ferment is related to the trick that lost us in the Motherwoods. Perhaps these items have some clues to what is fashioning itself in this world we inhabit. If so, I cannot read the runes.

"So I am sending you some more of the objects that have fallen into my hands. Look for six parcels coming separate ways, three by barge, three over land," said the letter. "These articles have considerable power, and do not lend themselves to being thrown into one big trunk and craned onto a barge. Some require distance from each other; I don't need Amran-an to tell me that much."

Morat looked over at the package Am was holding. "Am, tell me. What do you think it is?"

The wizard had sat down on the steps and had the bundle partially unwrapped in his lap.

"I don't know," Amran-an continued to examine the inner case, murmuring soft runes while his hands almost caressed the wrappings. These cloths were not faded or tarnished, and gold and silver and crimson and black threads shone almost with a light of their own in the dimness of Highrune's Great Hall. Finally his wizarding fingers found a seam, an edge, and the bindings reluctantly came partially loose. "Wood . . . but not wood . . . the runes say something . . . Prince of the Dark of the Moon, I think . . . something . . . something . . . here is a small sign of the unicorn."

Morat turned back to the letter. "Send word by the birds

when you have received all six," Heller wrote. "I warn you—keep a watch that these packages reach you. I have placed what wards and protections on them I can, and the articles themselves have their own protections. But I would not like them to fall into careless hands.

"I will continue to send whatever comes to my hands that may seem to have bearing on this mystery. I have a foreboding soul, my friend High-Lord, inherited from the darker-skinned and sea-born side of my family tree. A storm is brewing, just beyond the horizon, a heller of a hurricane. I have a feeling we will need everything, objects of power, runes of strength, and any understanding we can gather, in the days coming upon us."

A gasp from Amran-an made Morat look up again from the letter.

"It could be an original print, Morat! Of the Tale of the Black Prince! I thought it was just part of the legend, that the story was laid forth in hand-cut wood block prints."

Amran-an was reading more with his fingers than his eyes, like a sightless man reading blindman's runes. But the innermost bindings held fast, resisting his searching. "I cannot open it further now. I am afraid I will harm it. There is power protecting it." With a deep sigh, he closed the wrappings around and opened his eyes, looked up at Morat.

He shivered. "But this, this bundle which Heller has sent us, if I can ever completely unwrap it . . . I think it is one of the original woodblocks from which the print was made. It's like having a fairy tale—such a dark one, Morat—come alive."

"I don't think I've ever heard of this tale," said Morat.

"Ah, I'm not surprised. It's a dark, dark story, Morat, the story of the Black Prince. It's not something you'd tell the children. It was supposed to have been set forth originally in the old way, in a series of woodblock prints cut and printed on the old handmade mulberry paper by one of the most legendary artists in the history of Som-a-Nissen. She was supposedly one of the Black Prince's victims herself, a character in her own artwork. I never thought she was real, just part of the story."

"Will you tell me the story?"

Amran-an sat for a long time, very still. Morat thought perhaps the wizard would refuse to share the tale. That made the High-Lord very uneasy.

"The Prince of the Dark of the Moon, or the Black Prince, was a punishment to the land of Nissen. The details of their crime were long forgotten . . . something to do with a woman's cruelty to a man, or more probably, some High-Lord's cruelty to a maid. I . . . I think it was something about a queen come to wed the land's lord, but he took her wealth, and abused her, and cast her out to starve. But the people had not stopped the cruelty, and the land was to be punished. It was the right of the Black Prince to come at any time and take any maiden, no matter her station or to whom she was promised. And she was lost to his unspeakable cruelties.

"Sometimes one came back, was found wandering in the forest, maddened and hopeless, and so the people knew just enough of the specifics of his cruelties that the terror of him remained and did not diminish, so the land's punishment was in the anticipation as well as in the taking of its fairest and finest daughters.

"When the squire rode into the village of Trees of Paper to warn them, his horse lathered and near exhaustion, Yu-nikko was sixteen and at work on her masterwork. She had been apprenticed to Master Chen-yi at the age of nine; she knew nothing except his kindness. The harshest discipline she knew was only that which straitened and focused her life so that the artistic flower might blossom.

“And in a few moments, it was all shattered.

“Tana-Cho’s daughters and nieces were already running, the indigo dye-pots abandoned. ‘Look to your apprentice, Master Chen-yi,’ cried the squire, and rode on. But Yu-Nikko turned back to gather up the woodblocks and proofs of her masterwork.

“And the Black Prince, the Prince of the Dark of the Moon, rode into the village, and the light dimmed.

“His three outriders rode through the work compound, right through the drying mulberry paper. Their hooves cracked through the drying boards with horrible sharp sounds, and fragments of the drier sheets of the paper flew about in the air like pale, translucent butterflies.

“The Black Prince himself rode right through the knot of women, and Illicho, third niece and the prettiest of the maids, was a bundle of rags on the ground, her blood running into the dark purple of the overturned indigo dye vat.

“‘Rabbits!’ he spat at them, looking down. ‘Nothing here but rabbits.’ And then his glance fell on Yu-Nikko. ‘Except for this one,’ he murmured. ‘Here’s something more than a rabbit.’

“She stood petrified, her woodblocks and proofs clutched to her breast like armor.

“‘I’ll take this one,’ said the Black Prince.

“Master Chen-yi grabbed the girl and turned her away. ‘You cannot! She is a master apprentice! She does her masterwork! She has a rare gift . . .’

“The Black Prince’s only answer was the hiss of steel as he drew his long sword from its scabbard. His horse stamped restlessly.

“‘No, Master,’ Yu-Nikko said softly. ‘He’ll only kill you and take me anyway.' Already the sound of her doom was in her voice. She handed her woodblocks and proofs to her master. 'Keep these for me. For when I return. So I can finish them.'

"He let them slide from his hands. 'Yu-Nikko, daughter I never had, much more than daughter . . .' He hugged her to him, all the master's dignity gone.

"The Black Prince made an impatient sound.

"Yu-Nikko and Master Chen-yi released each other. He took the netsuk on its silk cord from around his neck and put the image of the god of longevity/good fortune/happiness around her neck. They bowed, in the old way, apprentice to master and master to apprentice. Then Yu-Nikko turned to face the Black Prince. She swallowed, wiped her hands, sweaty with terror, on her dress, and walked to the Prince, one slow step at a time, not for dignity, though it looked that way to Tana-Cho and her daughters and her nieces, but because it was as fast as she could go with all the fear.

"The Black Prince grabbed her roughly and pulled her up to the saddle in front of him. That close to him Yu-Nikko felt the light dim another step or two, and the air was hard to breathe. The outriders fell in behind him, and the horses sprang into an instant, hard gallop that jounced her painfully. But his arm, hard with armor, held her tightly and painfully against the armor on his chest, and she did not fall.

"They had ridden for what seemed like hours to Yu-Nikko, and she was sore and bruised from the jouncing gallop, when the Black Prince finally slowed the horse to a walk and spoke to her.

"'Well, rabbit,' he began, 'Na, you are not a rabbit like the rest. What shall I call you? Have you a name?'

"'I am Yu-Nikko, sire.'

"He laughed. He had a rich, beautiful voice, and a laugh that held gold, not blackness, though she would learn that both voice and laugh could change, change infinitely. 'Beautiful,' he cried, delighted. 'No rabbit, but a unicorn! Perfect! I shall call you Unicorn!'

"And he threw her roughly from the horse and pushed her down on the cold earth and the damp leaves under the dark forest trees, and tore the image of the god of good fortune and happiness from around her neck and threw it into the leaves.

"And thus began the first of the Unicorn's seven ordeals.

"Master Chen-yi found the image of the god, in the matted leaves and the blood, where it had taken him two days to track what the horse had galloped in hours. He knelt and wept for Yu-Nikko and wrapped the netsuk in silk and hid it in his shirt next to his heart. But he found no further trace, despite months and months of searching the forest. It was as if the Black Prince, and Yu-Nikko with him, had left the earth where mortals walked, for lands of deeper terror."

Amran-an looked up at Morat, emerging from his story as if emerging from deep water. Morat shivered.

"As I said, I'm not surprised you haven't read this tale," Amran-an said quietly. "It's definitely not the kind of thing you'd leave lying about for youngsters to find. It's a brutal, terrifying piece of writing, explicit in its sexuality and its violence. That was the vow Yu-Nikko made to the Prince, and the condition of her release. For in the seventh ordeal, she redeemed him from his blackness and gained her release, promising to make a new masterwork that would tell the world of his brutality and all the details of the punishment he inflicted so that he would no longer have to enact it.

"One version says she came out of the forest leading a child who grew to greatness and ultimately to sainthood. Another says the child was the son she bore to Master Chen-Yi, having discovered her love for him during the seventh and most ambiguous of her ordeals, and to whom she returned when she won her release from darkness. That version says that together they created the masterwork that redeemed the Black Prince.

"Morat, I thought it was just a parable, you know, about the suffering that an artist had to endure to give birth to truly great art. It's always described as such in the critical theories. I never dreamed it could be fact."

Amran-an continued to work at the wrappings, but there seemed to be some reluctance in his fingers. Amran-an was a gentle person, and it was obvious to Morat, with their deep friendship like a subliminal rapport, that curiosity and the desire to be of help warred with some inner instincts in the quiet wizard to leave the darkness undisturbed.

"Leave it be," said Morat quietly, kneeling down by the wizard and placing his hand on Amran's fingers.

"But it may hold some clue, some portent we need—"

"Leave this one be, for now, Am." He shook the moment of premonition from him and went on in a lighter voice, "Besides, when Heller's trunks arrive, you'll have more than enough to keep you busy. Here, look at his list!"

CHAPTER 10

"Ahhah!" cried Ranna. "Sire, you have arrived at just the perfect moment!"

"Just what have I walked into?" Morat asked, raising an eyebrow and looking around. The chairs were spread all around the floor in some kind of pattern. Wayland sat on a bench, with a lute. Redd, Ranna, and Willow had their shoes off. Willow had her skirts tucked up, baring her legs to her knees. Morat found himself smiling appreciatively at her trim ankles.

"Dance lessons," groaned Redd. "Oh, no, Sire, don't leave. I really need some help with this bunch!"

"We're trying to teach Willow the dances for the Winter Year-Turning. We did all right with the 'Festival Figures' . . ."

"That wasn't so different from the Woodwaynim 'Winter Walk,'" said Willow. But this 'Weaving of the Evergreens' is just impossible!"

Tresses of her hair were falling down; she pulled them back out of her eyes and repositioned the hairpins. Her cheeks were glowing with the exertion. By the Runes, Morat found himself thinking, she's beautiful! So alive!

"Wayland keeps saying it's my fault we keep losing our place in the steps," said Redd, "That I'm all left feet. But we haven't enough of us to set up the full Ladies' walk-through. So they put me to do the Lady's part." He sounded outraged. "How am I supposed to know *those* steps?"

"He's not exactly graceful," said Willow.

Redd glared at her. "*I'm* not supposed to be graceful. It's supposed to be enough that I'm tall and handsome and don't have sweaty palms or bad breath."

"I put rune marks on the floor for her to follow," said Ranna. "I thought that might help."

"So I see," said Morat, touching his toe to one. "Not permanent marks, I hope. I'm sorry, I'm too busy—"

"No, you don't!" cried Ranna and Wayland simultaneously.

"Don't you bolt for the door so quickly, cousin," cried Redd.

"Oh, no you don't!" cried Willow. "You're not going anywhere until I get taught this dance. Do you want me to shame you in front of your whole kingdom?" She grabbed his fingers, pulled him to the first set of marks on the floor. Ranna pulled Redd into position, motioned to Wayland, who struck up the tune on his lute.

"Left foot forward . . . hands high . . . now twirl her, Sire," instructed Ranna, and they moved through the paces of the elaborate dance.

It was growing dark enough to need candles lit. They'd danced the afternoon away, moving from the 'Weaving of the Evergreens' to other elaborate group pattern dances, and eventually to dances for couples.

"I don't know how I am going to dance this in a long festival gown," said Willow as she tripped and fell against Morat.

"You're doing splendidly," he said. "That's why the dresses the ladies wear for Year Turning have those slits up the side. I'm sure Ranna is hard at work on a dress that will set you to shining above all the other women there."

"Of course she is! And you'll have to wait until the festival to see it! No previews!"

He laughed, spinning her in a series of turns that took them away from the others, off behind a pillar. He held her, wanting to tell her how wonderful it felt to feel her in his arms, how the feel of her hand on his shoulder warmed him through, how right it felt to hold her waist.

Willow looked up at him, breathing rapidly from the dancing and, Morat suddenly knew with certainty, from being close to him. His own breath was lumped in his throat. He pulled her close, and she came without protest, and he kissed her, and she didn't move away, and Morat thought, half dizzy with delight, that Wayland's lute music had never ever sounded so magical.

*****

Willow was glad to see an intermission in the dancing. Her feet were sore from the dancing and she was glad for the chance to leave Morat's side and the glare of everyone's eyes upon her. Besides, the last few dances had been long and intricate ones that had taken her far from Morat among so many strangers. Strangers except for Evmorat. Somehow the dance had turned him up twice as often as anyone else as her partner in the closer movements, and her fingers seemed still to feel the pressure where his had held them. She was glad this pause in the dances took the women to one end of the hall, to sample fruit juices and light wine and iced refreshments, while the men retired to the far end to slake their thirst with stronger meads.

Highrune's ballroom was splendid. Candlelight from hundreds of candles reflected in the mirrors that lined the long walls and glinted in the polished and gilded stone of its ornate carvings. Pennants from all the Portions hung heavy with gold braid and many-colored embroidered symbols. Garlands of greens were hung everywhere in graceful arches, festooned with glass baubles made specially for the event by the Artisan Guild's best glass blowers; Willow had marveled at their delicacy as she helped Ranna and all the others hang them. Even the men and boys had joined the women and girls to do the decorating. Morat himself had helped Willow hang the winter-rune chimes she had made to add her own special touch, whispering into them a few thoughts of faraway Woodway.

Morat's sisters, their husbands, and their children had arrived at the last moment, delayed by early snows and forced to travel by sleighs part of the way. Morat had introduced Willow to them, and she had fallen in instant love with the children, cheeks rosy from the cold, as she helped them take off their scarves and mittens. A quick afternoon of cakes and hot cider by the fire, and then everyone was off to dress for the dancing.

Willow had felt entirely glamorous in the gown Ranna had helped her into. The little maid and her mother had sewn up a glorious garment, deep green that set off her yellow hair, embroidery at her neck and bodice of lovely little flowers and birds. And the slit down the side that allowed Willow to dance, as promised. Morat had laughed with delight when he saw it, spun her around to admire her, and pinned at her shoulder a corsage of greens and small jasmine flowers from the Glass Garden, now roofed over again.

Now, as she sipped her cool drink, Willow saw Evmorat come up to Morat; he held two wine goblets. He handed one to Morat, gestured with his cup as if in toast, and drank. Morat laughed and drank, too. Willow watched Evmorat slap his brother on the back and whisper something to him; both threw back their heads in uncannily similar gestures and laughed. It made Willow shiver, for some reason, to see them thus together.

Yet Willow was glad to see Morat enjoying himself so freely. The last few weeks had been full of long hours of work and worry for him. The harvest had been gathered in all over Rune, and it had been plentiful, but not up to the bounty of previous years. Here and there strange rusts and wilts had blighted with the onset of cool weather what had weathered well the hot, threatening seasons. In Proven Portion a series of strange storms had leveled hundreds of acres of wheat with hard hail. Weird accidents had befallen the harvests on the road to storage or destroyed silos and granaries. There had been an unusually large number of squabbles over distribution.

There would be enough, Morat had told her, for the winter that had whitened Rune early this year. Enough to keep the stores up, even against a bad year next year. But it hadn't gone smoothly, hadn't been good. Had taken its toll of the High-Lord of Rune, whose inner being harkened to the restless, disturbed runes of his land with something almost akin to Amran-an's wizardry, all the time his mind had to be bent to task after administrative task.

Willow was glad he was enjoying the Winter's Turning. She knew he had enjoyed very much having her beside him. His eyes had a special shine in them when he looked at her; she could feel his pleasure at her in the touch of his fingers on her arm when they had made their entrance to the hall already filled with the high folk come from all over Rune. She watched him now, across the hall, raising his cup to toast Redd and the other men, young and old, who crowded around him, saw him smile as they all laughed at some jest Evmorat made.

At her end of the hall, the ladies gathered now like clusters of bright, chattering birds, eager to renew old friendships after seasons separated by all the miles of Rune, to share gossip, and to eye the men. The young ladies had come to the festivities to be paraded on the arms of fathers and brothers, shown off eagerly by proud and matrimonial-minded mothers. Not a few of them were looking sideways at her, wondering who she might be who had stolen the coveted place at the High-Lord's side. She knew they were only being curious, not vicious, but she felt deeply uncomfortable being stared at. She had no older sister or aunt to introduce her to their circles; she stood alone.

Wayland was supposed to be with her when Morat could not, but he had been waylaid by a large and very loud lady who seemed to know him better than he knew her. She saw him glance her way and try unsuccessfully to disentangle himself.

As quietly as she could, Willow withdrew into the shadows.

The intermission was ending. The music was starting up again. The young men were crossing the hall to take ladies to arm for the next dance. Willow drew further back into the shadows.

Ranna almost ran headlong into her. The waiting-maid was out of breath, distraught. Her eyes were wide.

"Lady! Thank the gods of Rune I have found you! Please come away with me! You must hide!"

"Calm yourself, Ranna. Hush, they'll hear you," whispered Willow, drawing the maid back into the shadows. "Hide? Where? Whatever for?"

"Please, oh, please! Come quickly!" The maid tugged urgently on her hand. Bewildered, Willow yielded and followed. They slipped behind a heavy curtain, through a doorway into one of the narrow corridors that honeycombed the castle giving the servants quick passage to meet the needs of their masters.

Under a guttering torch, Willow made the girl stop. She held her by the shoulders, looking at her steadily until Ranna took several deep gulping breaths and grew still.

"Now," ordered Willow. "Tell me. From the beginning."

Ranna looked anxiously down the corridor, both ways, then up at Willow. "Lady, you must hide," she cried. "They are drunk. They are looking for you!"

"Who?"

"Morat. And Evmorat."

“Morat? Drunk?” Willow laughed. “I can hardly imagine that. But, after all, it is Winter-Turning.”

“Morat is . . . is crazed. Lexin was serving the wine for the men; he told me he saw—”

She looked down, shuddering.

“He saw what?”

“Evmorat put something in Morat’s wine. He taunted him, under guise of drunkenness, that he had not yet announced his coming marriage, and what better time that Winter-Turning . . . and while the lords crowded ‘round with questions, Evmorat put something in Morat’s wine.” The rush of words subsided into sobs.

A chill came over Willow deeper than the chill of the rough stones of the narrow corridor, runes of insight passing up her spine. She feared the devious nature of Evmorat. He would enjoy greatly not only doing a devious deed, but also leaving all kinds of clues beforehand, to crush his victim even more effectively by a knowing helplessness. “If only I had seen!” the victim would cry. “If only I had heeded!”

With an icy, thin voice she commanded Ranna, “What? What was it Evmorat put in his brother's wine?”

“Lex said—” The girl choked. “He said it was a vial of Midhe’s-tears nectar. The color—it's unmistakable—”

“Oh, dear Mother-of-All!”

Ranna was tugging at her; she felt as if her limbs were lead, she was a tree rooted to the spot like any aged oak in Woodway.

“Come, Lady! I can think of only one place that might be safe. Come!”

“Where?” Willow felt panic rising in her.

"My chamber. It has been empty since Lord Morat made me come sleep in your anteroom. Even if they should think of it, I doubt either Morat or Evmorat know where it is. They are the mighty folk, who would never come walk the servants' warrens."

Through narrower and narrower corridors behind the great walls of Rune's high halls they fled, through walls within walls, ducking into storage alcoves and rush-broom stalls to avoid servants laden with platters of food and skins of wine to replenish the festival tables. The servants' voices echoed hollowly along the bare, cold stone corridors like jeering blue-jays as they passed from pool to pool of torchlight.

Ranna and Willow passed into quieter halls, narrower and less travelled; the servants who were not busied in kitchen or in serving had crowded to the balconies above the main hall to see the bright crowd of lords and ladies. Ranna pulled Willow behind her into a small room. The waiting-maid drew a door shut, then fumbled about in the dark.

"The lamp is gone. I must fetch one, my Lady. Sit you here, quietly, and rest." She guided Willow to her cot, helped her sit in the dark, squeezed her hands comfortingly. "It will only take a moment. I'll be right back."

In the darkness the moment stretched out into a forever. Willow hugged herself, stifling back a sob. "Oh, Ranna," she prayed, "please come back to me."

She gasped. Was that a sound in the corridor? The thick stone muffled some sounds, let others ricochet far ahead of their makers. It was all Willow could do to keep back a scream.

The door opened slowly.

Willow did not dare to breathe. She waited, then unable to be still any longer, she whispered, "Ranna? Is it you?"

Light flared, blinding her. She raised a hand to shield her eyes, blinking. And now she did scream, a despairing cry that echoed around and around the tiny chamber.

Morat held the lamp high. His eyes glittered in its small light. With great deliberation he set the lamp in its niche. Then he stood looking down at Willow, a statue with madness in his eyes.

Behind him Ranna struggled in the grasp of Evmorat. His hand was clamped tightly over her mouth.

CHAPTER 11

Willow's eyes fixed on Evmorat, standing calmly at the door to the chamber. He stood almost arrogantly still; though Ranna was a small fury struggling determinedly in his grasp, he held her easily. "Quiet, little waiting maid. Give me no more trouble now," he purred, "and perhaps I will reward you a little later in the same manner as my brother now serves your lady."

"No," whispered Willow. "No." She struggled more desperately in Morat's hold, her will fired by white anger, by green sorrow. "No, Lord Morat!" she cried, knowing he didn't hear her. "I might have yielded to you." She sobbed. "I might even have yielded gladly if you'd given me just a little more time to know my heart's changings. But not now. Not like this. Not with him watching, mocking us, warming himself at your drug-instilled lust, turning my yielding to shame."

Her hand fell upon the belt at Morat's waist; her searching fingers found the hilt of the knife in its sheath. They closed on it.

Morat's breath was hot on her neck, his groans loud in her ear. His hand tore at the front of her dress, fingers tangling in the lace. She twisted, pulled away, freeing her arm. She raised the knife to strike at him. She didn't want to kill him, only to drive him off; her blow was hesitant. The knife blade glanced off the jeweled leather beltings that crossed the breast of his festival-fine jacket.

Morat laughed coarsely and knocked the knife from her hand. He threw her down onto the bare wood bed. And he knelt to her, smothered her cries with a kiss that strangled her breath on her lips. His embrace crushed her. One hand tangled in her hair, held her mouth to his; the other reached down her side, pushed her dress aside, caressed her thigh.

She felt the knife beneath her, hard and cold. She struggled to pull it free.

Willow looked into Morat's eyes. He had drawn back to stare at her, breathless from the kiss. She saw something stir in his eyes, some scrap of his real self struggling to be free of the drug-driven lust of the Midhe's-tears potion. His hands gentled their hold of her; he touched her cheek, a light caress of his fingers, as if he were surprised to find tears there. She felt him shudder, draw in his breath.

"That's it, my brother, my great High-Lord," crooned Evmorat. "Show her the impatience of a man put off too long." His hand was clamped tight over Ranna's mouth, strangling her cries. The hand that held the struggling girl's body was cupped over her breast. The beastly thing that leered out of Evmorat's eyes was no brother to Morat.

Morat shuddered, groaned. His hands closed tightly on Willow again, hurting her. She saw the lust rise again in his eyes, drowning whatever else had been there.

With a great, heaving sob, Willow got the knife free—got the hilt firmly gripped in both her hands—and whispering a prayer to the Mother-of-All, plunged it into her own breast.

She clung to it grimly, feeling the pain of it fine and exquisite under her fingers tightly twined on the hilt. She felt the clean, cold metal pierce her heart, opening it so that the anger and sorrow could drain away. The knife was the center of her world, axis upon which she spun gently in the winds of immortality. She clung to the jeweled hilt with all her strength, holding it to her breast while Morat drew back from his biting, lustful kiss, and looked down at her in shock. She clutched the knife to her, though in dawning realization, Morat began to tear at her fingers, trying to pull them from their bloody grasp on the hilt.

She clung determinedly, with all her will, to the clean, fine pain as her vision grew cloudy. Then all she could see was Morat's face, the lust fading from it, the grief beginning to rise in his eyes, and Evmorat's face beyond, the same features like an echo, a white mask deserted by the beast that had leered forth from its eyes, leaving it to its own uncomprehending shock.

And then there was only the keen-edged, fine-bladed pain in her bosom, the song of a wind-rune keening in the forest wind.

Blood welled over Morat's hand, streamed onto the festival finery of his shirtsleeve like rare and precious dye. It was a long moment before he was able to move. Clumsily he cradled up Willow's head, gathered her limp body in his arms.

He whispered her name over and over as the storm subsided from his body, leaving him weak, confused. He felt like he had been somewhere else, in some other body, and been called back too suddenly to know who he was. He did not understand why Willow should be so limp in his arms. He didn't understand why there should be so much blood.

"Willow?" He touched a finger to her white cheek. Why did she stare so sorrowfully at him? Why were there tears there? His fingertip left a smudge of blood.

He looked around as if for signs to give him a hold on understanding. Willow's torn dress, his own disarray, the small, bare chamber he had never been in before, all were runes he could not read. Confusion numbed his throat.

His eyes fell on Evmorat. And the confusion was gone, wiped clean by a white heat of understanding that shook him from head to toe. He remembered drinking the wine Evmorat gave him; he remembered downing the entire glass of it at Evmorat's urging, despite the strange off taste in it. He remembered running through the corridors, afire with lust and Evmorat's taunts at his manhood. He remembered coming here, led by Evmorat, and cornering Willow, and laying hands upon her.

He roared, a mighty cry of pain and rage that threatened to crack the stones of the small room. It rolled reverberating around and around the bare stones.

Evmorat quailed before him, white-faced. "I never thought —" He babbled in a voice high with fear. "Morat, I thought she would come around, afterward, and accept what was done. I only wanted you to have what you wanted—"

Morat ignored him. He laid Willow's body gently on the waiting-maid's cot. He closed her eyes, wiped the smudge of blood from her cheek, smoothed her hair. He laid her hands at her side, paused to draw her torn dress closed. Only then did he rise from her side to face his brother.

The bloody knife was now in his hand.

Evmorat backed away. "I never dreamed she'd rather die—"

Morat stepped toward him. He quaked with rage. It filled him like fire from his deepest soul to the highest corners of his brain. It was a fire that made Midhe's-tears lust pale and cheap beside it. It was a fire that almost made his fingers drop the knife.

Evmorat felt his back touch the stones. "Morat," he pleaded, "I am sorry. I never thought it could come to be like this. I would undo it, oh, by all the gods of Rune, and by the Mother, and by the Year, and by our shared blood, how I wish I could undo it." His voice had dropped to a whisper.

Morat raised the knife.

Evmorat stood straight in the face of his death. The deviousness seemed to abandon him, at the last. He stood straight and quiet, looking directly into Morat's eyes, and Morat looked back as if in a mirror. "Morat, I am sorry."

The last word was broken upon the knife that struck him in the throat.

CHAPTER 12

Redd burst in upon Morat, drew himself hastily to a stop before the High-Lord. He panted heavily, with more than exertion, and his chest heaved with words that would not fall into an ordered pattern and be a sentence.

Morat looked up at him bleakly.

Redd heaved a huge, gasping sigh and settled himself to stand at attention, dutiful squire and cousin to the High-Lord. "My Lord," he said softly, the effort of control clear in his voice, "Morat, she is gone. The . . . the body of Willow is gone."

He stepped back quickly at the sight of Morat's hands gathering themselves into fists.

"We stood by the bier, Lord, Amran-an at her head and myself at her feet. We watched over her to honor her and you, as was fitting. But in the deepest part of the night, the candles began to gutter and go out. We drew our swords; fumbling in the darkness, we called to each other. I felt a wind on my brow, a cold but . . . but sweet wind."

His young face took on a clear but far-seeing look, as the happening took hold of him again. "It smelled of earth, sweet spring earth. It calmed our fear. We waited.

"There came to be a . . . a glow . . . in the dark. It grew brighter and almost solid-looking. It moved to stand by us at the bier, and we could see the Lady Willow clearly by its light, looking as if she only slept. It . . . he touched her hand.

"'You shall not lay her in stone,' he said. Then he gathered her up into his arms and turned to go.

“We could not move, neither Amran-an nor I. Our arms just would not move; our weapons fell to the floor, our hands would not grip them. We could not cry out.

“He was gentle, my Lord. But strong. We were powerless to stop him.”

The young man looked steadfastly into Morat’s eyes, not flinching. “We tried to prevent him. We could not. This I swear to you.”

Morat buried his face in his hands.

“When the darkness fell over us again, we . . . we slept.” Shame flushed his cheeks. “Amran-an sleeps still, lying at the head of the bier, his fingers still straining for his sword. I came as soon as I woke.”

“Who was he?” Morat asked. There was something in his voice that seemed to say he already knew the answer. But he asked.

“The spectre . . . he wore a green cloak . . . with . . . with dark stains upon it. And a Mother’s amulet at his throat.” Redd spread his hands.

“Rowan.”

Redd nodded.

“How fitting.”

Redd flinched from the bitterness in the High-Lord’s voice.

*****

Morat sat motionless, leaning his brow on his hand, elbow propped on his knee. The cloak draped over his shoulders against the chill trailed gold braid across the ice-white skin of his arm. The thin gold circlet of his High-Lordship lay in his lap, leaving his brow bare and white under the disheveled dark hair. He stared down at the locket in his other hand. His eyes were dark, unseeing, oblivious even of the finely wrought wooden piece of jewelry split open on its tiny hinges, its heart lying open in his palm. The one chamber held the lock of white-blond hair Rowan had put in it before he gave it as betrothal gift to Willow. The other side held the fine, softer gold wisp of Willow's hair which Morat himself had taken from her dead body.

For countless hours Morat sat thus, and his eyes no longer saw what his heart could not leave hold of.

No longer did the tears well forth, silent and unmanly down his face, at the inward vision of Willow in his hands, clutching his knife to her breast with that desperate, small whimper of pain. No more did he gnash his teeth in hatred of Evmorat, come to stand before him again in the darkness, the mockery still on his ghost's face, the cup in his hand, strange blue-green scum on the surface of the wine, jeering, "Drink, Morat, I dare you, drink and find here the heart you lack to take what should've been yours long ago!"

No longer did Morat tremble at these inward visions and leap to his feet to pace the darkened chamber with helpless, hungry hands closing again and again on empty air, bereft of power to rescue love from death, power to rewreak revenge.

No longer. Morat had grown still, as still as the shadows wrapped around him. Stillness radiated from him like a powerful, subvocal rune. Even the single flame in its brazier did not dare to flicker. Morat had taken to himself the cold of winter, let it steal over him and freeze the waters of his awareness deeper and deeper until only the most still, most cold waters of grief lay cupped at the core of his being. Morat had become his grief and was no more anything else.

The only movement in the chamber was the faintest billow of tapestry, its heavy folds stirred by the icy blast of the winter gales whistling through the cracks between the casements. Occasionally a latch would rattle at an especially belligerent thrust of wind, but the tapestries smothered the small sound as completely as they did the thin, winter-strangled daylight.

Morat would not have heard anyway.

He must have taken food, water from someone's hands. There must have been someone tending the single brazier. Perhaps Ranna came, stealing silently into the room to stand before him implacable, not even shivering, despite the chill, until he took the bread and chewed it absently, drank the wine without tasting it. Or no, not wine, never wine . . . water. Ranna would know the unsealed ways, the servants' ways, secret, honeycombing the thick walls of the castle, reaching even to the High-Lord's chamber. She would come where no other could, for Morat had sealed his doors behind him when he came to seclude himself in his grief.

Ranna would come. She would claim the right to come.

But Morat would not see her, or taste the food he ate from her hands, or even remember that she had been there. He would have thought, in his still, silent madness, that grief was bread enough to sustain the body as well as the soul.

He would have sat and stared at the locket far past even seeing that token of his grief anymore.

It took Amran-an, with everything of the wizard's lore left to the land of Rune, to break open Morat's door and wake the High-Lord. Amran-an, who came struggling across the winter-locked land from his House in Deld, to pound on Morat's chamber door.

He pounded until his fists were sore, scraped on the etched metal. He pounded while the ice that had frozen on his eyebrows and beard melted and dripped down his thin, gaunt face. Melting snow ran from his cloak and pooled around his ice-worn boots.

He pounded in vain.

Losing his cool control completely and entirely for the first time in his life, he drew back, muttering angry words that smoked his breath red in the chill air, his hands fists at his sides. Then, throwing his head back, he uttered a great Shout. From his out-thrust, stiff fingered hand, fire laced to Morat's door.

The shouted Rune rumbled through the castle. In the main Hall, the dark-bronzed shields of Rune's elder High-Lords rattled against the stones on which they hung. The pennants of each Portion shuddered their emblems, and some fell in a heap of braided cloth to the cold floor stones. The crossed pairs of the halberds of the Six Silver Warriors, battle-ax heads on six-foot long poles, fell crashing to the floor from their high hooks, scattering servants. Everywhere along the corridors, strong metal hinges exploded, metal and wood doors alike flew open. The torches went out, all along the corridor outside Morat's room, and servants rushed to rekindle them, thankful for a pretext to vacate the vicinity of the angry Wizard Lord of Deld Portion.

The rumbled roar of the Shout washed against Morat's doors; they rattled, held—then flew open with a crash.

The High-Lord looked up at Amran-an. His face was white, his eyes blinking. Amram-an looked at the bemused Morat, struggling to wake himself to his surroundings again; and a sheepish look came to Amran-an's face.

"Forgive me, High-Lord. I didn't really mean to Shout. But I had come a long way through the cold . . . and found your doors closed to me . . . and . . ." His voice faltered.

Morat rose stiffly. He stuffed the locket into his shirt and wiped his hands on his thighs. He came stiffly to stand before his friend. His eyes were still strange but clearing of their glaze.

“You came—” Morat had not used his voice for too long. It emerged rusty from his throat. He coughed and struggled for his voice.

“The Winter, High-Lord. I came because of the Winter.”

“The Winter?”

“Haven’t you looked at all upon the land? Haven’t you felt the land-runes? Haven’t you marked at all the moon’s measures of the Year-turnings? Tallied the clock of the rising stars against the great Runestones on the Runegrave Height?” He paused, then answered himself. “No, you have not.”

His shoulders slumped; the straight formality dropped from them. He looked at Morat not as a liege of Deld, but with the sad eyes of a friend. “Morat!” he said, pain in his voice. “The Moon of Hard Ice has come—and gone. The Melting Moon has come, too —and gone. And the Land-Kindling Moon. The Plowing Moon is upon us. And still the Winter locks our lands in cold and ice and snow. The Sun stands in a second solstice, the stars’ runes stand awry, the declination lies halted.”

He saw comprehension dawning at last in Morat’s eyes.

“Even in Deld Portion, where I have struggled with the little skill left to me by my wizard forefathers, the rivers do not melt. The ice will not leave the land. The early flowers haven’t pushed up through the snow. The blackbirds haven’t appeared from the south to flash red shoulders and take possession of the marshes. The earth, ah! the earth does not grow warm for seeding.

“Morat! The Year has stopped Turning!”

CHAPTER 13

"No sign of Tellit?" asked Morat.

"None, My Lord," answered Hallon. To himself he thought, the High-Lord looks terrible. He doesn't need the worry of this wayward boy, with all that he has on his hands. "We've searched throughout Highrune . . . even using the hounds. The pages and Guards have searched the woods, as far as we dare go in this strange weather. Beasts are prowling closer to the city than ever before . . . wolves . . . bears. Word has been put out into the countryside in all directions, asking of him, but no one reports seeing him."

Morat drew his cloak around him tighter, shivering.

"Are you ill, Sire?" asked the hound-master.

Amran-an drew Hallon away, leaving Morat to sit. "It's a deeper chill than the flesh he's feeling, my friend . . . he's feeling the land, as he always has. It's cold, and so he is, too. No fire will warm him. Did the boy take anything? Provisions? Equipment?"

"Nothing that we've discovered. His clothes, his blankets, are all still in the pages' dormitory, though his sword is gone. But then, he'd be wearing that, wherever he went. No cornuas or ponies are missing. I—"

"Yes, Hallon?"

"I'm afraid he's dead."

"As am I. But Morat doesn't want to assume that. He feels guilty about the boy."

"So do I, my Lord. I didn't know what to do with him. He was growing ever more . . . strange. I—I failed him, didn't I?" He gestured, holding his helplessness in his upturned hands. "I'm a man who works with his hands," he said, looking to the wizard in appeal. "I can calm a horse with these hands . . . train a hound with leash and touch and a few words. But I couldn't touch Tellit, couldn't lay hands on what was pulling him away from all of us."

"He talked to Evmorat, didn't he?"

"He talked a lot to Evmorat, those last few months since Autumn, when Evmorat came back here to Highrune. It gave me hope that Evmorat was going to acknowledge him, take him under his protection. I thought if that happened, Tellit could stop fighting for a place to be, and rest a bit, and let himself grow up."

Hallon seemed to want to talk, unusual for the hound-master, thought Amran-an. Perhaps we are all feeling cold and alone, Amran-an thought, and we want to draw nearer to each other than we usually do. The wizard drew him over to the fire, gestured for him to sit. The large hound that dogged Hallon's footsteps, silently padding ever just behind the man's left heel, looked to the hound-master, who made a small gesture, almost automatically, with his hand. The dog dropped neatly to lie at his feet, looking majestic, like one of the statues guarding the smaller gates to Highrune.

"It's a hard time for any of them, these young men," Hallon said, shaking his head. "I watch them, the pages . . . the city boys who were born here in Highrune . . . the farmers' and craftsmen's sons who come here . . . to train for the High-Lord's Guard or to apprentice in the household. They are boys struggling to grow into men; their bodies grow faster than their minds and their hearts, and we forget, because they are taller than we are, and have deep voices, and are growing their beards, that in some ways they are still children."

He scratched the dog behind the ears, absently.

"They can do strong physical things with their new muscles, and it makes them feel powerful. But it takes them a lot longer to feel so strong about who and what they are. And a lot longer to understand what others are feeling or needing. Empathy isn't a strong point; competition is. They climb over each other like a pack of puppies, nipping and barking, wanting to be top dog. Do you remember how it was?"

"No, Hallon," Amran-an smiled ruefully. "So much has happened, it seems so long ago, the time when I felt that young. And I was a loner, because of the wizardry. My good luck was to have the friendship of Morat."

"And then there are the girls," chuckled Hallon. "Teasing at them, pulling them toward and pushing them away . . . seems like this generation's got a lot more flirts than I remember. Or maybe I found my Belda early, may her soul rest in peace, and just didn't notice what was going on with the rest of them after that.

"But it was especially hard for Tellit. No sure station . . . promise of it, being Evmorat's son . . . promise enough to make him attractive even if he weren't handsome . . . but without a clear place of his own in the ladder of the world . . . aaagghhh! No wonder he was so hostile half the time, so angry, even violent."

"You can't think of anything that might hint at where he's gone?"

"Nothing. Only one who might know is Evmorat, and . . ."

"Yes," said Amran-an. He bent and poked at the fire in the fireplace and added another log. "I hate to think of Tellit out there somewhere in the cold. It's cold enough in here."

*****

Unobtrusively Redd entered and made his way across the chamber, taking care not to step on any of the books lying all over the floor, and replaced the empty flagon with a full one of warmed wine. Morat would partake of it, he knew, only for the sake of warmth. But Amran-an needed it to keep his fingers from cramping. He tiptoed out again, trying not to attract the attention of Morat and Amran-an.

He need not have worried. The reek of stale old knowledge had gotten to their brains. Morat sat slumped forward, leaning on his elbows, palms of his hands pushed against his eyes as if to block the sight of the sea of parchment sheets, dried and cracked and glowing softly in the firelight. Amran-an leaned back, head against the high back of the old chair. Without looking, he closed the book on his lap, letting its heavy leather-bound cover slam of its own weight upon the fingerprint-smudged pages. Dust rose in a cloud, and he stifled a sneeze.

"I wish that other book had not gone obstinate," the Wizard muttered. "The one that Evmorat had fooled with, the one by the Wizard Maara-ap-nan. I can't get it open any more. Something doesn't want to let us have a hand at shaping something that might start the year Turning again."

"Of course unshaping seems more at work," Morat said, a taste of sarcasm on his tongue. "Of course. Which is why we are here, stirring up the dust, looking for something else to try."

He took up one of the older books and opened it. His lips twitched into an almost smile. "Perhaps there is some magic left in this one, after all. I can still smell the earth—or maybe it's the barnyard—on it." Indeed, the crabby notes scrawled in the margins of the illuminated text were blurred with strange stains that gave off faint odors of soil, and grain-bins, and new mown hay, that rose to stir an image in Morat's brain.

"I can almost see him," Morat mused, "High-Lord Agri Tennon. They called him 'Land-Guard.' I can see him, against the insides of my eyelids, in a low-ceilinged, wood-beamed hall; Highrune was little more than a manor house . . . he probably had shoulders like the oxen who pulled his plows. Rune was still mostly farms and the land fell sick. He tasted the soil on his tongue, mixed it with pots of liquids, crumbled clods between his fingers. He wrote these notes. He read the runes of the soil well enough to catch the soil-sickness early before the blight reached the heart of the land."

Morat reached for the wine flagon, refilled his cup, raised it with both hands to his lips and drank it dry. "If it weren't for him, Rune would lay as waste as the Maia, a desert too poisoned to bear a single leaf. But he found the right rune-words. They came to him, as they should, he was a true High-Lord.

"Nothing comes to me," Morat said softly.

Amran-an reached across to put a restraining hand on the High-Lord's arm. Morat stared at him defiantly.

"My friend," said the wizard softly, "I have never seen you drunk."

"There's a first time for everything," he snapped back. He closed his eyes, and a small cry escaped his lips before he could steady himself and fight down the memory back to a manageable place. His voice dropped to a hoarse whisper, and the flare of sarcasm died into apology. He looked away from Amran. "The second, actually. You were fortunate indeed not to witness the first time."

He refilled his glass. "Drink!" he cried. He motioned at the litter of books. "Drink with me to my ancestors—all those lawgivers, lore-gatherers, warriors, leaders, keepers of the land of Rune.

"Drink to High-Lord Telden Terranold. He put the fear of

the gods and of his own raging temper into the hearts of the Hundred Chieftains, forced them to Council beneath the High Stones and to make an end to the endless small wars that were ravaging the lands. He put the land under one rule, laid the runes of peace on it, and named it Rune.

"Drink to Trimnorix Telden-an, his son's son. He turned back the last of the huge worm-beasts that crept out of the wastes of Maia on your own Deld Portion, and slew it on its own sands, with his runes of power and with his sword. They say you can still see its huge bones, petrified into the rock towers of Edge by the power of his incantations.

"Drink to Haellena Lunan, his son's ten generations' daughter. She founded the smelteries in the western mountains, unlocking the rocks with new-found lore-runes, making the earth of Rune yield its rare metals. She brought a new age to Rune, with the birth of crafts and industries to add to the farming. In gratitude the people brought quarriers to hew the stones of those mountains, to build the highest halls of Highrune, and it became a city of rune-patterned stone.

"Drink to Temparr Lunan-an, Lawgiver, who set the courts of appeal in place . . . to Nendarinn the Beautiful, who founded the Guilds and brought the arts to blossom in Rune . . . the runes of beauty that were woven in stone, and sound, and cloth, and pigments, in her name!

"What rune words they had!" He raised his hands high above his head, stared up at his own fists raised in the posture of incantation and power. Slowly he opened them, let nothingness drain out, brought his empty fingers down before his face, turned them palms out to let Amran-an see. He laughed drunkenly.

"I thought I knew so much. What really hurts my heart is that I thought I was doing well by Rune, by my people. I thought I read the honesty on their faces, or the guile, and found it easy to make my judgements. Reading their hopes and dreams, I found it easy to lay down laws that fostered them. I know it wasn't magic; I don't mourn the loss of an old magic I never really had. But I cared, and I loved, and I thought that was enough in the way of runes.

"I thought I knew Evmorat, but I never dreamed of the betrayal he could hatch . . . they say Wayland has written a new song, the 'Three Dire Deeds of Evmorat.' I thought I knew myself, and I found myself in love with a woman I had widowed . . . and . . . a few drops of a stupid nectar from a twisted sea-dune vine, and I . . .

"I shall be remembered as Morat who stopped the Year-Turning . . . as Morat the Runeless. That is, if I am remembered at all . . . if there is anyone left to remember."

*****

Amran-an fingered the woodblock, still stained with its inks. It had been strange how it turned up in the library study. It must have been buried in all the clutter of books, but then, after all the books had been read, and no answers found to the halted Year-Turning, there it was, where Amran-an stumbled over it, the package from Heller Jade, with the masterwork of Yu-Nikko of Su-Nissyen. It had taken him several days to untangle the dark seals on it, and he grew pale and sickened toward the end of that work, throwing up what he ate.

This day it had taken him a long time to read the text wrapped within. While the wizard read, Morat had sat motionless, staring into the growing shadows as what small daylight coming through the casement waned into night. Finally he had lit a few candles, and he stared fixedly at their motionless flames while Amran-an turned over the last page and laid it face down on the table, with shaking hands.

"It's a different version than any I have seen published, but those were all second, third, even fourth-hand," began Amran-an. He sounded tired and bewildered. "She died! Yu-Nikko died, according to this, during the seventh and last ordeal."

Morat sat up abruptly. "What did you say? She died? But how, then, did she come back out of the woods? And bring the child with her who became the Saint Chan-yo?"

"That's what it says. I never heard this version of the tale before."

"What? What brought her back out of the woods? What brought her back?" A strange light sat in Morat's eyes, something more than the reflection of the candle's still flame.

"The Black Prince, he had been changed, under her influence . . . she was working on his heart. But it frightened him, to find himself losing the evil that was the only way he knew. He killed her, to prevent his redemption. But then he could not stand the loss of her. He went and brought her back from the Land of the Dead."

Morat blinked, once. Amran-an looked up at his friend, puzzled at the small sound Morat had made. Morat stared into some distance Amran-an couldn't reach, and in his eyes, the reflection of the candle flame flickered.

*****

"Am, you must do this for me. You must take the High-Lord's seat for me and hold it until I return." Morat was handing the servant the list he'd written of things he wanted gathered for his travel.

The tall, thin wizard didn't actually step back, but it seemed so, with the demurral in his voice, his eyes.

"My Lord," he said softly, "I am not of the High-Lord's line, not of the blood. It would be presumption . . ."

"There is damn little of the High-Lord's line left," Morat retorted. "The blood has grown thin, the lore gone from it."

"There is Redd—"

"Who is young and inexperienced in any kind of rule. But he is strong in valor and in faith. Am, where I am going—" his voice cracked, recovered. "Where I am going, I need a clean, uncynical sword at my side."

"My Lord, Morat, I must ask you again to reconsider. I have no High-Lord's blood."

Morat looked at him sternly. "But I must ask you again to do this thing, nevertheless. I know you want to go with me. But you would not dare to deny your High-Lord three times, would you, Am?" Slowly the sternness turned to a sad, bleak smile. "If I, who bear only High-Lord's blood in my veins, must have hope enough to take up a quest fit for a wizard, can't you, who have wizard's blood, do a smaller thing, and try to be a High-Lord for a while?"

CHAPTER 14

They stumbled into the lee of a huge outcropping of rock; here the snow didn't fall in such blinding sheets, and the wind did not whip it across their faces like stinging slaps. There was a deep recess in the rocks, a hollow under an overhang that formed a kind of cave, and a stand of low-branched young pines shielded it further from the storm. They stumbled into it gratefully.

Redd pulled the pack and saddles from the cornuas, while Morat pushed away some of the snow so that the animals might huddle under the pine branches, too. Redd went back out into the storm and returned dragging firewood and poles he had cut. "We'll be sheltered enough here, I think, with a little ingenuity," he said. He propped the poles against the rocks. Morat handed him the canvas from the pack, and together they rigged themselves a lean-to to supplement the shelter of the rocks.

With numb fingers Morat built a fire out of old dry pine needles and dead branches they broke off the tree trunks underneath the feathery evergreen boughs. He coaxed flickers of flames to life, sheltering the fire from the almost purposeful seeking gusts of wind with his body, and using a few drops of the oily substance Amran-an had packed into their packs, in a stone beaker stoppered with wax, wrapped up with the fire flints. The fire licked up the oily stuff eagerly, then bit into the wood.

"Amran-an's modest wizardry can be quite useful at times," Redd remarked dryly as he cautiously fed larger sticks to the growing firelet. When Morat didn't answer, the young man looked up to see the High-Lord standing motionless, ungloved hand laid bare on the cold stone of their covert.

"My Lord?" Concerned, Redd began to rise.

Morat shook his head. "I'm all right. It's just that . . . these mountains seem to be haunted with visions. I saw . . ."

Redd stared at him, concern on his face.

"I see Willow," Morat explained. "Here. Cowering. I feel her fear." He motioned with his hand to dispel Redd's protest before it left the younger man's lips. "And on the crest of that rise," his gaze rose to look out through the pines at the crest of land almost invisible through the falling snow, limned only by the ghosts of pine trees fading into the whiteness. He gestured. "The hounds . . . and Tellit. She knows now that Rowen is dead." He stared out, eyes wide in dismay.

Redd went to him, took him by the arm firmly, drew him to the fire and made him sit. "Look into the flames, my Lord, and see, and see for me, too, the hearth at Highrune, and the warmth of summer spreading out over the land."

Morat looked up into the earnest young face, and was himself again. "I am glad, my young cousin, that your vision is so clean."

On an impulse he reached down and picked up a small stone, round and dark, and tucked it into a pocket.

They brewed a hot way-brew to drink, with melted snow, laced it with the restorative powders Amran had packed, and drank sparingly of it. They nibbled at their provisions, breaking in half another star-shaped amrita fruit and sharing it between them, crunching even the seeds and licking the red juice from their fingers. The richness of the fruit almost made them drunk.

They lay down at last by the fire, nestled in the pocket of warmth between the flames and the rock wall, Redd with the pile of wood ready to hand. "I will watch, Lord, for a while; then you."

It was an old argument. "It doesn't matter, Redd, if we both sleep. There is only so much wood, and the cold will wake us if the fire dies anyway. And nothing will be going about in this storm."

"Nevertheless . . ."

"As you wish. Wake me, then, for my watch." He drew up the cloak and blankets around him, nestling his face into them so that the warmth of his breath would not be wasted upon the cold air.

Halfway through the night, Morat woke from fitful, disturbing dreams. The snow still fell heavily, and the cold gave the air a heavy weight. He looked across the fire, now dwindled to embers, at Redd. He smiled. The young man slept, his hand still upon the pile of wood. But he lay peacefully in the arms of his exhaustion. Morat leaned across the fire, drew Redd's blanket over his arm, and laid the remaining wood on the embers. He fell asleep again, watching the fire flare up to warm and light his young cousin's clear, peaceful face.

Morat woke with a start to the thin light of dawn. Around himself and Redd, just within the bourn of the sheltering pines, squatted four figures.

It was still snowing, but lightly, fitfully, so that it was possible to see again the individual flakes sifting down the air instead of the stinging, solid sheets. Morat looked at the four figures. At first, he had thought they were animals or only half-men, so swathed in furs they were. From the snow upon their hoods and capes of fur and upon their brows, he guessed they had sat there for a long time. He looked steadily over the blanket-wrapped, sleeping form of Redd into the green, unblinking eyes of the one across from him, the one who sat a little closer, and who seemed to have placed himself so as to be the first thing Morat's opening eyes would fall upon.

Morat noted the blond hair poking from beneath the furred

hood, the blond-brown beard. He noted the wooden spear that the man leaned upon, the green-dyed cords wound about its shaft and binding the gray metal head to the shaft. He noted the bow slung across the man's back, short and recurved for power, power enough to bring down the great, shaggy, antlered horn beast whose furs he wore, with one arrow through the heart.

His eyes moved back to the face, and he saw the small crescent scar, the Mother's mark, high on the left cheekbone of the craggy-featured face. A peculiar sense of relief washed over him. The face was mature, knowing, lined with experience, not young. Not young.

"Woodwaynim," Morat whispered. "Woodwaynim," he said more loudly, like a salutation, clearing his voice of a catch in his throat. Redd stirred beside him; Morat heard his surprised indrawing of breath, laid a hand on his cousin's shoulder, holding him still. He did not take his eyes from the face of the Woodwaynim.

The green eyes blinked, but the expression on the face did not change; it was knowing. None of them moved, where they stood or hunkered hemming Morat and Redd in against the hollow of the cliff, as if it were no effort at all to stay so for hours, as if those muscles knew no cramping, no weariness.

Morat thought of the tales he had heard, that Woodwaynim could turn into trees and back to men. Even in the thin, cold daylight of this unending winter that illuminated Morat's breath a visible cloud in the cold air, the burnt-out black embers of the fire, Redd lying motionless, snow drifted atop his blankets and against the pack, the cornuas shuffling unrestlessly beyond, limned all with harsh tones of cold reality, Morat believed the tales.

"You. High-Lord Morat of Rune." The voice was peremptory, stolid as the creaking of great tree limbs in the wind. "Come." The Woodwaynim rose from his hunker in a smooth motion.

"Who are you?" Morat asked. He made no effort to move, though as if at a signal the other three rose and moved in on him and Redd and silently began gathering their gear together.

"You are to come."

"Where?"

The Woodwaynim pulled the blankets from Redd, spilling the night's accumulation of snow from them; they lifted the young man to his feet and handed him his cap and fur mitts. Their movements were not threatening, only inexorable, and Redd, shrugging, did not resist. They made no move to take his sword.

Meanwhile, the leader looked at Morat, a steady gaze just short of a stare. The Woodwaynim moved toward Morat. He waved them aside, got up of his own accord, dusted off snow from his cloak, and pulled on his mitts, keeping his motions slow and calm. The other Woodwaynim looked at their leader; he nodded, and two moved off to saddle and load the cornuas.

Morat finished pulling on his mitts and stood staring at the Woodwaynim leader as openly and calmly as the man had stared at him. Something quivered across the leader's face, at last a trace of expression other than the knowing closedness. It softened the craggy features for an instant.

"I am Burr Oak," he said gruffly to Morat.

One Woodwaynim came, unslung a bundle from his back, and knelt to undo it. He handed something to Redd. The young Runerin held them carefully, but with no understanding on his face. "What are they, Lord?"

They were large, flat affairs of netted thong and woven wood, wide rounded at one end, trailing to a narrower curve at the other. There were straps trailing from the center of them. The Woodwaynim knelt, lifted one of Redd's feet, laid the object under it, and laced the straps over Redd's boots. He rose and motioned Redd to tie on the other.

"Snowshoes, Redd," said Morat, taking the pair handed to him and kneeling to lace them on. "The snow is too deep for the cornuas, I think, but these netted things will hold us atop the crust."

He stood awkwardly, took a few tentative steps, almost stumbled to his knees. He looked up at Burr Oak, a wry smile on his face. "Well, my friend, lead the way."

The other turned to climb out of the covert, slipped deftly between the trees. Morat, following him, loosed a small avalanche of snow from the overhanging pine boughs. Cold wetness piled onto his head, a bit down his neck. He heard Redd behind him utter a protest as snow cascaded onto him, too. Two of the Woodwaynim fell in behind them as Burr Oak led them up the rise and crossed the slight valley to take an upward-rising way among the trees. Morat saw the last Woodwaynim move off downslope, leading their cornuas.

The trek was long and cold, and Morat's stomach ached with hunger, his calves and thighs were sore with his efforts to master the snowshoes, when they made their way down the last of a series of steep slopes and around yet one more shoulder of a mountain to look down on Woodway nestled in the bosom of the Mother's Mountains.

It was a many-colored, intricately textured splendor of wood that lay like an exquisite carving amidst the white of snow, the black and dark green of rock and pine. From the height it looked to Morat like one more of the fine-carved, intricately inlaid, multicolored plaques of wood he had spotted from time to time on a tree or in a niche of rock, finding them easily once Burr Oak had shown him the first one or two, stopping to wipe away the snow with a reverent touch. Some were fixed like signposts, others hanging free to chime and sing in the wind.

Did they point the way? Were they icons to the Mother (whatever the intricate pattern of design, they invariably bore her crescent-sign)? The Woodwaynim's concrete, carven version of the Runes of protection and guidance, like those familiar ones patterned into the stones of Rune? Or just the overflow of exuberant joy in fine crafting and worship of wood? Morat wasn't sure which of these the Woodrunes were meant to be—but he saw the city of Woodway as one more, greater, even culminating Woodrune bearing all the purposes of its microcosmic miniatures scattered through the Mother's Woods. Or perhaps it was the pattern for all of those others.

Woodway spilled down the mountainside in a cascade of wooden towers that looked far too frail to resist the mountain gales. The city hung above an abyss, a chasm that dropped to a mighty river that was a silver thread far below. Towers and parapets and archways and bridges rivaled and twined with the trees that grew everywhere among its courtyards and winding pathways. The towers were windowed with rare-colored panes of glass that sent flickerings of light rebounding from one tower to another like secret signals even in the wan light of the cloudy winter day. Morat's heart ached with the imagination of how it must look in summer, set to glory by the sun.

And the trees, everywhere the trees! Spirals of paths, wreaths of walls wrapped around them and led the eye and the heart to them as if to shrines. Even bare-branched in winter undress, the trees complimented the textures and colors of Woodway's artificed wooden towers in a way that reached the highest art. Morat saw elm etching its vase shape of fine, gentle black lace against the light silver of weathered balconies, and the harsh, twisted, yet noble lines of oak rearing against a fittingly rugged mass of arched gateway. He saw the contours of many trees that were unfamiliar to him, and raised awe in his heart; perhaps here, in winter guise, lay the trees of legend—the famed ginko tree, brought from the far lands that lay even beyond the

Mother's Mountains. Or the gold-fruited love-apple tree, grown from a cutting of that famed original that is said to twine its limbs beneath the earth itself, holding it steady beneath the churning mill of the sky.

Morat felt strange, almost drunk, with these thoughts—that came, it felt, from somewhere beyond himself and took him beyond his usual practical vision despite himself. He felt, for an instant, as if something—something that felt like the wispy lock of Willow's hair—brushed his cheek, as it had once, when he had stood still behind her, close, close, and she had not moved away. His face felt flushed despite the chill air.

They descended, dropping out of the wind that roared across the shoulder of the mountain and into the protection of the valley. And with ears cleared of that rougher noise, Morat *heard* Woodway.

He stopped in his tracks. He closed his eyes, closed out the visual splendor of Woodway, and abandoned himself to its sound. Gentler winds blew here, on the southern slopes. And they played upon the towers and arches like a vast flute.

Woodway was an aeolian harp, its soul a song called forth by the winds, played upon the thousand stops of its windows and doorways. Great sonorous bass tones boomed through the main gateway, the Xyl Gate, forming a basic rhythm of sound upon which built the tenors and high flutings. The east towers, above the gate, were reeds upon which the wind's lips played ornate, tart, oriental filigrees of oboe notes. The center of the city, a nest of concentric circles of archways, were the soundboard for sweet flutings, thrilling higher and higher until the ear could no longer contain them.

Morat could have stood and listened, enraptured, until the cold had taken him entirely, snuffed the spark of his life, and left him an ice statue to stand forever in a never-ending winter. Tears started from his eyes and froze upon his cheekbones when

Redd came and took him by the shoulders and shook him hard, making his head jog loosely, and woke him.

He had heard the same notes, plucked somehow from a harp by Willow's fingers. How inadequate an instrument she had had to make do with! Even the many-wooded harp he had found for her. He understood as he never had before why she had cried sometimes, over her harp, and laid it aside, refusing to play again for days. How could a harp ever satisfy, when one had heard an entire city played by the Mother's wind?

How heavy and silent the stone halls of Highrune must have been to her!

"Willow!" sang the city of Woodway to Morat, all the time it took for Burr Oak to lead him and Redd down the mountainside to the great Xyl Gate. "Willow," sang the city, as they made their way through the winding ways, carefully swept clear of snow, up and down and around tree after tree, and under arch, and over bridges that rocked slightly underfoot and made Morat feel as if he tread on the wide arms of tree branches swaying in the wind. Around the circles to the heart, and into the great Heartwood-Hall and up to a small chamber with round, protecting walls, and warmth shed from glowing stones in the center, and food and wine were brought, and soft cushions covered with fabric woven of lluria fleece so that they might sleep.

"Willow!" sang the city, the wind song now muted through the closed windows with their panes of colored glass and filigree mullions of rich-hued wood, though base notes like sobs of grief seemed to rise like vibrations through the very floor of the chamber, as Morat closed his eyes and gave himself up to exhausted sleep.

*****

Morat stood at the center of Woodway, in Heartwood itself, the culmination of centuries of Woodwaynim artistry. On all sides, columns rose, covered with carven life: leaf and vine, flower and fruit, bird, animal, some few familiar, most unknown to Morat, a few so fantastical they awed him. The flickering of some kind of light globes—not torches, never torches here, never fire at the heart of everything wood—teased the ornate carvings into near-life, almost-motion, and bewildered Morat's eyes.

Up and down the columns rose and reached arms to each other in vaulted arches and intricate coigns. There was a teasing irregularity to the distances between the columns, the sizes of the curved petal-shaped surfaces of the arches; no two measurements quite alike; no pattern quite completely repeated—it all teased Morat's perception. The randomness of the ornate complexity, the sheer play of artistry, seemed nevertheless constrained in an order; a ruling force hinted its presence.

But he, who did not possess the tree-runes of the Woodwaynim, felt his brain only painfully enmeshed in the coils of the woodcraft. Until suddenly an insight, a flare of vision, licked at his mind like a hot tendril of flame. He felt that he stood at the heart of the earth, at the dark center of all things. And he saw that each whorl of twig and vine that marked each dome was also a circle of roots reaching *down* from each tree, searching with patient tendrils for the mystery at the core that sustained all life.

And standing where he was, he stood at that core. He made a sound, half groan, half sob, that stayed in his throat to choke him with awe. He wanted to reach up his arms, join fingers with the reaching root-fingers of the trees.

A sound broke his reverie, the rustle of feet, the scrape of wood chair legs on wood floor. Morat drew his gaze down from the ceiling and across the hall, adjusted his eyes to focus on the ranks of the Xyl of Woodway.

They sat in high-backed chairs, a long arc of table before them; it was a huge slice of tree-burl, flat surface polished and gleaming, edges swirled and roughened. Whorls and streams of grain flowed across the surface, glowing in the light.

Burr Oak had warned Morat of the expected courtesies. Morat bowed deeply, stood erect again with hands at his side, open toward them.

Nine Woodwaynim, the foremost masters of wood magic and tree-rune, leaders of the Woodwaynim crafts and hearts and mysteries, sat staring pointedly at Morat.

"Morat High-Lord of Rune . . . Runerin . . . why do you break again the peace of the Motherwoods?"

Morat could not tell from which lips the words fell; all nine seemed to speak with one voice which the recesses of the carved ceiling caught and sent at him from all sides.

Morat considered an instant, decided not to protest the accusation, but to go at once to the heart of the matter. "The Year has stopped turning, O Xyl," he answered loudly, putting all the force of rune and wordsmithing he could into his voice. "I wish to seek out the Mother, the Giver of Spring."

"She sleeps."

A voice separated itself from the skein of nine voices and added, "Nothing in the Mother's realm, not on Mother Mount, nor in Mother Woods or in Woodway itself, nothing *here*," a hint of emphasis on that last word, "stopped the Year-Turning."

Morat searched the nine faces, to see who had spoken. But he could not tell. Green eyes, pair after pair, stared back at him. The faces all had a sameness, whether male or female he could not tell; none wore beards, and their robes were all of one style.

He answered their challenge.

"I did not say the cause lay here; I only come here seeking a remedy. The cause," his voice fell into roughness, "the cause was made in Rune."

"We would know the cause. And why you think the amends should lie in our land's heart-place."

"Willow Lythew of Woodway is dead."

The words seemed to ring up into the intricate coigns of the hall and echo. Morat balled his hands into fists at his side; he felt unsteady on his feet, as if he could feel the forces of the windsongs of Woodway groan through the floor beneath his feet, swirl upward through his body.

"Willow," he groaned, "is dead by her own hand, though not of her own will. I loved her, and she is dead." He felt the words tumbling out, beyond his control, and he almost sang them to the dire song he felt around him, humming in the air, vibrating his bones like the strings of a harp.

"She is dead through the dire deed of Evmorat my brother, who made me his tool." He raised his open hands to them. "And his slayer." For the thousandth time rage and shame shook him like a storm, choked off his voice.

One of the nine threw arms across the table, burrowed face in hands. The air thrummed tighter, nine fragmented voices babbled from the spaces of the carven ceiling. After a few moments, the Xyl raised her face again, looked at Morat. "I was her mother. I will require of you the way of my daughter Willow's dying. You have made me a tree without branches."

Morat's face felt hot, his heart cold as ice. "I loved her," he whispered. "I will set the Year turning again in her name, or die trying." The deeper, more overreaching desire he kept locked secret in his heart.

The Xyl voices wound together into a tight, unfrayed cord again. “The Mother sleeps,” they repeated. “She does not hear us, and Woodway lies as locked in winter’s grip as Rune. Why should She hear you, who do not serve Her as we do? Who do not live upon Her very breast? You who hew wood and cut stone without first asking Her permission or blessing?”

“I will make Her listen.”

“Have you such Runes?”

“I will make Her hear me. I am High-Lord of Rune, and I grieve.”

“We wish you good fortune.” The nine’s voice was not bestowing permission on him, but mockery. It added, almost as an afterthought, “The Pass is blocked with snow. Even if you should find it, you will not get through the customary way. There is another way, but it is not possible for the likes of you, either.”

“I crave the indulgence of the information anyway.” Morat's voice was edged with sarcasm answering their own.

“You can descend the steep breast of the Mother Mountain and enter the Earth’s Doorway from below instead of above.”

The Xyl rose from their chairs as one, and filed out of the hall, green robes furling like leaves behind them, leaving Morat to stand with his fists at his sides, quaking like an aspen in the wind of their hostility.

CHAPTER 15

"Rune-Lord, this will not do."

Morat looked up at the Woodwaynim who stood as firm and stolid as the oak that was his namesake.

"I am grateful to you, Burr Oak, for returning our packs to us." He bent again to the sorting of their contents into the bare essentials.

"Lord, forgive me if I am wrong—but it is my guess you have never climbed a mountain."

Morat looked at him questioningly.

"Those packs. They are the wrong kind; they will not stay balanced well on your backs. You will need harnesses, and ropes, and rock tools. And mitts of leather, not fur, and tighter shoes with chamois on the toes, not those heavy boots, for surer grip on the rocks."

"I will have to make do."

"Rune-Lord—"

Something in the man's voice, something not formed of oak rune, made Morat look more deeply into the green eyes. He saw flecks of red and bronze, the colors of autumn-tinged leaves: sorrow. The man could not offer; but, Morat realized, he himself could ask.

"Burr Oak, will you help us?"

The man nodded, heaved a sigh of relief. "I will. I can. I will get proper packs, and harnesses and ropes."

Morat stood up, grasped the Woodwaynim by the shoulder to keep him from going. The muscle felt as hard as wood beneath the shirt.

"Why? Why would you defy the Woodwaynim Xyl to aid us?"

For the first time, Morat saw the man smile. "You owe me a debt, Rune-Lord. I wish to see you live to make payment." There was no coldness, no threat to the words. Yet Morat felt a chill grow within him.

"What debt?"

"The life of Rowen Oakbranch, woodrune wizard."

Morat's cheeks flushed despite the chill in his breast. "I did not mean to kill him."

"I know. He was young, and overconfident of his skills. And youth does not know, as experience does, the worthlessness of battle-arms in untangling subtle problems. But Rowan was of the Oak clan, son of my sister. I have no son of my own; I loved him as my own." It was a long speech for the Woodwaynim.

"You want to kill me, then, in your own way, rather than have me die on the Mother Mount." Morat's voice was a whisper, but steady. Behind him he felt rather than heard Redd reaching for his sword.

Something new passed into Oak's green eyes, amusement, perhaps, mixed into the knowing, experienced look that had returned to them. "It is foolish to think one can restore a forest by uprooting still more trees. By the looks of you, you would make only fair wood for winter fires, much less for woodrune carving."

"Yet you have a use for this particular wood?"

"A secret intention flows in you, Rune-Lord, like the sap

locked in the roots of the maples. I share it."

Morat started. He looked at the Woodwaynim, feeling a hot shock burn down his spine. But Oak stood straight, unmoving, a small smile still on his lips—not amused but knowing. "But first, to wake the Mother."

And he turned and went to get them packs and tools.

*****

The rock was black and cold and slippery with ice beneath Morat's fingers; he could feel its chill even through the leather mitts, thin and flexible as any hide Morat had ever seen tanned, but double-layered for durability, lined with lluria wool for warmth. The shoes he wore were similarly thin and flexible, and they let his toes work more effectively into niches in the rock than his boots ever would have. Burr Oak had been right about proper equipment.

He clung determinedly to the face of the cliff.

They had hung their snowshoes in a tree at the edge of the cliff, he and Redd and Burr Oak, wrapping them and securing them under the overhanging pine boughs, to hang under the watchful eye of a carved plaque-shaped woodrune's grinning mask where Woodwaynim travelers in need might find them. It had felt to Morat like a kind of farewell to the forest.

Just before they had slipped over the edge of the cliff, Burr Oak had drawn from his pack a short, tube-shaped carved piece of oak wood. It was hollow and pierced with holes, but bore the same swirls and whorls of carving, the same crescent Mother-sign, as the other Wood-runes Morat had seen. The Woodwaynim had held it in his bare hands, whispered a few words over it that had sounded like the rustle of dry, autumn-bronzed oak leaves, then hung it on a thong from a bare, gnarled branch overhanging the abyss. The winds from below swirled through it, and called forth a piercing, low-tuned note that modified itself into a plaintive two-noted windsong. The song wound through Morat's brain until the wind changed it; it made him feel light-headed as if he were a bit of thistledown, able to float on the wind.

Carefully, guided by the Woodwaynim, he had strapped on the harness around his waist and thighs and attached himself to the rope anchored to the tree at the top of the cliff with the large figure-eight knot through the ironwood clip, as Burr Oak instructed him. He had watched carefully as Burr Oak checked the harness and knots on Redd.

He had looked over the edge, into a sea of mist broken by towers of rock rising blackly from it. It baffled his eyes. With a shrug he had made himself take a firm grip on the rope and lower himself after Burr Oak into the unknown.

After that, his world had narrowed to foothold, foothold, handhold, the secure pull of the harness around his waist. After the first cold anxiety passed, it did not seem as difficult as he had feared. The cliff was not as sheer as it had looked from above, but was abundant with niches and crevices and ledges and protrusions. It had been a trick of perspective that fooled the eye into thinking the cliff dropped inward rather than sloping outward.

Often there were ledges where Morat could stand, catching his breath and massaging the cramps from his arms and legs, while Redd slithered and slid to stand panting beside him. Burr Oak would already be hammering the ironwood pegs into the cracks in the stone, muttering woodrunes over them to assure their firm placement, securing the ropes to these new foundations. Morat would smile at Redd, wiping from his brow with the back of his mitt the sweat that formed despite the chill wind.

An odd happiness began to steal over Morat, a mood that

mixed his fear of the heights with a thrill of self-satisfaction that he was even there, inching his way down the face of an immense mountain. The ache of his muscles became an exhilaration that warmed him from the inside out. The courts of Highrune, the rune books of his ancestors, the inactive body trapped in the habits of mental endeavor and the administration of the affairs of Rune, the worries about unshaping forces, all seemed blown away in the soaring wind, to leave him with an enlarging sense of the feel of himself as a concatenation of muscle that was stretching itself to new limits and new accomplishments.

He began to feel euphoric. It lasted well through the first few hours of the descent. The wind that blew in fitful sighs upward from all points of the abyss below seemed like the exhalations of the mountain itself, and Morat inhaled it and was intoxicated. He was in motion; at last he was taking action against the paralysis of his grief.

The clouds that rode the air on all sides of them, sometimes above, sometimes below, would part here and there to give the climbers glimpses of masses of ragged rock that were revealed truths to Morat, a powerful new kind of rune. The face of the cliff they toiled down grew smoother and less hospitable to hand and toe seeking secure hold. But Morat's exhilaration held despite the growing difficulty of the descent, especially when the rags of cloud parted above and let him see how far they had already come.

But the Mother Mountain did not permit him to retain his hubris. Eventually she turned her flank inward, undercut the contours of the rock like a hollow beneath her breast. They clung above it, while Burr Oak explained again and again the maneuver with the ropes, patiently, wearing away at the fear in Morat and Redd at the very idea of swinging loose on ropes over emptiness.

Redd looked at Morat, swallowing dryly, the whites of his

eyes showing just a little more than usual; Morat looked away, at Oak's hands fixing the ironwood pins and rings, looping and knotting the ropes. He knew how his young cousin felt. It had not occurred to him either that he would have to give up even the meager security of the feel of the rock under his hands and toes.

And then the moment of decision was upon him, and he hung beneath the outward-curving mass of rock, the ropes taut around his chest and waist and between his legs. He could feel the rope vibrating in his hands, as Burr Oak paid it out over the edge of the rock.

He swung in the wind, buffeted by a great gust of cold air that whirled up from the abyss below, carrying cloud with it like the steamy breath of the wintered earth. Tendrils of mist, tasting of ice crystals, lashed at his face and rose past him, suddenly obliterating from view the rocks, Redd's face peering over the edge, even the rope.

He dropped slowly, steadily, bit by bit, into white oblivion. It cut him off from the reassuring presence of Burr Oak and Redd far more effectively than the bulging mass of overhanging rock.

Morat swung in the mists, feeling utterly alone. "Redd!" he cried, "Oak! Re-edd!"

The wind snatched the voice from his throat, moiled it into the swirling white mist and lost it. He leaned back, craned his neck to look up, desperate. The rope disappeared into mist. He felt as if he had gone blind. All he could see was whiteness; all he could feel was the humming tenseness in the rope, taut with his weight, and the small hollow bubble of vertigo in his chest.

He closed his eyes and breathed deeply and deliberately, trying to still the fear that was rising in him like this cursed mist had risen from below.

His legs banged suddenly, painfully, into rock; his body

bounced against rough hardness, then slid past into emptiness again. Morat loosed one hand from the rope, scrabbled with fingers for a hold on the outjutting rock. He kicked his legs, reaching for a toehold. The rope jerked with his motions, and he swung wildly. He froze in panicky immobility, gasping for breath in the rare, cold, ice-crystalled air. The outjutting of rock was lost above him in the whiteness. And still he felt himself inching downward as Oak paid out the rope.

What if that had been the ledge Burr Oak had pointed out to him? The one he was supposed to reach? What if he had missed it, and Oak reached the end of the rope? Could he and Redd pull Morat up again? He had the sudden, nightmarish conviction that the Mother Mountain had swept away Redd and the Woodwaynim, and dangled him herself from whimsical goddess fingers, like Burr Oak's carven flute of a woodrune whistling mournfully into the wind.

Clutching the rope desperately with numbing fingers, Morat swallowed down the sour taste of panic and looked down. At the moment he did so, the mists parted, and he looked freely down into the abyss.

Great black slabs of rock dropped converging verticals to the depths. The opposite face of the chasm visible far across an open space loomed closer and closer to the face on which he hung as the abyss deepened and perspective seized his vision. Beneath him and to the side spires of rock reached upward. At their bases, which almost converged with the base of his face of the abyss, flowed thin ribbons of the great white flowing river of the glacier that wound between the cliffs, scouring an inexorable way down out of the mountains that were the Rim-of-the-World.

The glacier debouched from its valley beneath him, its outpouring of ice ending in a white wall across the bottom of the abyss. A lake lay cupped against the wall, a glittering pool that looked tiny in the rocky bowl the glacier had scoured during one of its advances eons ago. Tiny as the bowl of a wine goblet it looked, the lake—until Morat realized that the white flecks floating like foam on its surface were great chunks of glacier ice calved from the ragged wall of the ice river.

Suddenly his brain caught hold of the true scale of the scene below him. He exhaled his breath upon the wind, and tears blurred the view until he could barely make out the thin silver thread of river that ran from the far end of the lake, the Mother-smilk, that curled around the base of the Mother Mountain, between the high crags beneath Woodway itself, and beyond, winding down out of the mountains and across the Simmanlirl Plains to join with the Rune River. His head roared, his brain faltered, his eyes' vision, unable to encompass the vastness, blurred, and he wept.

What woke Morat from the heart-stopped paralysis of his awe, brought him back to awareness of his weight swinging slowly in the cold air, was the impossible glint of green in the depths of the abyss. There, where ice and rock and lake and river met, where only white ice and black rock and silver water could be, glowed the true, undeniable new green of spring.

Just a glint; just a tiny patch—if such a green could be, here at the heart of the wintered world, even though the Mother slept, then, Morat whispered to the wind, then She will not let me die on this Her mountainside.

And he grew calm. The hammering of his heart faded, the sweat dried from his brow. The heaving of his chest against the rope and the straps of his pack eased. The mist curled across his vision, a merciful blotting of the vision into whiteness that gave his soul back to him. His eyes cleared, focused on nearness again, spotted the ledge he sought; his feet found it, his hands scrabbled, then took hold firmly of rock. He pulled himself onto the ledge.

Morat slumped on the ledge, struggling with numbed hands to loosen the rope, tugged on it so that Oak could draw it up again, let it slide out of his hands, and sat like a child, arms on his knees, head resting on his arms. By the time Redd appeared out of the mist, dangling on the rope, to land beside him, Morat had finished his weeping, soft but without restraint, and sat immobile, head buried in his arms.

CHAPTER 16

Soft as a velvet cloak, the green of the moss billowed over the glacier-rounded boulders at the mouth of the cave.

They had trekked along the river. At first, they had been unable to speak over its deafening roar, working their way upward against the rise of the land as the water bounced and plunged downward in huge solid splashings over the rocks. The air had been filled with wetness, and the spray had iced on their furs and their eyebrows.

They had clambered over rocks newly released from the hold of the glacier ice, rounded and scratched with the ice's wearing. They had trudged along beaches of gravel and coarse sand flecked with golden glints of mineral treasure and dark green of jade. Morat had taken up one agate in his hand, polished by ice and water to smoothness, touching its pearly veins and strange inclusions, and tucked it into his pocket as a talisman.

But as they moved uphill against the flow and toward the source of all things, the melt of the false-spring fell behind, and the cataracts of water diminished to a less noisy rush. It became a stream that stepped down huge blocks of ice and boulder, and finally a trickle that ran down the face of gray-white ice. And then, at last, they faced into the full force of the unturning, frozen year.

And now, paradoxically, they stood in the midst of that incredible patch of green that Morat had seen, like a sign for his quest, hanging in the high wind on the breast of the mountain. No water moved; it was frozen into stillness. It was silent.

Redd stared around him, catching his breath after the hard exertion. His eyes held questions.

Burr Oak knelt, took off his mittens, and gently touched a bunch of tiny, white flowers that had pushed up out of the ice. Unexpected tears glistened on his cold-toughened cheek. He took out of his shirt the small carven Woodrune he wore on a cord around his neck, and head bent over it, he prayed. Morat couldn't make out the words.

Morat looked at the mouth of the cave that yawned blackly. Its mouth hung with huge icicles; oddly shaped humps of ice stood on guard at its threshold like some kind of frozen animals. But the green moss led like a carpet toward it, starred with the white flowerlets.

Morat stepped toward the cave.

Redd protested. "You can't go in alone! You have no idea how deep the caves go! How many branches there may be!"

But Morat felt like a lodestone, drawn and directioned by some spiritual magnetism blossoming amid the greenness. He didn't have the words to explain his feeling.

"I won't get lost. I know it."

Redd just shook his head. He reached down to take up his pack.

Oak rose and came to stand between them.

"The Rune-Lord is right. It's his path, now, his alone."

He sounded regretful. "I wish . . . this is such a holy place . . . we Woodwaynim seek it always, all of our lives. . ." He shook himself. "But I can feel it is not my time to enter here. She is pleased at what I have done to bring him to this point of the way. But She will speak to Lord Morat alone if she speaks to him at all."

He knelt and dug in his pack. He took out a package and

unwrapped the furs from around it with gentleness. It was a glow-globe like those in the Xyl's Heartwood Hall at Woodway. "I kept it next to my body for warmth; it's a living thing, you know. She will not allow fire or torch in there."

Morat looked into the eyes of the Woodwaynim, realizing the generosity and forethought of the gift. "I thank you," he said softly. "And I'll be carrying your purpose as well as mine into the Mother's darkness, with this lighting my way."

Oak nodded, satisfied.

He reached again into the pack, pulling out the makings of a tent. "We will wait two days here, then climb back out."

Redd moved to protest.

"No, young Runerin, I doubt greatly that he will return this way, especially if he does succeed in reaching the Mother's heart and getting her to listen to him. Don't worry. I will get you safely back to Woodway."

Morat gave his young cousin a brief, hard hug. He stood back, his hands still on the young man's shoulders, and looked at him, noting how his fine facial features were filling out, how his body felt bulkier under his hands. He realized how the trek had been toughening the youth.

"Go with Oak. Be safe. That is what will help me the most, Redd. I'll find you. Your clean heart will be a beacon for me, believe me. Trust this."

Redd returned the hug, then stood back awkwardly. "I'll wish strongly for the path to be clear for you, cousin. And Rune needs its Lord back."

"Bring back the Spring, Runerin," Oak said. "Bring it *all* back."

And with that Morat turned toward the darkness of the cave, the glow globe in his hands.

*****

Morat's sense of the passage of time was gone. He had long ago lost any sense of how long he had been in the cave. It simply felt like an endless present. His body moved in a strange, disjointed rhythm as the difficulty of the path changed.

The path had been tight and tortuous at first, uneven underfoot, icy patches making the way slippery, the walls closing in on him from time to time until he had to turn sideways and squeeze through. He held the glow globe in one hand and supported himself with the other against the rough rock wall from time to time, to make his way over the boulders that lay in the path. Rounded like the glacier-worked ones outside the cave, they glinted green in the light of the globe, somehow covered in living moss, despite the darkness.

His shins were bruised. His shoulders ached.

There had been passageways opening off to the side from time to time, but they had not tempted him. Somehow, he was being drawn, and he felt like he had a clear sense of the direction to take.

After a while there were no more side passageways. Only the one way, and Morat walked it almost automatically. Now he was walking easily through a large, airy gallery, aware of its size only because of the echoes of his footsteps, seeing only the one nearby wall visible in the small circle of the light. Then the passageway narrowed again.

He stopped suddenly and blinked. He knelt and held the glow globe out to see more clearly; something seemed familiar in that cluster of spears of rock he had just stumbled on. There—that scuff mark! It was a mark from his own boot, where he had stumbled before. He stood, listening hard into the silence, as if he could somehow aim his ears more acutely and listen further into the void. He heard nothing. A thought teased his brain, blossomed.

How *could* he have been traveling in circles? He had never turned aside from the main way!

Morat sat down where he was, laid the globe down, and held his head in his hands. His mind was clearing a little bit at a time.

What had he been doing? Wandering! Without focus. He felt unutterably tired. Weary to the inner places in his bones. He had let his confidence in the importance of his quest, his certainty of his own intentions, take him along down the wrong path entirely. The sense of direction had been a trick.

He wanted to weep.

"She has a gentle side, the Mother," he said to himself softly. "Gentle ways to protect herself from stupid interlopers."

And in center of the small sphere of light in the darkness he started to try and remember everything he had ever learned about the Mother-of-All.

She was the mother. . . the source of all things. She gave birth to the earth, its rocks were her bones, the soil was her flesh. All things came from her.

Rune's lore had moved away from the Mother's Way long ago in its history. They had kept the letter of her laws, especially the women, doing the ceremonies at the Turning Days and cross-quarter days of the turning year, but mostly the Runerin folk had overlaid it with more masculine, more "rational" ways of thinking. They had built up systematic schools of wizardry and bodies of learning, chemistry and mining and stone-lore and metal-lore. He thought about the gridwork streets of Rune, the orderly rows of furrows in the fields, the gardens of Runehall tamed and pruned. Even the agriculture, the cultivation of living things, had meant the taming of the wilds.

With his fingers he traced the rough, uneven texture of the stone he sat on, its natural roughness, and compared it to the memory of the feel of smooth, polished, inlaid stone of the balcony railing he had held to as he looked down on Willow, watching her play the harp.

Did this have something to do with the waning of power over the generations that Amran-an felt? That Willow had seen in the dwindling of the generations of Runehall? He remembered how Amran-an struggled with the fading of the wizardry, the older body of learning. The lore they had taken such pride in had waned. Unshaping impulses had been allowed to emerge, causing trickery and diminishing and decay. Was it that so much time had gone by? Or that they had overlaid their natural instincts with so much encrusted stone?

The memory of Willow's music made him think of the sound of Woodway . . . its subtlety, complexity . . . the vision that had overcome him in the Xyl Hall, where up and down, branch and root, had become echoes of each other, become one, endless variety fusing into one incredible unity that had taken him by force, through the gateway of his perception, out of his ordinary state of mind.

What happened when the soul, the heart, saw instead of the brain?

Had the clouds moved across the moon that night he had been riding from the Well of Urthumna toward Willow, riding to overtake Evmorat? Or did the moon and sky turn against the stationary clouds . . . it had felt like the sky itself turned, churned by his anger and his anxiety, in his dizzy, headlong riding.

He let his thoughts wander as his feet had through the tunnels within the Mother's thick mountain.

His thoughts turned to the objects that had been turning up, sent to him by Heller Jade or brought to him by the messengers from the Portions, from the mines and smithies. He thought of the metal that was poisoned, prematurely rusting. Of sickness. Of accidents. He thought of the other side of peculiarity that had happened, of the rare objects that made themselves encountered, that cried out for examination.

Was there a message in the antique block prints of Yu-Nikko Su-Nissyen, the brutal story they told? There was a betrayed wedding at the root of that story, that had set free too much of the worst brutal side of the male principle, and let it take Yu-Nikko into the wilderness. It was something she did, her feminine principle, that redeemed the bestiality. No, that felt too simplistic. Was it her artistry? Something she did that blended thought and dream, conscious decision and technical control with impulse and intuition?

Was it something else? About the way intention got bent in the realization of the artwork? Hadn't Amran-an told him how making a woodcut held a special challenge for the artist in the inherent reversal of the image? You made the image with the cut of chisel into wood, with an intent in your mind . . . and then when you printed from wood to paper, the image was reversed. There was always a surprise, he said Master Chen-Yi had written, despite all the conscious design you committed.

The shaping took on a life of its own.

Did we need to let the conscious design of our acts get balanced by something beyond our control?

Blighted marriage . . . how terribly, horribly astray had gone his design to wed Willow. As had her intention to wed Rowan. What was loose in the world that was turning aside their best intentions?

That thought held him still for a long time, in the glimmer of the light globe. Unshaping . . . Unshapers?!Did we let them walk?

Give them doorways into our world?

Tellit. Tellit flashed into his mind. Oh, grief, the perversity of Tellit.

Andellienne . . . oh, beautiful and warm 'Ellienne . . . he had loved her so much, but he had been so young . . . he had been enamored of his new authority and responsibility as Rune Lord . . . he'd figured he had plenty of time later for love . . . he had been too busy, ignored the opportunity to reach out for a soulmate. And she, also so very young, and yearning, feeling crowded out of his sight, had turned to Evmorat. A seduction . . . and Tellit had been the result. Evmorat had been right. The failure of fatherhood had been his. What unshaping had they three let free?

The glow globe flickered unexpectedly, and gems of ice—or diamond—twinkled like stars in the darkness of the cave. Morat drew Willow's Woodrune necklace out of his shirt and fingered the carved wood. He closed his eyes, and like a brief nightmare, the sight of Willow lying dead in blood, blood on his hands, flickered against the insides of his eyelids, to vanish in a flare of pain that shook his body and tore a small cry from between his lips, as it always did when he let down his guard and remembered.

His thoughts turned away desperately . . . he opened his eyes and stared hard past the edge of the sphere of light into the dark.

The Mother was mother of everything . . . not just the feminine, though it was the women who had kept her ceremonies. It wasn't just the excess of some "masculine" rational order that perverted things. She was the Mother of male and female, of all sides of all dichotomies. She was oneness . . . the joining of all those disparate and broken halves into a unity of passion.

The right kind of passion.

Morat felt a huge despair come over him. Had he missed

every opportunity to express the right kind of passion? Maybe he needed to let go of his need to reason things through, be methodical, if he were to achieve this quest. After all, the ultimate goal he had secreted deep in his heart was a mad one, wasn't it? He had to find how to lose the distinctions, break down the barriers, and let the chaos through—but oh, by all the runes he knew, let it through in a purer, unsullied, unpolluted way that defied unshaping. Let the flutter of a butterfly wing on a parapet of Highrune Hall be free to send the clouds running down on the lands from Deld to Kai-Haluu, and the wind flying to find and tune the aeolian harp of Woodway!

Let go of the surety of control. It wasn't possible for it all to be held tight, like reins, in his hands.

He picked up the glow globe and dashed it down on the rocks, and he stood up in the darkness and listened with his soul, with the surface of his skin, and felt the tiniest push of moving air against his bare fingertips.

And stumbling occasionally, tears flowing down his face, whispering Willow's name like a prayer to the Mother, he moved forward into darkness.

A while and a while. The air lost its silence, though he heard nothing. The small scent of a rare, tropical flower insinuated itself like a tendril out of the darkness to his trembling nostrils. It sat like a taste on his tongue as he opened his mouth and breathed in.

Morat dropped the pack from his shoulders.

He followed the scent, drinking it in, savoring it on his tongue. His eyes were closed even against the darkness.

He stumbled on. He unpinned his cloak and let it drop.

The scent grew green and a little salty, like the grass at the seaside. Oh, how he loved the seaside. Why hadn't he gone there each summer, as he planned, instead of staying tied to Highrune hall?

He shed his clothing, piece by piece, as he went forward. It was cold, but that didn't matter. At the last he wore only the necklace he had taken from Willow, around his neck, the Woodrune betrothal necklace carved by Rowan for her. It felt hot, alive on the skin of his breast. He clutched in one hand the stone he had taken from beneath the pines where Willow had hidden, and where Burr Oak had found him and Redd. He clutched in his other hand the agate from the doorstep of the glacier.

He tripped, again and again, and he didn't try to steady himself against the cave walls, but moved out into undefined space. His knees were bloodied. Cold seeped up through his feet and legs into his torso.

He felt the edge of the abyss before he fell, but he did not hold back. He launched himself into the dark void as if he could fly. He cried out, not in fear or regret, but in acceptance of the certainty of destruction, his passion a green streak flaring against the insides of his eyelids.

It was a long fall, at first through empty air. Then he hit stone, fell again. It felt like he slid through an icy tunnel. Slippery ice buffeted him from wall to wall, and finally he came to rest, hard, bone-jarring.

Moss cushioned his impact, but he lay sprawled and feeling broken at the bottom. The chill of the stone bit into his back, stung the cuts and scrapes all over him. The pain was immense, and he groaned it out into the darkness before he could get his teeth clenched over it. He scrabbled fingers in the gravel, shivering. His arm was broken for sure, and probably his leg. Something didn't feel quite right beneath his ribs. But he could still move fingers and toes. In time he would try again to move.

For now, he spat out blood and let his head whirl.

"Oh, Mother, Mother of All," he prayed. "Here I am, come to you at last. Hear me. Hear me, please."

And a light blossomed in the darkness, a scent uncurled on the dank air, that exotic tropical floral sign again.

With it came a gentle sound of soft bubbling. He turned his head and saw a pool, boiling, a hot spring. From where he lay, he couldn't see into it, but a strange, green-tinted glow was shining up out of its depths to light the mist that wreathed above it, condensing where warmth met cold.

The mist grew denser, wreathed itself more tightly. Slowly it coalesced, grew into a figure, robed, face hidden. The figure turned to him, folded back the robe from her face. It was the face of a young girl, just budding into womanhood, eyes large, luminous, long-lashed, slanted slightly over cheeks smooth and rose-tinged like finest porcelain, finely sculpted chin, delicate nose, fresh lips slightly parted. Her breath was perfume, she was a harpsong.

Morat sighed. She looked nothing like Willow but held everything in her features that had ever drawn him to love. The light from her figure shone down on his pale, bruised, naked limbs, and he felt warmed as if by sunshine.

"Rune Lord," she spoke, with a voice full of flowers and bees humming and birds singing far off in spring-flowered trees, "Rune Lord, you have fallen far and deep."

"Mother of All, I have come to you as best I could."

"Sa, you have." Her voice held pity.

"Mother, the year has stopped turning."

"Sa."

"Everything is frozen. Nothing is growing. We—all the world—will starve."

She regarded him silently.

"Will you start it turning again?" He felt frustrated that he couldn't find a more polished, persuasive way to lead up to the request. But he was faint, breathing perfume and light from her, mixing with his pain.

She came closer and knelt down by him. The air was warm around her, scented, aglow. She reached out and touched him, lightly, on his arm, and the pain faded, then on his leg, and the pain faded there, too. But it wasn't gone entirely. She wasn't healing him; he was still broken open to her.

"Have you nothing more personal, more immediate to ask of me? Poor, broken Rune Lord?"

He considered, forced by her question, how desperate his situation was. He'd never be able to climb out again, not on a broken leg, not with a broken arm. He'd freeze, naked as he was. Something inside him hurt, and he spit out more blood.

"I don't care about myself. I came to ask—"

"Yes, I know, for me to start the year turning again. For Rune, and for Woodway, for Redd and Amran-an and Burr Oak, for all the world." Mockery was green in her voice.

Anger flared in him. He struggled to raise his head, pushed himself up on his sound arm.

"Yes, for all the world. I am Rune's Lord. I am steward of my land, caretaker of my people. Who else is there who should speak for them?"

And he realized he meant it. That this was his own truth, however out of balance responsibility might sometimes be, in him, over personal need; care for others was how he was anchored to himself, how he expressed his own soul. This was what hung from the other end of the balance beam from the crazy, impulsive dive into the darkness he had taken.

"Evmorat said I always had to fix things," he muttered.

She rose, turned away from him, wrapped her face in her robe again. Her voice was muffled, "Yet it was your deed that stopped the year. You took to rape. You killed."

"Yes! Yes, I did!" he screamed. "Mother, forgive me, Willow, forgive me, I did. With the best of intentions, the most loving of hearts, never in any corner of my soul wishing anyone any harm, I did." He buried his face in his arm and shook.

Her fingers touched his head, and he looked up. The robe was set back from her face again, but that face had changed. It was fuller, eyes softer, tender, glistening with near-tears, brow lined gently with concern, lips smiling in a special, gentle way, and he remembered—as he had not in many, many years—his mother, holding him to her, kissing away some small injury.

"I know, I know. I know all, remember. Of course you loved them, 'Ellienne, and Willow, and even Evmorat."

"Of course."

"And that's the paradox that makes you, and all of them, human . . . and the world such an imperfect place."

Morat had no answer to that. He lay on the rocks, the incredible moss, bathed in the glow of Her and in the soft, bubbling sound of her warm wellspring, and pain washed over him.

"I'd give anything to undo their deaths. You know how far I have come. You know that is why I am here. Can't the depth of my love win some redemption? What can I give you, who are the source of all things? You have my body, if pain or death will pay the price . . . I've shown you already I mean that . . . I'll pay anything you ask."

"I can give you spring again . . . but I cannot set the year turning beyond that."

Morat was surprised at the sorrow in her voice.

“Long ago I birthed my children. And like any truly loving mother, I taught them to stand, and walk, and then I let them free to take their own way. It’s up to them, now—to you, Rune Lord, and the likes of Burr Oak, and Redd, and my Xyl, and all the others, to make the choices and move the world forward again.”

Again she turned away, pulled the robe across her face. Her figure seemed to shrink, the bubbling of the spring grew quieter, and the glow dimmed slightly. The scent in the air became dried roses, faded blossoms.

Morat was dismayed.

She turned back to him one more time, and she was old. Her hair was lank and gray around her face, which was deeply wrinkled; there were myriad lines at the corners of her eyes.

“There’s something more, however, out there. Amran-an, your wizard friend, is wiser than he knows. The powers—including mine, are waning. Something else is moving upon the face of my beloved world,” she sighed. “Something that unmakes, unshapes. It turns aside the best creative impulses.

“Morat, I give you a special gift. Know this: the consequences of your deeds were not your own fault. They were not deserved, not earned.” She reached out a hand, gnarled like an old oak branch, and touched his breast, and a hot glow spread through him. “Your heart is true; your hand only was turned aside. Trust yourself. Forgive yourself."

For a long moment, her fingers lay on his breast, and warmth filled him. He felt a peace unlike anything he had ever known.

She stood back. “I ask something indeed, in exchange for giving you spring. I ask that you hold to the purpose that sits within you, that goal which you have spoken to no one.” He reached, and she let him touch her hand, and he looked up at her in surmise.

“Yes, I see where you would go, if you are freed from my Mountain’s heart. “Do you swear to this task? In exchange for the spring?”

“I promise. I will go onward. I will go and find Willow in the land of Death and I will bring her forth again. I swear it.” His chest heaved; it terrified him to put his secret desire into words at last, especially before the Mother.

“Go with my blessing. Unmake the work of these new-emerged Unshapers. Bring my best beloved children back to the world.”

She touched the Woodrune locket that lay on Morat’s breast.

“Will you give me that? As token of your pledge?”

“Aaieeh! It is all I have left of Willow!” he cried involuntarily, then felt ashamed. He scrabbled at it with his unbroken arm, trying to pull it off over his head. “It is your sign, oh Great One. Come home to you. I’ve only kept it for a little while.”

Amazed, he saw, under her fingers, the wood of the carving soften, bend, and lift itself up. It became a seedling, unfolded two small green leaves. She cupped it in her hands, then laid it back onto his breast. Roots sprung from it, and reached through his skin, into his breast. He almost panicked, but there was no pain.

“I give you the spring you asked for,” she said, drawing back, away from him. “Let it grow in you.”

And he lay still, as the small tree grew upon and into and through him. He felt his broken bones knit together. Warmth filled him, and greenness, and singing.

“I’ll tell you where to go next, and what you must do . . . as far as I may.”

She whispered into his ear, then backed away and stood tall, shedding her agedness, queenly again, goddess. She smiled down at him, her arms held out to her sides, and her figure grew larger and larger, merging with the walls of the cavern. It was all illuminated now, by her glow, and Morat saw through tears a million gems and precious minerals shining crystalline around him. He lay in the heart of a huge geode.

There was a flash, an incredible, explosive blast of light and sound that shook him; the jewels rained down on him. The wellspring bubbled up and over its rim, metallic-smelling hot water. Cold water broke free from cracks in the wall and ran down to join the flood of water from the hot spring that poured over him. Mist tumulted everywhere.

Morat rode the torrent like a leaf on the surface of a mountain stream, like a fish plunging down a cascade. He was tumbled and buffeted, without air. Huge explosive concussions shook the mountain, thundering through the water to buffet him. It was bright and green, a tide that washed out through an opening of the Mountain to pour down the riverbed. It carried flowers and leaves and greenness; it poured balm and breathy spring out over the rocks, melting away the ice.

He rode the tide down out of the heart of the Mother's Mountain, feeling how the spring spread out, green and new and blossomed, into the valley, flowing toward Woodway, growing into a huge tidal cascade.

His lungs ached, then exploded with airlessness, and blackness overtook him.

When Morat woke, he lay curled like a baby into a carpet of ferns and flowers. Droplets of fragrant moisture jeweled everything, like morning dew, including his skin. He felt newborn.

A bird sang, and he looked up to find it, and found above him the tree that had been rooted in him and grown through and out of him when the Mother touched him. Now it sat rooted in the earth, many-trunked, and bent blossomed boughs gently over him, brushing his cheek with white petals, it roots curling around his shoulders. Hanging down from its heart was the necklace that had been Willow's, the Mother-signed Woodwaynim betrothal rune. On his chest, where the tree had been rooted, there were scars; he ran his fingers over them, expecting pain, but they were silvery and healed. They formed the same image, on his breast, that was carved into the necklace, webbed branches within the crescent moon sign of the Mother. The tree itself might stand free now, but its mark was on him forever. And like the necklace, he was and would be a sign of a promise before the Mother-of-All.

Morat found his clothing and his pack on the ground nearby and he dressed. He took his knife from the pack and cut one of the tree's branches into a long, straight staff. He gathered spring vines from the base of the tree and wound them around the staff; he reached up and took down Willow's locket and tied it at the staff's crown. He picked flowers and ferns and wove them around it, knowing somehow that they would not fade as long as they were twined upon the staff with Willow's woodrune.

Still in an otherworldly state of mind, seeing and feeling and hearing the spring around him, but through eyes misted with tears, body awkward with being remade, holding his staff like a hiker's walking stick, Morat walked its green, flowered path toward Woodway.

*****

Redd fairly danced around him like an excited child.

"It was unbelievable, Morat! The Mother's Mountain burst open, and the water poured out, and everything it touched turned green . . . flowers sprouting out of the ice everywhere . . .

It was like a river of green . . ."

He fell still, looking into Morat's silent face.

"My Lord! Your eyes!"

"Redd?"

"They're changed, Sire. They . . . they are *green* . . ."

Burr Oak came forward, taking Morat by the arm, and stared into his face. "She touched you, Runerin," he whispered.

But Redd couldn't hold back the flood of words for long.

"You were gone so long. It got hard to tell the number of days, with all the cold and the ice and the mist, but finally Burr Oak made me come away from the glacier with him, and we climbed the cliff again, and they found us and brought us back to Woodway.

"We were frostbitten and out of food, but Oak set the woodrunes singing as we went along. They must have been signals, because the Woodwaynim came quickly and helped us back to the city."

"The boy fell ill," said Burr Oak. "We made it up the cliff, but by then he was in fever. But he kept going, until they could reach us through the deep snow."

A smile creased his weathered face, as he looked at the young man. "He'd make a good Woodwaynim. He can have a place in the Oak Branch if he ever wants it."

"But Morat! You succeeded! You found the Mother! You got us spring!"

"Sa, I did." Morat's voice sounded strange even to his own ears. He had been wandering in greenness, following the cataract of spring down the valley toward the city, watching it unfold before him like some kind of unrolling carpet of flower and warm air and blue sky until it outpaced him and left him behind. He leaned on the staff and looked up at Woodway.

Woodway was alive with color, scarves and banners flying in the warm breeze. The trees that mingled with the buildings were gorgeous with spring blossoms. Its sound rang bright, hopeful, ebullient.

Woodwaynim were crowding through the high Phloem Gates, which had been opened all the way to their full height, not just the small winter doors Burr Oak had taken him through an age ago. They wore silks and finely worked hides, not furs, and almost everyone had decked themselves with flowers.

Morat leaned on the staff. He felt unsteady in the face of so many people crowding toward him. He felt the need for wilderness like a wildness of heart rise in him, and he swallowed it down and tried to focus his eyes on the people and away from the green distances where his mind had been wandering.

Redd saw him sway, and suddenly the attentive squire again, went to his side and put Morat's arm on his shoulder.

"You must be sore fatigued, My Lord. Lean on me if you will."

*****

Once again Morat stood in the great Heartwood Hall before the nine Xyl elders, so sexless and same in their robes. Redd stood beside him, an attentive honor guard.

The young squire was subdued since he had helped Morat to a chamber and helping him to strip and bathe, had uncovered and seen the scars on the Rune Lord's chest. The staff and the scars and the greenness in Morat's eyes had made him a stranger to his young cousin. Something a bit magical, awesome.

But something he was determined to serve as he had always,

with steadfastness and youthful determination.

Together the twined voices of the Xyl spoke: "My Lord High Rune, we are eternally grateful for the gift of this spring you have won from the Mother. We are in your debt. And we bow down before the favor she has shown you."

As if they were arms of a single body, they rose and bowed to him. One figure—was it the same? Willow's mother?—came around the huge table and up to him, holding out a ribbon embroidered with leaves. It matched the ones they wore, but it had all the different leaves of the Xyl Branches on it, while each of them wore only one.

"We welcome you as one of our own."

Morat didn't take it.

"The year hasn't started turning yet," he said firmly. We have Spring," he said, "but the bigger part remains to do."

"Nevertheless, we would bind ourselves to your task with you in whatever way we can."

Morat stood still.

The Xyl hesitated. Then she stepped up and tied the banner to the staff in Morat's hand. The staff sparked a small bit of static when she touched it, and she flinched, but she completed a complex knot before she stepped back.

Without a word, Morat turned and went, followed by Redd and also by the Woodwaynim, Burr Oak.

CHAPTER 17

"Don't worry, Am. This time you go, too," said Morat. "And Heller, too," he turned to the large seaman, "if you will come."

Heller fingered the blade of his axe that he was turning in his hands as he sat, with the sharpening stone and the oily rag in his lap. He was searching patiently and thoroughly with his experienced fingers for signs of dulled edge or roughened metal.

"Of course," he grinned. "You know I'll na pass up a chance for a bit of adventure. And though I am glad to have spring, and the ice and cold gone, I would have true summer again, and fall, and all of it, and I would follow you to the gates of the Land of the Dead if it will fix this cursed world."

Morat turned sharply, fixed his newly greened eyes on the seaman.

"What?" said Heller, responding to the intensity in Morat. "Is that, then, where we are going?"

"To the Land of the Dead?" asked Redd, astonished.

"Ah." said Heller. "Of course." One bushy eyebrow went up.

"He's not joking, Heller," said Amran-an.

"Of course he isn't," said Heller steadily. He looked back down at the axe, put the sharpening stone to the edge, carefully keeping it angled correctly to hone the edge properly. Softly he whistled a sailor's tune.

Redd looked at them, from one to the other, eyes wide.

Amran-an was sorting some bundles Morat had laid across the table, trying to decide how to fit them into a pack.

"Here," said Morat. "You'll need to bring this, too." He handed the wizard a small, old book.

"What is it?"

"Don't you remember? It's the Book of Unshaping by Maara that strayed from Deld at the beginning of all this business. However Evmorat opened it, it's still closed down and inaccessible now. But it was there on the table in my library again this morning. Asking to come, maybe."

Amran-an looked at Morat sharply, but Morat just shrugged. "You can work at the bindings as we travel. And pack this as well."

"And that is . . ."

"A piece of stone from the cornerstone of Highrune Hall."

"What? Not the entire stone itself? And don't give me that green-eyed stare, Morat. What about the rest of this stuff? Why are we bringing all these odd objects? I thought I was the wizard here," Amran-an said, exasperated. "But I swear every time I think I have it all packed, something else just *turns up*."

Morat handed him a double handful of small packets, neatly wrapped.

"Sorry, my friend," said Morat, a small smile crossing his lips. "It's just that . . . well, it keeps popping into my head that we'll need this . . . and that . . . I can't explain it. I just have the feeling these will be needed somehow. My fingers itched until I found them and packed them up."

"Well, I sincerely hope they stop this itching soon. Just how big a pack do you expect me to carry?"

He turned the backpack over and dumped it out again. "All

right, let's see if I can fit them in—what's this? I *know* I didn't put that in there!"

Redd was picking up objects. "Piece of metal?"

"Forged in the mountains of High Havenn. From the best ores in Rune."

"A vial of sand?"

"From the Wastes of Maia, at the border of Deld Portion," said Amran-an, a bit embarrassed. "It has a fossil seashell in it. Did you know the wastes were once an inland sea?"

"And this? A piece of wood? Wrapped in paper?"

"Don't handle that, Redd," Amran-an snatched it away anxiously. "It's a piece of the woodblock from the Tale of the Black Prince, and a piece of the print made from it. It might . . . might hurt you."

Noise came from the doorway, argumentative voices. Wayland pushed his way in, followed closely by Ranna and Lexin. Wayland handed something to Morat.

"What's this?" Morat looked at the small scroll of parchment, tied with a striped ribbon, to which a medal was attached. "Isn't this the medal you were awarded?"

"Living Treasure or something like that," Wayland shrugged. "I want to go with you, but I've got too many years on me to make such a trek. Let that go with you instead."

Morat turned the scroll in his hands. Some instinct told him to keep it tied as it was.

"It's my unfinished poem. My best work, I'd hoped. But I've worked it and reworked it, and I cannot seem to find the right last line. I think . . . I think it's out *there*. Find it for me."

And then Ranna stood before Morat. He thought he'd never

seen her so . . . so unmovable before.

“I’m going with you.”

“Child—”

“I’m not a child, begging your pardon, My Lord. And I have the right to go. I was there when—” Her voice choked, “I tried to protect her, but—”

She saw Morat flinch, and the pain flash across his face quickly before he got it under control.

Behind her, Lexin looked over her head into the High-Lord’s eyes and shrugged. “She’s going. Nothing you or I can say or do will stop her. And she goes nowhere I don’t follow.” He took her hand. He held out his other hand. “Here. This is for the rune you are going to build.”

Morat and Amran together stared at the young gardener’s apprentice. “So that’s what all these things are for,” whispered Morat.

Ranna looked at them as if they were stupid. “Of course. Willow told us. It takes a Finder, a Maker, a Binder, and a Tuner.”

Amran-an looked even more puzzled.

“To make a Mother’s woodrune,” explained Lexin. He held out a package to Morat. “It’s dried blossoms from the sensitive tree. The one in the garden where we sat together. Her favorite.”

“Wrapped in the best square from the marriage quilt I was making,” added Ranna, her small chin up, stubborn. “One I embroidered with the special purple thread.” Her eyes were bright, however, with tears.

*****

“It’s still following us,” Redd said softly, gesturing slightly at the cornuas' ears. Heller nodded.

"I know," Morat whispered back as he worked at the pack knots. "Their ears have been twitching all day. Don't alarm the others. Redd, get them setting up camp. Heller and I will check it out."

Loudly, Morat said, "Here, Redd, you and Am get the tents set up; Ranna and Lex look like they're going to drop in their tracks." He handed the tent bundles to Redd. "Here's the firepot, Ranna," he said. "I'll find some wood for a fire. Heller, you look for some over there," he pointed to the far side of the clearing.

Redd took the tent bundles to the center of the clearing, handing one to Am and the other to Lexin. They started to put them together. The tents were compact affairs, easy to set up. Amran-an had made the framework poles from some strange trees from the south, soaking them with chemicals and marking them with runes to make them stronger and yet flexible enough to bend without breaking. He had threaded the poles with cords and marked all the pieces so they almost fit together of their own accord, when they pulled them out of the bag and he said a rune over them.

Morat stamped heavily off into the woods, taking every opportunity to step on branches that cracked sharply. Redd smiled after him, then turned back to the tents. The ground was hard, and he silently blessed Am's ingenuity once again as he inserted the poles into pockets sewn in the canvas. The tents stood by themselves, and only needed a few rocks at their footings to anchor them.

Morat's noise faded into the wind.

"Make sure you bring back lots of dry kindling," Redd called loudly in the direction Morat had taken.

Morat crept silently up behind the figure crouched in the darkening twilight under the pines. He hadn't heard a sound from Heller, but he knew he, too, was circling to join Morat. It was amazing that the large seaman could move so soundlessly in the woods. But he'd seen him do it often. Once, when they'd been much younger, he'd watched Heller, on a dare, creep up on a unsuspecting horn beast and actually lay a hand on its haunch before it exploded away in startlement.

Morat was surprised, though, at how easy it had been to circle around and come up behind this intruder. It was such a simple ruse; he hadn't expected it to work. He even had the disadvantage of height, having had to come up a gradual slope to a small cliff overhanging the interloper, and having trouble keeping his silhouette low against the last light in the darkening sky. It couldn't, then, be a Woodwaynim, not that unwood-wise.

The figure was clad in rough furs, but appeared human, though Morat couldn't see anything that enabled him to distinguish its identity.

With sword unsheathed, Morat leapt down onto the crouched figure, knocking it flat to the ground. It struggled under him until the cold metal of his sword blade touched its neck, then lay still. Heller's bulk was suddenly beside Morat, ready, but he motioned the seaman to stillness. He turned the figure over, still keeping the sword to its throat.

"Who are you?" Morat cried, "Why are you sneaking around behind us?" And gasped in surprise as the furs fell from its face. "Tellit!"

Redd had come up by this time. With the fire-bowl as a lantern he lit the boy's face, white and frightened in the light.

"I thought you gone," said Morat. He helped the boy to his feet, steadied him.

"Where would I go?" Tellit whimpered.

The boy was shivering, but mostly with fear and shock rather than cold, Morat thought. He and Heller helped Tellit back through the woods to the clearing and settled him down near the tents. Heller moved off to help Redd set up the wood for the fire, while Ranna and Lexin came to stare at the newcomer. Ranna rooted in a pack, seeking food that could be eaten without cooking, and brought a small way-loaf filled with dried fruit and nuts to Morat, who gave it to Tellit. Tellit grabbed it greedily, stuffed it in his mouth, barely chewing it before swallowing and reaching for more.

"Bring some more," Morat motioned to Ranna. "Looks like he hasn't eaten in days. Am, how about breaking out one of the amrita fruits? He could use the restorative. He's in bad shape. We're four days out from Highrune, and he's got no pack, no food."

Tellit continued to eat, staring at them, still shivering.

"At least he had sense enough to steal Hallon's old winter hunting furs so he didn't freeze to death," said Redd.

"Morat," said Am, bringing the cut pieces of the precious fruit, "I think he's been in the forest a lot longer than four days. You know he's been nowhere in Highrune for weeks."

"I know, I know. Where *have* you been, boy?" asked Morat gently. "We did look for you."

Tellit's eyes were fixed and unblinking, as he watched Redd uncork the small vial of fire-starting fluid, pour a few drops on the wood, and light it with an ember from the firepot. The light of the blossoming fire danced in the darkness of the boy's pupils.

"I felt the year stop turning," Tellit whispered. "I sat outside your door, my Lord, hoping you would open it, but you didn't."

Morat looked away.

"It was my fault, the cold and the stillness."

"*Your* fault? Tellit, that's not—"

“I gave my fa—Evmorat the Midhe’s Tears.”

“*You*?!”

“Sa . . . I had it from an old peddler who called to me in the marketplace on the eve of the Year-Turning festival. The voices made me go to the marketplace . . . and to seek out that peddler.”

Amran-an came closer, knelt in front of the boy. “Voices, Tellit?”

“I’d been hearing them for a long time.”

“When did you first hear them, Tellit?” Amran-an’s voice was gentle.

Tellit looked at the wizard, his dark eyes troubled. “I’m not sure . . . it’s been a while . . . think I heard them first the day we got lost in the Motherwoods . . . telling me to cry out when I spotted that white horn beast.” Tellit looked up at Morat. “I’m not crazy, My Lord,” he flared. “They’re not *that* kind of voices . . . not like old crazy Mikka hears, who helps clean the stables. These are *real* voices!”

“Tellit, what do you mean, ‘real’?” asked Amran-an, handing the boy more pieces of the fruit.

“It’s hard to put into words, Sire,” said the boy slowly, “But it’s like the people speaking are really there . . . it’s just that I can’t *see* them. Like they’re one step away from us, in some other world, really close to ours, but not the same.”

“I wanted to tell someone . . . I tried to tell Hallon, but it scared him, and he wouldn’t listen. I tried to tell Evmorat when he came back to Highrune.”

The boy looked at Morat with such deep unhappiness in his eyes, that it choked Morat.

“*He* listened! And then he got a look in his eyes . . . it gave him ideas, you see. He wanted to know more, wanted me to tell him everything they said."

"What *did* they say?"

"When they came most clearly, they suggested things . . . they talked about how things could change . . . how Evmorat could be High-Lord—and then someday, I could . . ."

He looked at Morat, panic in his eyes.

"I wouldn't listen to that part, Lord! Honest! But they told me I could have a father—"

A groan escaped Morat, coming from deep in his chest. Heller put an arm around him.

"I know Evmorat was my father. All *I* wanted was for him to say so . . . he didn't have to do anything else more than that. Just say I was his."

Tellit gripped his hands tightly in his lap, as if trying to hold himself together.

"But he was more interested in the other things the voices had to say, about power, and magic, and ways to control people and events. I thought the things the voices said could be done were more often harmful than good . . . but . . ." He wiped his hand across his mouth, reached for more of the star fruit.

"But I was so angry . . . at Evmorat . . . I was angry at Hallon, who said I was bad . . . at everyone! I was angry at the other boys, who knew so surely who they were . . . where they were going. I was angry at the girls who teased me, and then laughed at me, pushed me away and called me a bastard. I wanted to hurt everyone for hurting me."

He sighed, a huge breath that shook his entire body. He looked up at Morat, his eyes dark with sorrow.

"And every time I hurt someone, the voices got easier to hear . . . and now I've killed my father."

"Na, boy, na, that wasn't you," said Morat, trying to keep the pain out of his own voice, trying to calm the boy. "That wasn't you."

"I ran away . . . not from you, Sire, or from Rune, or even from what I did . . . but from the voices. I waited by your door, High-Lord, until the voices got so loud I couldn't breathe, and then I ran."

Ranna put a cup in Tellit's hands, a cup of warm way-brew, steeped on the now blazing fire. She put more way-bread, a slice with cheese on it, on a cloth, on the rock by his side.

Morat watched as Tellit put both hands around the warm cup, breathed in its vapors, eyes closed. He seemed to settle a bit. The boy was coming back to them, he thought, from some extremely distant place where he had been, in body and mind.

"Where *have* you been, Tellit?" asked Amran-an. "We did search all of Highrune, and we sought word throughout the countryside. But it seemed like you had vanished." His voice caught. "We thought you were dead."

"I've been in the forest."

There was a long pause in his speech. They watched him, and Morat held his hand, as the far-away look welled up in his eyes again, and he struggled visibly, though motionless, without breathing, to bring his focus near again.

"I think I lived with the wolves . . . it's hard to remember, the voices were so loud in my head. But there were wolves . . . and I think they let me be with them because I wore a wolfskin."

He looked up, staring at them, as the memory seemed to come clearer, himself surprised by what he had said. "They let me eat from their kill and sleep in their den . . . like one of their cubs. . . like one of their *children*! And for a while, the voices were quiet, and I felt safe."

Tellit took up the cup of way-brew again, and he sipped it.

"But the voices found me again, finally. Told me where to find you. They want—" His hands tightened on the cup, as he fought to keep them from shaking, and the brew sloshed in it, the vapors twisting.

"What do they want, Tellit?" asked Amran-an, his voice as gentle as the fingertips he laid on Tellit's arm.

"They want . . . they want to finish the unshaping . . . to stop you. They want to stop the year turning forever, stop things from being born and growing . . . to keep things from taking on shape, good and clean like they ought to be!" he exclaimed angrily. He looked up at Amran-an, then at Morat again, and said fiercely, "But I want to help you." He stared into Morat's green-turned eyes, put a hand out to Morat, pleading, "I want to go where you are going, Sire. To find my father."

His voice dropped to a whisper.

"To be with him. If I have to die . . . to be with him."

*****

They came to the rise from which they could look down into the little valley, and for a moment, the strongest feeling of déjà vu seized Morat, and he had to stop at the crest and take hold of himself, consciously try to quiet the pounding of his heart. He sat the cornua, the staff tingling in his hand, its ribbons blowing gently in the chill breeze. He sighed deeply, and the ever-fresh flowers twined about the staff put a sweet scent to the air that clenched his chest as he breathed it in.

The still pool was as dark and mysterious as before, not even mirroring the sky. Although spring had touched here, as elsewhere throughout the land they had crossed, it had touched it only lightly, and there was still primarily snow and dark rocks and dark green pines to be seen.

A woodrune hung from a carved pole set in the cairn of rocks that marked the grave of Rowan of Oak Branch, Green Wizard of Woodwaynim. The chilly wind twirled a feather tied to the rune and called forth a sad, moaning tone from it.

A dark shape, that Morat had thought was just another rock, or maybe a tree stump, stirred, moved, rose to a man's height, and it was a Woodwaynim, emerged from a stillness Morat could barely imagine. It raised an arm in greeting.

"It's Burr Oak," said Redd. "I am glad to see him again."

"A chilly wait he's had," Heller said with a grunt.

"Not for him," answered Redd. The young man moved his mount forward, taking the lead down into the small valley. He dismounted, and he and the Woodwaynim exchanged an embrace.

"Can you have grown so much, in these few weeks, lad?" asked the Woodwaynim. "I think I need to reach up at least an inch more."

Redd ducked his head, blushing, pleased.

Burr Oak turned to Morat. He nodded, and it was almost a bow, coming from him. "Rune Lord."

Morat took his hand. "I hoped you'd come."

They gathered around the cairn of stones, listening to the moan of the woodrune hung above it. Morat, Amran-an, Heller, Redd were all silent, remembering. The others stood back a bit, daunted, as these faced the ghosts that were their memories alone . . . of a confused battle . . . a mischance killing . . . wild grief. Morat knelt and brushed a finger over one of the rocks they had piled into the cairn, touched one of the flowers that grew up between the stones. The flower broke at his touch. Morat raised his fingers to look at the sap, red as blood, on them.

A wind shook the pines suddenly, tossing shadows at them. A hawk cried high above, startling Ranna, and Lexin put a protective arm around her shoulder.

"The realm of the Dead lies very close to ours here," said Amran-an. "But if this grave is the gate, how do we open it?"

Ranna shivered. "Would the book, the one you have been working to open, have any clues?"

"It might, if I could open it. It still resists any runes I can devise."

"Let me see," said the little maid.

Amran-an, surprised, took it from his jacket, where he had been carrying it, next to his heart.

The Book of Maara had remained clamped tight shut since they had found it in the library, somehow unopenable after its single use by Evmorat to send them astray so long ago. Whatever had been released then had sealed it, as if fighting against releasing any countermeasure to that unshaping. Yet Amran-an had felt a need to bring it along, had been hoping, in some crazy way, to *feel* his way through its locks with his body, or his soul, though his conscious mind had hit an impasse.

Ranna turned it over in her hands. Lexin, coming to look over her shoulder, pointed to a leaf embossed in the pattern on the cover. "I've seen that leaf before," he said.

Amran-an remembered the young man was a gardener's apprentice. "I didn't recognize it," said the wizard.

"It's not common down in the lowlands of Rune. See how it's shaped a little like a hand? How it wraps around the stem? That bud? It's the alpine bloodroot, and it's found only in the mountains, only in the early spring. The plant puts its shoots up through the snow, and blooms, and dies down as soon as the snow is really gone and the weather starts to warm. Its root bleeds, Sire, if you break it." He touched the stain on Morat's fingers, then touched the leaf embossed on the cover of the book.

And the book fell open.

Amran-an and Morat gaped. "How—?"

The Woodwaynim smiled. "Maybe the time wasn't quite right. Or maybe it took the touch of these innocents. The boy does have a bit of the Finder in him, and the girl has a bit of the Maker in her. Maybe it needed the two of them."

"And a little of the actual blood of the root."

Amran-an fidgeted, wanting to take the open book into his hands, but the Woodwaynim put a restraining hand on his arm. "Wait," said his green eyes. "Wait."

Ranna sat down on a rock, and paged through the book in her lap, turning the old pages carefully. "Here, Sire," she said, handing the book to the wizard. "I think this is the page you want. I can't read it, but this picture . . . I think it says something about what we need to do."

Amran-an took the book, and he and Morat looked together at the page Ranna had picked. The picture on it drew a soft whistle from the Rune Lord. It showed a figure dressed in green, a young man, with a crown of the bloodroot leaves and flowers around his brow, and the sign of the Mother-of-All, crescent moon and branched tree, on his breast. He held a flowering branch in one hand, and a cup in the other, and was pouring it, and the liquid that was spilling from it was painted red on the page . . . as red as blood, thought Morat.

The characters below the picture were meaningless hieroglyphics to Morat. "Can you read it?" he asked Amran-an.

"I think so . . . but it will take a while to tease it out."

He took the book and went to sit on a rock by the fire.

"It says it will take blood."

"I thought it might," said Morat dryly.

He had been sitting by the fire as well, eyes closed, resting his brow on the staff he held planted in front of his feet. He'd felt something coming up to him through the staff, out of the cold earth, almost a humming, something so barely sensed he didn't even consider telling Amran-an that he was feeling it. At times it almost took on the sense of voices, and when it did, he had looked over at Tellit.

The boy sat still, eyes unfocused again, and Morat knew he was hearing his voices again. Were they the same voices?

"Blood." Morat repeated. Were they, he wondered, about to do something that fed the wrong voices? "Whose?"

Neither of them even bothered to suggest it might be animal blood, not human blood, that was required.

"Rowan was of my branch. Of the Oak." It was Burr Oak, come silently up behind them. "My blood he will heed, before any other."

"That fits the words that are here, Morat," said Amran-an. "*'Branch of my branch, tree of my tree,'*" he quoted, "*'Earth of my birth, I will harken to thee.'*"

"But that isn't enough, Rune Lord," said Burr Oak.

"Na, I didn't think it would be. It will take my blood as well, won't it, Am?"

The wizard read on, "*'Sign of my failure, seed of dire deed, breath of my death, lend blood to this need.'*"

The others came forward, summoned by the intensity of their voices. Morat stood holding his staff in his left hand, needing it to hold him standing and steady. He reached to his waist, took out of its sheath the small knife he always wore. "Are we ready?" he asked them. One by one, they nodded. He held the knife up to the Woodwaynim. "This was the knife that shed Willow's blood and Evmorat's. It still has the stains of their blood on it."

"It will do," said Burr Oak, taking it. He pushed the furs up to bare his arm and slashed at his wrist. The blood ran from the cut down his arm. Ranna gasped.

He handed the knife to Morat. Morat bared his arm, still holding to the staff, and slashed his wrist in the same place.

The two, Rune Lord and Woodwaynim, put their bleeding wrists together, so that their blood ran down onto the staff, the rivulets of it braiding across each other, mixing. Morat felt the staff tingle as the blood ran on to it. The vines twined on it rustled, the flowers moved, a scent rising from them of funerals. He let the blood run down onto the cairn of stones, tensing as it touched them.

Nothing happened.

Morat lifted the staff and struck the cairn of rocks with it.

Nothing happened.

Then Tellit pushed the others aside and grabbed the knife from Morat. Before they could stop him, he slashed his wrist and pressed it, bleeding, to the staff. His blood mingled with theirs.

A concussion shook the earth, knocked them all sprawling. The pool exploded, geysering dark water. Rocks and snow tumbled down the cliffs on them, from all sides.

Ranna cried out; Lexin threw himself on top of her, shielding her from the avalanching rocks. Heller was on his knees, axe raised, looking around wildly. The rest rode the bucking earth flat on their faces.

“Yes,” cried Morat. “Oh, yes,” he pleaded, feeling the staff under him flaring with energy, feeling the sign of the Mother on his chest burning, burning. Burying his face in the blood mingling with the flowers on the staff, he prayed. “Please,” he prayed, with all his being, for the gate to open, the gate to the Land of the Dead.

The ground gave one huge lurch and buckled open beneath them, dropping them into darkness.

CHAPTER 18

Morat sat in the glow the staff was giving off. He had planted it in the ground, and they lay in the small circle of its light, and he was clinging to it with both hands to stay upright. His ears still rang, his head was still filled with the thunder of the concussion that had opened the cairn of rocks and dropped them through. Into what? He had no idea what lay outside that circle of dim green light.

Amran-an tore a strip of cloth from his shirt and came to wind it around Morat's wrist for him, to stanch the bleeding.

The Woodwaynim was pressing his fingers to his own wound, muttering runes. When he took his fingers away, the bleeding had stopped.

"Tellit," gasped Morat. "Take care of Tellit."

The boy lay sprawled on his back, arms thrown up over his head. Amran crawled to him, touched his brow.

"He struck his head. He's unconscious. Burr Oak, can you do that same trick on his wrist? He's too wasted to be able to spare much blood."

The Woodwaynim crawled to them, touched the boy. Something made him pull his hand back for a moment. "Boy's got something in him," he muttered. "Something I don't want to touch, bless the Mother." But at the pleading look in Morat's eyes, he reached again.

Morat took a piece of cloth from his own shirt and after the Woodwaynim had stopped the bleeding with his words, the wizard bound the boy's wrist. He bunched his cloak under

Tellit's head, lifted his eyelids, fingered his brow. "Doesn't seem to have a concussion." But he sounded worried.

Heller Jade sat up and groaned. He'd fallen heavily, with all his bulk. He ran his hands over his body, sighed when he found no broken bones. "I feel like I did when that top-spar fell on me, years ago, during the storm that near wrecked the Whale-Dancer. Thought lightning had struck me, back then."

He reached around in the darkness, found his axe. "Feel like lightning struck me again," he groaned.

Morat looked around anxiously. "Redd!" he called. "Ranna! Lexin!"

He heard sounds from the darkness, moans. "Here. We're here. It's dark!" Redd's voice sounded a little panicky.

"Come to the light. My staff is giving us some light. Can you see it?"

"Just barely. But I can find you by your voice, so keep calling."

Redd and Lexin stumbled into the circle of the light, holding Ranna between them.

"High-Lord, I think she's hurt," said Lexin. "Please, Sire?"

"Here," said Amran-an. They laid her gently down by Morat and the staff. Amran-an touched her cheek, and she opened her eyes, looked at him with a gaze that was rapidly focusing.

"Take more than a drop into Death's Land to put me out," she said tartly, struggling to sit up, then falling back with a cry of pain.

"I think that arm is broken, little one," said the wizard. "Just lie still and let me see." When he touched her forearm, she cried out, and Lexin flinched and almost pushed the wizard away.

"You'll have to splint it," said Burr Oak. He reached into the furs on his back, handed Amran-an several of the arrows that went with his bow, long and straight, made of wood. "These will do, won't they?"

Amran-an took the arrows, after staring into the Woodwaynim's calm green eyes for a moment, imagining how many injuries he'd splinted on the trail over the years for him to be so matter-of-fact about it. He shook his head slightly, then bent to the task of splinting Ranna's arm. It wasn't a bad break; it hadn't broken the skin.

"You'll have to be brave, little froglet," said Morat gently. He touched the staff to her arm and willed its warmth and peace into her. "This will hurt."

"Lexin," said the wizard, "you'll have to help her stay still while I set the bone straight." Lexin's face was white. "Can you do it?"

"Of course he can," Ranna said, but her voice was small and shaky. She looked at Lexin, and he looked back, a long moment, and Morat saw the exchange: his concern and fear of hurting her . . . her trust in him. She didn't want anyone else to touch her, and she let him see that.

Lexin put his hands firmly on her shoulders.

"Here, little one, bite on this." Burr Oak offered a piece of wood, the woodrune he wore around his neck, to put between her teeth.

"She can cry out all she wants to," said Amran-an crossly. "She doesn't have to be that brave." But Ranna took the woodrune and smiled at the Woodwaynim.

"Ready?" said Amran-an. And he pulled to straighten the bones. Ranna cried out, around the piece of wood, and her voice echoed out into the darkness. "It's all right, Ranna, it's done." And Redd helped the wizard tie the splints tightly to her arm, while Lexin stroked her brow, and she gave one or two small whimpers before she got herself back under control.

Heller was dragging their packs into the circle of light. "Our gear fell with us," he said, "some of it, anyway. It's scattered all around, but I can find it."

"Be careful," warned Morat. "Don't get lost."

"I won't," said the seaman, "as long as you keep that staff glowing like that. But I think we need to rest a while here, and we might as well do it with food and a fire. I've no idea what's out there. Can't see. But I *can* see we're not going anywhere into it very soon," he gestured at Ranna and at the still unconscious Tellit, "and not without some kind of light."

Tellit was babbling. "He's delirious, Morat," said Amran-an.

I don't think it's nonsense that he's speaking," objected Morat. "Listen."

Tellit tossed his head back and forth. Sweat glistened on his forehead. His lips moved, shaping words. Morat leaned close to hear them.

"They're close, Sire, they're close . . . the Unshapers. They're angry that we've made it this far. Be careful . . . Father? I'm coming . . . I can see you . . . but so far away . . . it's dark . . . who's the lady? She's so beautiful . . ."

Heller and Burr Oak were finishing up the redistribution of their supplies into packs they could carry. There was no clue yet about what lay in the darkness, but they wanted to be as prepared as they could. Food they had. Water would be a problem. But something else they needed even more.

"Light," said Heller. "What can we do for light? We haven't got much we can use for torches, nothing that would last long, anyway."

Amran-an was digging in the pack he'd been carrying, the one with all the odd items, the "itchy finger stuff," as he called it, making fun of Morat—and himself—for their strange compulsion to gather the odds and ends.

"I think I may have something. If it will just work as I think it might, with Morat's staff. Ah, here it is."

He took out a small, roundish package and unwrapped it to reveal a glass jar, well-padded and carefully sealed.

"Luminor. Extracted from fungi that glow in the dark, the one called 'witches' fingers.' It grows on dead wood, in the deeps of Runegladden. Took me a while, a few years back, to find enough to get this much of the essence concentrated from it."

"That's not what we call it, that fungus," said Burr Oak, with a mischievous smile totally unlike his usual expression. "Not fingers. But then, the sorcerers our legends talk about in conjunction with that fungus are male."

Morat looked at him in astonishment. Ranna blushed.

"Well, anyway," said Amran-an, flustered, "Try painting this on the staff, Morat. Use this tool to do it, don't let it touch your skin."

"It won't harm the staff, will it?" Morat asked anxiously.

"I don't think so," said the wizard.

"I think it will be fine," agreed the Woodwaynim. "We use this substance to make the glow globes last longer, and it doesn't harm them."

Morat held the staff in his lap and carefully applied some of the luminor to it at the top, pushing aside the flowers to seal it onto the wood. It flared at the contact, the luminor, and the staff vibrated in his hands, and Morat had a moment of near panic, but the greenish phosphorescence settled into a steady, clear, bright glow that pushed the horizon of their sphere of light outward a considerable distance.

They all stared. The glow touched pale shapes, revealed them on all sides. They sat in the middle of a circle of stones. They were the stones of the cairn that marked the grave of Rowan Green Wizard in the land up above, but transfigured, taller than them by twice, thrice; they were white, translucent, as if the light cast by the staff passed through them. They didn't cast shadows. They were covered with runes, degraded into softness as if by untellable age.

Amran-an stepped toward one of the pillars, touched the runes hesitantly, fingered them, then shook his head. His frustration was clear on his lean face.

Beside him, Burr Oak echoed the movement. "Not anything Woodwaynim, either, I'd say," he said softly. "Not that I know all the kinds of runes that wizards use, but there's nothing here that looks like anything I've seen before."

Beyond the stones they saw trees . . . pale ghosts of trees, trunks and limbs white. The trunks were wider around than any tree they had ever seen in Runegladden or in the Mother's Woods. The branches were gnarled and twisted, but not ungraceful. And the leaves . . . the leaves were large and shimmering with highlights in the light from Morat's staff, fluttering very, very slightly in some breeze they didn't feel, like white moths.

It was like looking through a circle of doorways. But they were all the same, in every direction. How to know which way to go?

The question was on all their faces. Amran-an shrugged, and took up his pack, held it up high, and dumped it out on the pale earth. He watched how the packets and objects fell.

"You know," he said, "they say that in the land of Yan-tse they tell the future by throwing down a pile of sticks and watching how they fall."

"Yeah," said Heller. "But the sticks have runes on them. And there are rules . . ."

"Well, some of these have runes on them, too." Amran-an sounded grouchy. "Got any better ideas?"

Morat reached over into the pile.

"Fingers itching again?" asked the wizard sarcastically.

"This. This might do the trick."

"That's the piece of metal from the smithy in High Havenn, said Redd. "But it was blighted, wasn't it?"

"It doesn't have any rust or flaking on it here," said Morat, turning it in his fingers. "Not in this light."

"Not in this world," corrected Redd.

Morat unthreaded a cord from his hood and tied it around the piece of metal. He held it up by the string, letting the metal piece hang free. It swung around, several times, then swung back, then steadied.

"A compass," said Heller. "Of course."

"Can we trust it?" asked Burr Oak. "It was blighted, wasn't it, up above?"

"That was the Land of the Living," said Morat, tossing the metal and its string in his hand. "This is the Land of the Dead. We'll go that way," he indicated the opening between the pale rocks to which the compass had pointed.

Tellit nodded, then fell back into his self-absorption, eyes glazed, listening inward to the voices that haunted him.

White winged creatures, like small owls or huge moths, flitted white and ghostlike through the branches, dipping and weaving with batlike motion, never quite touching any of the softly stirring leaves. Redd ducked and brushed fearfully at one of them that flitted low at his head, and it wheeled away, with a small piping cry. Sprays of blood-red flowers spilled down from the crotches of the branches, everywhere, glowing parasites on ghosts of the trees . . . fibers of moss and spider webs hung across their paths. Lexin, ever the gardener's apprentice, stopped to look at a low-hanging spray of the flowers. He reached out, but Amran-an pulled his hand away, shook his head in warning. They stared at each other for a moment, then Lex turned, taking up Ranna's hand again, and they walked onward after the others into the strange landscape, with Morat in the lead, his staff their beacon and their lantern.

Out of the silence a small sound was born, distant, a mere sigh in the stillness. Morat stopped a moment, staring into the grayness, and then they moved toward it without asking each other whether it was the right way to go. It was the only change in an endless sameness, and it drew them to it. It grew . . . became the sound of water, a small fountain.

It was Tellit who moved to the front, as they found a wall of vegetation before them. Unlike the rest of the landscape, it had a strangely familiar beauty.

"Roses," said Morat softly, reaching to touch one of the blossoms that crowded the hedge. "Roses."

Tellit reached, pushed aside the branches. They moved away before his fingers, no thorns touching him, and Burr Oak smiled. "Something is here that will not harm the boy, not even with the prick of a rose thorn."

The woman sat at the edge of the fountain, her hand dabbling gently in the water. The water was dark, a mirror, stirred only by the few ripples her fingers made. Her face was hidden by a veil, but she looked to be Runerin, by her clothing, and highborn.

"Lady," said Tellit, and moved forward to kneel before her.

Morat stood motionless, frozen. Amran-an, beside him, laid a hand on his shoulder, felt him trembling.

"Lady?" questioned the boy.

And she reached up, pushed the veil back from her face.

"You are more beautiful than the voices said you were," whispered Tellit. He reached . . . hesitated . . . and the woman took his hand in both of her own.

Morat made a small sound. She looked up at him, eyes large and darkly luminous in her very pale face.

"Elli . . ." he gasped.

"My Lord." She smiled, bowed her head.

"Aaah, Elli," he groaned.

She turned again to Tellit, looked intently into his face.

Burr Oak looked at their mirrored profiles, the one soft, feminine, pale in death, the other a bit more rugged, the chin fuzzed with the first beard of manhood. He looked at Morat, at Amran-an, at Heller, in turn, surmise in his green eyes and his raised eyebrow.

"Aye," said the seaman softly. "The boy's mother. Amandellienne."

"She died giving birth to him," said Amran-an softly.

"He's a fine boy . . . nay, a fine man," she smiled softly, speaking to Morat. "You are fine, my son . . . na, you are splendid," she said to Tellit, squeezing his hand. "I'm glad of you, however you came to be. I always was."

"You were?" gasped Tellit. He knelt at her knees, mesmerized, gazing into her eyes.

"Truly. I would sit in the sun, by the fountain in the garden, each day, and hold my hands over you, growing in my belly, and feel you move both inside me and beneath my fingers, and I was glad to have you growing there. Ever and always."

The smile on the boy's face was a beacon as bright as the staff in Morat's hand.

"I only regret I could not stay with you," she sighed, and her voice was echoed by the sad sound of the little fountain. "I would have watched you every moment . . . I imagined it all, you know: seeing your first smile . . . feeling your tiny fingers grasp my finger for the first time . . . watching you take your first step . . ."

"Elli, you mean—"

"Yes, My Lord Morat." She blushed, looked down, smiling to herself. "I loved you. Indeed I did. We all did. You were so young and earnest, and our hearts ached for you, taking on the Lord's crown so unexpectedly at the death of your parents. You were a strong light in a time that was dark for us all.

"Of course I loved you. You were the first love of my silly young girl's heart, and I pined after you! I set myself in your path and thought poems at you in the silence of my mind, and scribbled them on scraps of parchment, and tied them in packets with ribbons, like all the rest of the girls . . . but I loved Evmorat, too. I did. And it was something deeper than anyone knew."

"But Evmorat said—" Morat's breath was a gasp, remembering the pain of Evmorat's words.

"When, Morat, did Evmorat ever tell the truth?" she asked, turning her gaze to him. "He lied to you. Even he didn't understand why he needed to hurt you. He loved you like all the rest of us did; but his love was so twisted."

Tears welled up in her eyes.

Morat was shaking, and the light of his staff fluttered, moving the shadows at the edge of the circle of light, so that even the air seemed to vibrate with consternation.

"But even worse, Morat, he lied to himself. He spun his own truth in his own mind. He was just too set on having his way be painful, to accept what I was giving him. He couldn't accept that I loved him. Couldn't believe it." She shrugged. "Oh, Morat, it was so easy to love you! Everyone around you did. You radiated—oh, I don't know what to call it—goodness of heart, caring . . . the strength of Rune land ran through you, singing, and I swear I could hear it. It was harder to love him . . . but you know I was never one to take the easy path."

She reached up to touch Tellit's face. "I wanted *his* child. I chose to make you, my son, and I chose to make you with Evmorat. I didn't care that he'd never marry me. Morat can tell you . . . I was rebellious, *unconventional*." She smiled. "It was more important to me than any outward appearance of chasteness or *honor*, that I thought I could give him something that would change the world for him. It was more important to me that I could give him something to live happily with. I was so sure I could do it! But alas . . ." Tears welled up, slid down her cheeks. They all felt tears on their own cheeks, even Heller. "I died!"

The tears of the little fountain filled the brief silence.

"Oh, Tellit! I left you! To grow your own way . . . make your own path alone . . . it wasn't the shape of the things that I thought I was making! That was never the rune I thought I was weaving. I'm sorry! That is the only regret I have . . . that I couldn't stay with you!"

She took him in her arms, and held him close, and the boy clung to her.

It was a strange sight, thought Ranna, seeing his arms through her, as she wasn't quite opaque. "She's dead!" Ranna remembered, touched by the strangeness of it.

"Where is he?" asked Morat.

"Evmorat? He's there," she gestured.

Morat looked beyond the pool, the little fountain, into the gloom. A path lay there, fading into the darkness . . . a pergola whose columns were twined with death-ivy and roses, gray-white with the color of death . . . and in the distance, surrounded by bushes of rue and everlasting-flowers, a crypt. It was the mirror image of the mausoleum in Highrune, above in the Land of the Living, where they had laid Evmorat. Morat hadn't watched them bear him there; he hadn't seen the body laid with its ancestors. Hadn't given his brother any good-bye at all, he realized. Hadn't been able to.

Tellit looked eagerly where she pointed, but she laid a restraining hand on his arm.

"He's still asleep, my son. He won't . . . can't . . . even here he can't . . . accept any bit of happiness . . . or even peace."

"I came, mother, to find him," said Tellit fiercely. "I'll wake him!" He started to rise, move toward the mausoleum. "You're awake, aren't you? So he can be wakened, too."

"Tellit—wait. Some of us do walk here, it's true," Ellienne said. "Mostly because we have something we—we haven't finished. Something that makes us wakeful, even fretful." She looked toward the path to the mausoleum. "Others sleep . . . because they *want* to sleep. They don't want change, can't endure change. They—they're frozen."

Morat came to stand by the boy; he put a hand on his shoulder. "She's trying to protect you, Tellit. Evmorat will reject you. He'd rather sleep than face the possibility that he was so wrong about her . . . about you . . . about everything."

Amran-an nodded his head in agreement. "He may not wake. Or he may wake and do you terrible harm."

Tellit shook his head, put his hands to his brow. "The voices —"

Ranna, Lexin, Redd all put their hands to their heads as well.

"Can you hear them, too?" cried Amran-an. Morat took Redd's hands, tried to pull them away from the boy's head. "Are you all right? Redd, speak to me!"

"They're warning us away from Evmorat," cried Redd between tight teeth.

Heller Jade looked around wildly, confused, his axe raised. Clearly he heard nothing. To Morat the voices were becoming visible, a whitish eddy of wind swirling around Tellit, seeking out the others. Ellienne's veil was tossed in the wind of them, her dark hair pulled loose and swirling around her face.

"Don't listen to them," said Ranna fiercely. "Don't listen, High-Lord. Don't listen, Tellit." The wind seemed to be pulling at her hair, her shawl, her skirts.

"She's right," said Lexin, shaking his head back and forth as if trying to throw the sounds off, his hair flying. He was having trouble speaking, but he forced the words out, chest heaving, clinging to Ranna, trying to shelter her as the wind tore at her. "They don't want you to wake Evmorat, Tellit!"

"Then that's what we *must* do," cried Tellit. "Go, Unshapers!" He shouted into the wind. He steadied himself, and pointed his hands into the darkness, fingers spread. "Leave me alone! Leave us alone! Amran," he called. "Help me! Help me be steady!"

Amran-an came up behind Tellitand put his arms on his shoulders to steady him. He pulled the others to him.

Morat moved close to the boy, put the staff in front of them, gestured. Tellit placed his hands on it, over Morat's hands. The light flared brighter, and sparks shot out from the Woodwaynim medallion twined in the branches at the top of it, just above their joined hands. The sparks flared into the surrounding wind and seemed to suck up the turmoil of it. Slowly the din faded, and the pull at their hair and clothing eased.

And then it was quiet.

Tellit turned and moved in the direction of the mausoleum where Evmorat's shade slept, drawing the rest behind him.

"The gates aren't locked," said Morat, surprised. Up above, in the land of live Rune, there was a huge metal lock on the gates of the family mausoleum. It was crusted with age but kept oiled to open with ease on those few occasions when another burial required it. He remembered being told, as a child, during a ghostly tale told by Wayland in a creaky voice, that it was to keep the ghosts in, not intruders out.

"A sign of hope, perhaps," said Amran-an. "A crack in Evmorat's resolve not to wake, not to face truth."

Tellit moved forward, laid his hand on the gate's handle, and pulled. The gate creaked as it opened.

The darkness inside was intense. The boy motioned them back and moved into it.

Evmorat lay on the stone table in the mausoleum, looking as if he slept, his hands crossed on his chest. Tellit hesitated a moment, as if unsure what to name him, then called out, his voice wavering a bit, "Father. I call you Father. I call you to waken."

There was no motion, no sound.

"I have met my mother, and she has named you my father," the boy tried again. He took a step closer, straightened, standing taller, feeling insistence rising in him. "She named you the object of her love, and named me as the result of that love, and I give you now no further excuse to put me off. I demand you to attend to me."

Still there was no motion, no sound, though the darkness in the crypt seemed to lessen in its depth.

"The Lady named you the true object of her deepest love, and I call you, in her name, to rise and face the truth of her gift," conjured Tellit, finding words arising from within him like an incantation he threw in the face of the voices that huddled on the fringes of his awareness as well as in the face of the figure sleeping before him. The silence, after a lifetime of silence from Evmorat, angered Tellit.

He balled his fists, finding anger rising in his breast as it never had before, not on his own behalf, despite all the years of pain of placelessness. Anger rose in him, not for himself, but on behalf of the mother he had found at last here among the dead.

"All these years you, alive in Rune among us, you dishonored her in denying me," his voice grew hoarser in his anger. "Whore, your lie made her, who was truer to you than any of us knew. Whore, you let the world see her, who was dead and could not defend herself. You shamed her by denying me, letting the world call me bastard. I dare you to keep that dishonor on her, here, in this place, beyond the living. I dare you to face *your* shame in how you denied her, who had died in giving you the greatest gift she knew how to give.

"Wake and face your lie to her, if you will not face me."

The figure stirred, sat up slowly.

"Tellit," it said. It made a gesture as if in excuse. "She was dead. I didn't know how to care for a child."

“You do not deserve me,” declared the boy Tellit, spitting at the shade that stood before him, his voice bright with the sudden, new truth he found in that moment. “You did not deserve her, and you do not deserve me.”

The shade shook in the wind of the boy’s anger.

“I don’t need a father. I don’t need you.” And it was another layer to the truth the boy found emerging in that moment like a flame in the darkness.

“Son?” Whispered Evmorat’s shade.

“Na, not son of you,” Tellit spat. “Not son of your darkness. No son of your hateful twistedness. There was love always for you, but you met it with evil. Ellienne gave you love, and you shamed her. I tried to give you love, and you left me to bastardhood. And Morat, who loved you as a brother, you hurt most of all, destroying all his hopes.” He turned away, to move out of the darkness of the crypt. “I am not son of you.”

Evmorat’s shade reached, to hold him back.

“You try to conjure *me*?” said Tellit. “Na, I have no need of you.”

As the boy re-emerged into the light of his staff, Morat reached and touched Tellit’s shoulder, thinking there was need of comfort. But Tellit shook off his hand.

“I came to conjure a Father out of the Dead,” he said, marveling, and instead I conjured myself into being. All I wanted, all my life, and now that the moment is here, I have no need of him.”

“Morat,” came the voice out of the dark crypt. The shade emerged into the light, and Redd, Amran-an, Heller, Ranna, all shrank back. They were surprised, those who had known the living Evmorat, at the diminished shade of the dead Evmorat.

There seemed to be no sign of the wound that had slain him, thought Morat, looking past the boy at the shade of Evmorat, and he was glad of that little blessing.

“I am sorry,” said the shade, “I am sorry.”

“I think I forgive you,” said Morat, unsure how much he really spoke truth. His heart ached with the grief of his loss of Willow. His staff flickered, dimmed. He did not stop the shade as it started to turn back toward the dark crypt.

“Wait,” he felt his words welling up from some place deep within, remembering all that had been done to bring him here, to the Land of the Dead, and his staff brightened. “I am sorry for the loss of you, my brother. Sorry for *my* deed.”

The shade of Evmorat turned.

“I never meant—”

Amran-an spoke, trying to bridge the fragile space between them. “It doesn’t matter what you meant, what Morat meant, what anyone of us meant in the land where we were living . . . Let us leave our mis-shapings behind. Let us shape a new intention, here, in the Land of the Dead, and defy these shadows that turn us aside.”

And Morat reached out, took Evmorat’s hand in his.

CHAPTER 19

Morat stared, his heart a large, hot lump in his breast, his breast that ached from not breathing. "Willow," he breathed finally, exhaling his passion softly, stirring the flowers on the staff on which he leaned.

The nearest leaves on the tree stirred slightly, as if his breath had reached them. The tree was huge, the trunk wide, the branches thick and wide-spreading, the roots ridging out across the ground . . . and Willow stood encased in it. The wood of the trunk was almost transparent but not quite, and she appeared starred with the faint glimmer of its substance enveloping her. It made it look as if there were tears on her cheeks.

Her eyes were closed. Her hands were open at her sides, reaching so slightly, a small, beseeching gesture. Morat devoured her image hungrily with his eyes, from head to toe, noticing she still wore the dainty dancing shoes Ranna had embroidered for her. He hesitated, but let his glance travel upward again, and was glad beyond expression that there was no sign of the knife's wound on her breast. Her fine yellow hair lay curled down over her shoulders, and the ribbons of her ballgown bodice lay undisturbed.

He was drawn again to her face. It wore a slightly troubled expression, and Morat's own features moved in sympathy to echo it. "Willow," he breathed.

Amran-an asked the question for the Rune Lord. "Why does she sleep, Green Wizard?"

Morat repeated the question. "Why does she sleep, encased and entombed, when so many other ghosts walk free here?"

Rowan moved as if to get between Morat and the tree where Willow stood. He put out a hand to ward off the Runerin.

"You!" cried Morat. "You keep her asleep! So she cannot change . . . cannot turn away from you . . . so you can keep her changeless!"

"We're dead, here!" cried Rowan, his eyebrow raised in supercilious scorn. "What change can there be?"

"She doesn't have to be trapped like that!" answered Morat hotly. "Other shades move about, speak, rework the things that delighted and pained them during life. Even *you* do that."

Amran-an moved forward to stand next to Morat. "What are you afraid of, Rowan? It is written in the lore, spoken in the secret words of the Mother's rites, that sometimes souls here, after a time, may choose to yield themselves up to a new life, choose to be born again on the earth above. Are you afraid she'll turn from you?"

"Wouldn't you wish her to live again, if it were possible?" Morat asked.

"I keep her perfect, as she was! You!" Rowan pointed at Morat. "You come here and dare to criticize? Dare to try and wake her? You're the one who killed her! Do you want her to relive *that*!"

"The Unshapers killed her!" cried Morat, "Not me! *You* had as much to do with her death, in truth, as I did!"

"Me? How can you dare to suggest—*you*, who murdered *me*?!"

"Again, the Unshapers! You were the one who built that stupid, stupid illusion!" All the wildness that had smoldered in Morat's heart broke into heat of anger and passion. "Stupidity! Stupidity, Rowan! Back at the seed of all this is your stupidity! My accident! And the secret will of evil-wishing Unshapers!"

"You dare?" Rowan's eyes were green flame. It was only

Morat's staff, blazing in his face as Morat held it out between them, that fended off the enraged shade.

Morat wondered what would happen to him if Rowan touched him, if dead and living, so impassioned as they were, were to come into contact . . . here in the Land of the Dead. He held the staff out in front of him with both hands, though it was hot to the touch, heated with his passion and the proximity to the heat of Rowan's rage. For an instant he imagined striking the Green Wizard's shade with it, imagined it destroying Rowan in a flare of hot, green flame of living, plant-fueled, flower-driven energy.

Rowan drew the knife from his hip; crescent and sharp, it glittered in the green light of Morat's staff.

Morat gestured with the staff, warning Rowan back, to keep his distance. The staff flickered and sparked. "Do we beat ourselves down, use ourselves up, then, Woodwaynim, for our stupidities? Or do we turn this energy against the real evil? Look out there!" he gestured.

Tellit nodded, echoing the gesture. The boy stepped up toward Rowan, pointed. "Green Wizard! You have more power than any of us here . . . but you keep letting your hatred cloud your vision. Look there! They're all around us! Unshapers! I can see them, now, as well as hear their voices, in the light of your rage. They are taking on shape! Our wrangling, our waste of energy . . . we are feeding them!" He turned, pointing again and again. "They are so sure of victory over you. I can't blame them. Have you any idea what you look like, with that aura of hatred around you? It's like lightning! It'll blast us all to nothingness, and they will win!"

"What do you demand of me, boy?" cried Rowan, haughty, arrogant. "You're as misbegotten as they! You laid hands on Willow! You procured the poison that led to her death! Misbegotten, I say!"

Tellit flinched violently, as if he had been slapped.

"How dare you!" Heller Jade stood forth with his axe raised high. "The boy is as innocent born as any child born into the Mother's world!"

A stillness held the moment. Evmorat stepped into it, spoke softly into it. "You! You fine and splendid paragon of Woodwaynim righteousness! You're a posturing jaybird!" He spat, and the spittle sizzled at the feet of the Woodwaynim shade. "The boy had no choice at all about how he was born—any more than you or I or the High-Lord of Rune or that serving maid who stands there. We're all one and the same at that starting point, freshly born into the world, a rune with its own unique meaning to spin out over our lifetime.

"Even the Mother-of-All gave us the gift of forgiveness, freed us from the guilt of our intentions turned aside from what we meant to happen," said Morat. "And by her gift, here we stand, to undo the wrongs of the past, to shape something new."

Ranna stepped forward.

"I'm low-born, oh mighty Woodway Wizard. I only have the wizardries of sewing and household tasks in my fingers." She held up her hands. "But I'm here! Here in this place no living serving maid ever imagined herself to be. I'm here to stand for Willow and for my Lord Morat, in whose goodness and in whose love for her I believe. And I know this! Keep us fenced away from Willow by your blaming, and we'll all go down into darkness, everyone here in the Land of the Dead, everyone out beyond in the world of the living. The Unshapers will see to that, they'll unspin all the threads of both worlds. The year will never Turn again!

"Both of you loved Willow, I remind you." She stood challenging, and Lexin stood like an echo behind her, his hands on her shoulders, his eyes burning as bright as hers. "Are you willing to test that love? Wake her! Let her choose! I, for one, trust her woman's heart more than any of you posturing clods!"

Rowan laughed arrogantly. "Sa, fine words, little one. But I hold power here. Your *living* power isn't equal to mine, not here. Try to wake her if you will . . . but without any help from me."

The shade of the Woodwaynim Green Wizard flared, and they flinched. It was gone, nothing but a bright splash fading against their closed eyelids, his mocking laughter persisting in the air after it was gone. The leaves of the tree that encased Willow fluttered softly, white, a bit like waving hands, in the atmosphere darkened by the passing of the green-shining shade.

Morat stood motionless for a long, long moment, staring at Willow. He walked slowly toward the tree, laid his hand on the wood. Transparent as it was, he expected it to feel glassy and cold, but it felt like wood, like bark a bit rough, not chilly at all. He put one hand over where Willow's hand lay opened out to him, beneath the encasing substance, and then reached with his other hand, as if to touch her face. But he wasn't tall enough. He had to be content to put his hand over where her heart lay beneath the wood. He laid his cheek against the wood.

"Aiyeee! She's frowning! What if she is dreaming? Dreaming of her death again and again?" He crumpled, sliding to the ground, among the roots of the huge tree.

Amran-an and Ranna both moved forward as if to comfort him. Lexin touched the girl's arm.

"Let him be. He's exhausted. Let him be, Sire. Let *them* be."

Amran-an opened and closed his hands, frustrated. He took the cloak Ranna offered, put it over Morat's shoulders. "Come on," said Lexin. "We've got a rune to build."

*****

“We’ll have to fit the rune to Morat’s staff. But I think we can start assembling it first. I knew we’d need a woodrune to call to Willow,” shrugged Ranna as she brought forth the pouch that hung from her waist. She untied it, pulled the drawstring open, and dumped its contents out into her lap, skeins of thread.

Amran-an looked at the little maid, bemused. “Of course,” he whispered.

“We can tie it all together with this thread. It’s the purple thread from Yan-Tsse. And here’s green, for growing plants, and red and blue for High Rune’s colors, from the tapestry my mother and her ladies are making. We will have to be the Finders and the Makers,” she said, her voice growing firmer.

“And I think I shall be the Binder,” added Amran-an. “But Morat, you, I think, will have to be the Tuner.”

Morat laid his staff down on the ground, untying some of the things that were laced into the branch of its top so that they could incorporate them into the new woodrune.

“Here’s the piece of the cornerstone of Highrune,” he turned the small rock in his hands, thinking how far away from his home they had come.

Redd put a hand on his shoulder in comfort.

“Seeds,” spoke Lexin, like an incantation. “From the fields and meadows of Rune. From everywhere in our land. But also, and most important, from the forest, which she loved. I had gathered them for her, toward the coming spring, for a new garden. Spring Beauties, Maid’s Tresses, Foam Flower,” he named them. “Forest Rose. Twin-Hearts. Love-of-the-Woods.” And he looked at Ranna, and she caught his meaning from his eyes, “It was to be a brand-new garden that brought field and forest together. For the High-Lord and the Lady. And for us, too, Ranna, to pledge our love in."

He took a green thread from Ranna and handed the little packet to Amran-an to add to the construction.

"Here's Wayland's poem," Redd handed over the paper, crumpled from his pocket. "For all the stories and all the songs we shared. So many of them were sad," he hesitated, "Still, not all of them. But lest it be too much of Rune alone," and he took a small piece of wood from his pocket as well, "I cut a small piece from Willow's harp, the one from Woodway. It made a quite unmusical noise when I took my knife to it."

"It feels—well, unbalanced somehow," muttered Heller Jade. "Too much earth, not enough water. We haven't got any water from the Mother-of-all, from her ice or her river. But maybe she will feel the kinship with something from the sea to which her waters run."

He reached inside his shirt, behind his neck, undid a catch. He brought out a necklace and held it up.

Amran-an looked at him in surprise. "Never knew you wore that, Heller."

The large man blushed. "The Queen of the Pearl Divers gave it to me." He was quiet for a long moment, staring out into the darkness of the ghost forest, reminiscing, a small smile on his lips. "In the way of the Pearl Diver folk, she decided it was time to bear a child. There are no men on her island, only women . . . only women dive for the pearls . . . it's said the Ocean is a very male deity, and he will only let the women find their way to the depths where the pearls are born in their oysters."

He held the necklace in his palm, stroked the two baubles attached to the chain.

"So in the way of her folk, the Queen called a man to her island. She called me, and I was deeply honored to be chosen to sire her child."

Amran-an smiled, and Redd blushed.

Heller gave the boy a playful rap on the head. "Oh, come now, boy, surely you know by now what it takes to make a child.

"The Queen of the Pearl Divers is very beautiful. Even if she weren't, she is very wealthy, and it is moreover a great honor to be chosen by her. Most of the sea captains and fisher captains—and even the pirate captains—in the Lower Sea try to get seen by her or her messengers." He smiled, reminiscing. "She is *very* beautiful.

"When I gave her not one, but two children, twins, a girl to be her heir and a boy, she gave me not only the traditional pearl as a gift, but also an aquamarine."

He held up the necklace by the chain. A large, shining gray-dark pearl hung from it, and beside it, a smooth blue-green gemstone.

Ranna gasped. "They're magnificent."

Burr Oak winked. "Probably means he was, too."

Heller blushed again. It seemed surprising, for the large, blustering sea captain. They all laughed.

"She'll send the boy to me, in a few years, to be my heir. I'll be glad to have him!"

He handed the necklace to them. Amran-an took it carefully. "It's all right, Am. You don't have to worry. This aquamarine is a true love's gift; it won't crush, like the one in the story of Midhe's Tears."

"I bring Woodway to this rune," declared Burr Oak, coming forward, to the surprise of the Runerinnen so intent on their work they had forgotten him. "To counter the stone of Rune, I bring branch and leaf." And he held forth one of his arrows, to which were tied shafts of wood, a few with a leaf or two.

Amran-an took them, and looked a question at the Woodwaynim, feeling the power in the bunch.

"These are cuttings of each of the seven sacred woods of Woodwaynim," explained the Woodwaynim, his voice for once not roughened. "I bring them in hope of recovering Willow to the world of the living, and Rowan as well, restored to the Oak branch." Thus he stated, openly, his secret goal.

"And," he added, "I bring them as tribute to the need I see in Rune's High-Lord, and in the people of Woodway as well, to bring the year back to its Turning."

Tellit stepped forward, hesitantly. "I have nothing to give," he said sadly. "Except my gratitude that Willow was kind to me, and that you, too, my High-Lord, were kind. But I feel your need." He opened his hands, showing them empty. "I have only given unshaping, not a good thing at all to gift you with, and something I would not want bound into this rune."

"Nor have I anything to give," whispered Evmorat, "having given all the pain you have had from me. Nothing except the constant apology that fills my soul. And what can that possibly help, dead as I am?"

Morat stepped forward, took the boy's hand in his, and the shade's hand as well, his fingers showing faintly through its shadow. "Tellit, you bring a mother's blessing and the power of her truth that undoes unshaping. Evmorat, you bring the rue of a long-bruised heart and the hope of a changed soul.

"Am, are you finished with the Binding?" he asked.

"Sa, I am," said the wizard, awe coming into his voice, at the glow that began to form as he tied the last knot of purple thread, and laid his wizard's hands on the objects, and let his wizard's will knit them together and to the staff. "I have finished this

Binding! And it is fine to behold, for it is bound with all our love."

"Then," cried Morat, putting his hands, and the hands of Tellit and Evmorat on it, all together, "We shall Tune it. We shall Tune it with Hope and Fear and Need . . . And Love. Let us give this rune Shape."

Morat stood before the tree which encased Willow. It hurt him immeasurably to see her so frozen in its substance, her hands beseeching, her eyes so sad. How, he wondered, could Rowan not see how awful the fate he had chosen for her shade, to be so encased? How, he wondered, could the Woodwaynim wizard not see how alive she could be, free, even as a shade in the Land of the Dead? How could he call her his beloved, and encase her so?

Morat planted the staff firmly before him. Since the Binding and the Tuning, it had grown more leaves and flowers. There was no wind here, in the Land of the Dead, to blow through the windharp structure of the windrune at its top; nevertheless, it hummed a song, sad and sweet, perfuming the air with the sound of the hope and need of all of them who stood with the High-Lord: Amran-an, Redd, Ranna and Lexin, Heller, Tellit, the shade of Evmorat—and the burly Woodwaynim woodsman.

Rowan had come again. He moved to stand between Morat and the tree, mockery in his stance. The shade had taken on more substance, but even so, the tree—and Willow—were faintly visible behind him. Now he came holding a staff of his own, crowned with oak leaves, and with his betrothal amulet pinned at the top among them. It seemed to Morat a mockery of his own staff, a dead thing to his live one, remembering how his had been formed from the tree that had grown out of the flow of springtime force put out by the Mother-of-All. And he took confidence in the power of the gift from the Mother, and in the power of the rune that crowned it, feeling its song grow louder.

"You shall not have her," declared Rowan. He put out the staff in a wizard's gesture, to prevent Morat. "You shall not have her," it was an incantation.

Morat stepped aside so he faced Willow unblocked. He put both hands on his staff, closed his eyes, and willed. "Be free, Willow," he willed.

There was a whining sound, as Rowan's incantation took on power, and Morat felt his staff quiver in response.

"Be free, Willow."

And the tree that held her shook its leaves.

"Be free, Willow," conjured Morat a third time. And the tree that held her began to melt, bit by bit, while Rowan cursed and Morat hoped. Willow stepped forward, out of the last of its bindings, hesitantly, confusion on her face and in the hands she held out. Life came slowly into her eyes, as she looked from one of them to the other.

"Rowan?" She whispered. "Morat?"

And she looked at the gathering of the folk beyond them, puzzled at first, but gradually her face took on recognition.

"I died!" She whispered, and a groan tore from Morat's breast.

Before Morat could move, Evmorat came and bowed before Willow, kneeling, his shade a beggar before her shade. "As did I, my Lady, in payment for betrayal of you and of my brother." She looked down at him, memory crowding tears into her eyes. "And for all the world I am sorry for your dying, and I beg your forgiveness. I beg beyond any words that can be."

Willow shied from him, still confused in her emergence from her sleep in the tree. Her hands went to her mouth.

Morat's staff hummed softly in the long, silent moment.

"You came for me," She turned to Rowan.

"Dead also, my Betrothed," he answered, "I brought you here to the Land of the Dead. To rejoin me."

"So that is where we are." She looked around at the ghostly forest, at the dimness of the atmosphere, and a shiver went over her. "And you, Morat," she asked, turning to him, "Have you died also? And all of you, my dear friends? How sad!"

"No, dearest Willow," he said, unable to take his eyes from her. "Though I wanted to, wished I had, in my loss . . . and though the year itself stopped Turning for my grief."

"I wouldn't let him," cried Ranna. "I took care of him."

"She was stubborn that way," said Amran-an. "As was I . . . and he, being always himself and duty-driven, took on the task for all of us to bring Spring back to a world that was as frozen as Rowan had frozen you."

"And now?"

"Come back with me," cried Morat. "Come back with me to the Land of the Living!" And in a voice cracked with love and need, he cried, "Willow!"

She stood, like the fulcrum of the world, between Rowan's shade and Morat's living being.

"Rowan, hear me!" cried Burr Oak. "If Willow can return to the Land of the Living, then also can you! Son of my sister, almost-son of my heart, high scion of my Branch, I came here for *you*! I allied with Rune's High-Lord and folk for this purpose, to reclaim *you*!" The Woodwaynim reached out his hands to Rowan's shade, took the shadowy fingers. "By the Mother-of-All, who may—nay will—allow this, who has spoken her permission to the Rune Lord to raise Willow with the bestowing of her

Spring on the frozen world, I beg you, come with me!"

"Not if he would have Willow! That is not a bargain I will have, even with the Mother."

"Rowan!" The desire was naked in the voice of Burr Oak.

"Never! The Runerin shall not take her!" swore Rowan.

Rowan waved his staff at the tree that had held Willow, holding out in his other hand the Mother's amulet on its string. A flare flashed from the amulet, green and somehow hot, and Morat and the others winced away from it. Amran-an raised his hand to protect his eyes. The tree shivered under the blast. It trembled more violently, then suddenly collapsed in upon itself, its branches twisting. It shrank until it looked like a body, with hands clutched across its breast. A small, choked wail of fear rose from Ranna's lips, and Lexin tried to push her behind him.

"Na, Rowan! You must not do such a thing!" cried Burr Oak. "It's a *tree*! For the Mother's sake!"

Rowan laughed at the older Woodwaynim. "It's a dead tree, anyway, old man! Remember where you are!"

Burr Oak shook his head, dismayed. "No one of Oak Branch ever would dishonor even the *ghost* of a tree in this way! You were Woodwaynim! You were my almost-son! Don't do this!"

Rowan hesitated. Then he held the amulet out again. The tree had become an almost human-looking figure. It blossomed in the light, straightened, held up an arm on which a shield hung, carved with Woodwaynim runes. Its flesh was pale, as pale as the tree had been, but its shoulders were shrouded in the ghost of animal pelt, not leaves. It raised a sword in its other hand, glowered at them.

Rowan turned and pointed the amulet at another tree, and it, too, began to tremble and transform.

Morat motioned Ranna and Lexin back. Heller pushed Redd behind him, raising a muttered protest from the young man which he cut off with a sharp motion of his hand.

"Guard *them*," Heller muttered aside to Redd, indicating Ranna and Lexin with a thrust of his chin. The seaman raised his own axe, balancing it, one fist tight on the shaft of its handle, lightly supporting the heavy, double-bladed axe-head on fingertips of his other hand. The green light of Rowan's magic glinted on the high polish of the sharpened edge. For all his bulk, the seaman seemed light, balancing on the balls of his feet, surefooted and poised into the face of coming action like he might have stood balancing on a rolling sea deck, moving into a building gale.

A dozen figures now stood where there had been the ghosts of trees, armed Woodwaynim warriors bearing swords and pikes and spears. They moved restlessly, eyes aglow above ghostly cheekbones painted with war runes, woodrunes of battle and protection braided into their long hair, fierce intentions on their grim bearded faces.

Rowan lowered his hand. Sweat beaded his brow, and he trembled with the expenditure of his wizard strength. He leaned on his staff. But there was a look of triumph in his eyes.

"Burr Oak, do you still stand with the Runerin?" he asked softly.

"Mind your tongue, insolent one," the Woodwaynim barked back. "Have you forgotten all respect for your elders? For the Branch that bore you?"

"How can I respect one, born however high on the Branch, however close to my mother, who chooses to stand beside my murderers?" His voice was shrill, caustic.

"Rowan, my almost-son," said the Woodwaynim, sadness making his voice even deeper than usual, "This is the kind of foolishness that caused your death, not this Runerin." He gestured at the warriors who moved restlessly around Rowan, a rustling, insolent sound rising from them, not words, not runes, just a whine of sound.

Tellit moved up beside Burr Oak. "Those aren't wakened Woodwaynim warriors, are they?" he asked the woodsman. "Not your ancestors, not really."

Burr Oak looked at them closely, trying hard to see some face he could recognize. He shook his head.

"Unshapers, Rowan!" cried Tellit. "You haven't called up Woodwaynim!"

Morat moved forward. He clutched at the staff he carried, trying to restrain his agitation. "These aren't real Woodwaynim you've called out of the trees! No more real than those were you raised in illusion that day in the Mother's Woods. When you died."

"All you've done is given the Unshapers a way to us! To act openly!" Tellit waved his arms, frantic. "Unshapers! They couldn't shape themselves! They *used* you!"

The young Runerin looked at Rowan, and the young ghost of a Woodwaynim wizard looked back at him, eyes wide. Tellit nodded. "You *do* see what you've done. What you did that time. What you've done now."

But Rowan shook his head, threw off willingness to understand as he tossed the sweat from his brow. No way, his body said, as he straightened, drew back from Tellit. No way to turn back now.

Tellit sighed, a huge, deep sob of disappointment.

Morat stared at Rowan's eyes, watching them darken from green to something hot and glowing despite the blackness. Amran-an put a hand on his shoulder, muttered a rune at him.

"Steady, my friend. Don't let him trap you in that gaze. It's only the eyes of a dead one."

"Na, there's more than that in him now," said Evmorat, heat rising in his own eyes.

Morat felt giddy at the grip of his brother's fingers on his arm. It seemed impossible, he knew, but it was he who felt attenuated, thinned into a shade. He thought the others might even be able to see through him, while they, the truly dead ones, Evmorat and Rowan and the Wizard's phantom warriors, took on mass, solidity.

They could harm him, Morat thought in amazement. Here, in the Land of the Dead, they were real and he was the phantasm. These warriors in ragged pelts of beasts he couldn't name, with the teeth of these unknown carnivores strung around their necks and their biceps, and bones worked through nostrils and tied into their shaggy locks . . . these warriors could harm him as those phantoms conjured up above, by a young and mistaken Greenwizard by a dark pool surrounded by bloodroot flowers, never, never could have touched him.

Morat felt afraid. Totally afraid.

"Watch out, Morat," cried Evmorat, reaching to hold him standing, and Tellit on his other side muttered an endless string of broken runes, curse-like, angry, at his side. "Unshapers," he cursed. Redd cursed in echo, looking at the growing mob of warriors, moving to stand back-to-back with Amran-an as he had before, surrounded by phantom warriors in the Mother's Woods.

Morat shook off the sensation of déjà vu. He held the staff, not a spear. He reached down and laid one hand on a rock. He laid his other hand on the rune that Amran-an had Bound to his staff, feeling the piece of the cornerstone of Highrune embedded in it. And he closed his eyes and let himself speak, in his heart, a summoning, not a woodrune but a rune of Rune.

He understood what he had to do, but it wasn't something he could have put into words. It was an instinct that rose from the same place within his soul that had given him that sense of the land of Rune. It felt like that tide in his blood that turned when the seasons turned. It felt like the vertigo of unease he had felt when the year stopped turning. It felt like the dark ache he felt when he touched the soil of Rune that had been damaged . . . the metal that had been blighted . . . the sickness among his people.

He closed his eyes and poured his land-sense into the stone under his hand. The ghost of a stone under his hand. And the stone began to tremble, as the trees had under the flare of Rowan's power. And to grow, transform.

Morat opened his eyes. It wasn't a warrior that stood before him. Redd and Heller looked disappointed. Only Amran-an smiled, understanding and approval on his high cheekbones.

"Telden Terranold, Land Guardian," whispered Morat.

"Sa, boy. You almost got it right," answered the shade, flinging a cape back from his shoulder and taking hold of Morat's arm with a hand burly knuckled with toil and soil. "Now let's get to work in earnest."

Morat almost giggled to feel the firmness of the ghost's grasp of his hand. "Another stone, boy."

This time the shades that formed were definitely more formidable. Wulflin Swordwielder, Morat recognized, one of the Hundred Chieftains, and his cousin Alflin Axwielder, warlords fierce in battle among themselves but more so against foreign foes when Telden put the fear of the gods and of his own raging temper into them to form their alliance; weapons shining and sharp, burly arms bearing rings of gold and silver, brotherhood pledges . . . Trimnorix Telden-an, worm-beast killer, cleanser of the wastes of Maia, with his spear dripping the strange blue blood of the last ancient scourge . . .

Morat touched more stones and forms materialized . . . Haellena Lunan, female but brawny, hammer in her hands like a weapon to smite the earth, and smear of mineral dark on her cheek . . . and her smith sons and daughters, equally burly, wrestlers of rock and tamers of metal . . . Morat touched stone after stone, in his frenzy of inspiration, and a whole clan of masons rose up, waving rock hewing tools, builders of the highest halls of Highrune's rune-patterned stone . . . Temparr Lunan-an, Lawgiver, bearing the bound hyrax of law, raging . . . even Heller's mother, a sea queen with a vicious-looking cutlass and bolos, who winked at her astonished son.

"All Shapers," crowed Morat, and Amran-an and the rest of the Runerinnen cheered with him. "All Shapers I throw against your Unshapers.

"Behold, Rowan!" cried Morat, as his Shaping ancestors fell upon the Unshapers of the Woodwaynim's forming, with fine wrought swords and with crude smithy tools and with Rune words in their shouts. And Rowan's Unshaping forms were unshaped, and fell back, clouds that faded into the dark air of the shadowed Land of the Dead, despite the balled fists of Rowan, calling them with curses to stay.

"Behold, Willow," Morat's inspiration carried him into rapture, "see the future you could have. Come with me back to the Land of the Living, join with me. Join your Woodways with these my ancestors of Rune! Shape a future with me that bears the best of us both!"

And he conjured up, spinning out from the rune at the top of his staff, a vision he could have her—and all of the others—actually *see*: herself sitting enthroned with him, elderly but sound, with grown children standing tall and fair beside them, and grandchildren playing at their feet . . . laughter and song sounding through Highrune Hall restored to glory at a Winter

Turning celebration joyous and bountiful far beyond the terrible one they had gone through.

But Rowan saw it too, and it enraged him. "No, by all the trees of Woodway, by all the stones of the Mother Mountains, by the Mother-of-All herself, you belong to me, Willow! If you would return to the Land of the Living, do so as mine! Together we could take the Xyl as ours! Be the master Binders and Tuners of all! Rulers of all Woodway! Of all the green earth! Turn the Year our way! Let the Runerinnen freeze forever in their stone towers!"

And he launched himself at Morat, throwing him down, and grabbing the Rune Lord's staff, he turned it on him, its point like a spear.

Rowan stood over Morat, spear point pressing into the Rune Lord's breast, a small dot of blood welling forth under it.

Morat lay, feeling the symmetry of it, as the worlds whirled around him: the Land of the Living, a mountainside in the Mother's Woods, his own spear leaving his hand, thrumming through the humming, confused, misshapen air . . . and the Land of the Dead, feeling the spear about to enter his own breast, wondering what held it short of his heart.

"No!" cried Willow. She reached to Morat, a hand, a word stretching toward him.

"Willow!" cried Rowan, a scream that rent the air, as he realized his own act had turned Willow to Morat, perhaps lost her to him.

And Amran-an's leap took him against the Green Wizard, his cry a rune that carried all the power of his wizard's frustrated soul, his body striking Rowan and carrying him off away from Morat, his hands tearing the spear from his grasp.

A concussion shook the air, the ground, a green flare and a red flare meeting in an explosive flash that blinded them all.

Willow stood between them, a hand reaching to one of them, a hand reaching to the other.

"I was your first love," cried Rowan. "I was your betrothed." He reached hands to her.

"I came upon you later, true, but I love you with all the heart in me," said Morat softly.

"He caused you to die!"

"I went to the heart of the Mother-of-All for you. I came to the Land of the Dead to restore you to life."

"We were to be Xyl, I was to be Tuner to your Binder."

"I raised the dead builders of Rune for you. To send the Unshapers into oblivion."

"He stopped the year from turning!"

"With you I would start it turning again. With you I could."

"I would return to the World of the Living," cried Rowan. "For you, with the help of the Mother, I would do this, and bring you with me."

The moment stretched out, with all holding their breath.

"I want you!" cried Rowan.

"I need you!" Morat cried inside his heart and his soul. But he paused and did not say those words aloud. From his deepest heart came the truth in him, the love that helped him serve all of Rune, the caring that was the center of his bone and nerve and heart, as well as the love he bore for the woman before him. And instead, these words came: "I want you to be happy," he said. "Whatever your choice, I do not ask for myself. I ask only for you to be happy," he said simply.

He felt Willow take his hand in hers, small and warm and sweet around his bruised fingers.

And he felt the vertigo as the year started to Turn again.

CHAPTER 20

"And so it came to be," said Willow, "That your grandfather Morat came riding again down out of the Mother's Woods and appeared out of Runegladden, as he had before, with me riding before him on his cornua."

The children sitting at her feet shifted, emerging out of the depths of their concentration on the story. And they and their parents asked the questions, as they did every year since they had been born, on this, the eve of the Winter Turning of the Year, half answering them as they asked, for the story was known and its telling a treasured ceremony, as Wayland had written it long ago, before he himself had finally left the Land of the Living, his poem completed.

"And it only took two days, that ride, just as before?"

"Sa," laughed Redd, "Some magic was still at work."

And the Old Ones, the ones who built Rune so many years ago, they built the steps for you?"

"Indeed they did," answered Morat, "Tearing up the stones of the Land of the Dead, they piled them into fine steps, just as they built the steps lo so many generations ago that bring you up from the city into this our Runehall. And we walked up them, out again into the Land of the Living."

"And it was summer?"

"And it was summer."

"But you left the staff with the windrune behind?"

This time Tellit answered, handing off the wriggling toddler to his wife. "Sa, we did, to give light as a token of our love to Evmorat and to Ellienne, who remained in the Land of the Dead. But the tree that we grew from the seeds of its flowers blooms here, for us, every spring, and we remember that we are loved in return."

"In the Garden," asserted a young lass, whose braids were the very color of Ranna's in that day long ago, though the little maid was now gray. She put aside the embroidery she had been working as the tale unfolded.

"And you tend it, the Garden, out there where Rune's fields meet the forest, with mother and father and us," added one of her sisters.

"And Jarrian, too," smiled the lass, holding the hand of her betrothed, who came from a line of gardeners.

"And Rowan the Green Wizard, what became of him?"

"He came out of the Land of the Dead as well, to the great happiness of his uncle Burr Oak. It took all the persuading runes the Woodway woodsman could muster, for Rowan was not happy to lose Willow, and thought to stay dead. But he was persuaded, when he felt the year turning again and understood the rightness of the Shape that had been made by Morat. And he lives and reigns, high master of the Xyl and Binder and Tuner above all others, in the windrune city of Woodway, as you well know, since he sends you such wonderful carven woodrune gifts each year at Winter Year Turning."

"And the Unshapers are gone?"

"Truly they are, banished by High-Lord Morat and also by Evmorat, who took the book of Maara in their joined hands and destroyed it in the green fire of Lord Morat's staff," said Willow, "with the willing help of the Wizard of Deld. And thus broke the influence of that ancient wizard on this our world."

“Though it’s said that the spirits of Maara and of the Unshapers he had birthed still howl in the cold wind of the Winter’s Turning, if there is a blizzard,” said Ranna, mischievous light in her eyes, shaking a finger at the younger children, “and you hear them and are afraid of the dark.” She winked.

“Shame, Ranna, for scaring the youngest ones. You know they can no longer come into our world,” smiled Willow, “so, no worries.”

“And it seems that some of that strange self-wandering that objects were doing is also gone. So we have supposed that was a sign of Maara’s meddling, too,” said Redd. “So don’t look for that favorite bangle bracelet you lost to turn up by itself, daughter.”

“And the Year Turns?”

It was the final, ceremonial question, and everyone answered, in a great shout of old, young, and baby voices, “And the Year Turns!”

www.ingramcontent.com/pod-product-compliance
Lightning Source LLC
LaVergne TN
LVHW010543160826
845677LV00013B/2983